Thumbing It - 1967

David Done

"Coming of Age in the Summer of 1967" was the original title of this book. Thankfully I came to my senses and realized it was a clunker. "Thumbing It" fits well. It is about a hitchhiking trip I took during the summer of 1967. I have been working on this book for many years and there have been several versions. It has been hard for me to "get it right." I did a lot of editing and cut out a lot of the dull meanderings parts. It is my "personal" story, and almost all of it actually happened. I have to warn you there is no drama, and no one dies. I am a boomer, born in 1949 and this was conceived as a book for boomers. If I am lucky it will find a wider audience.

Table of Contents

Thumbing It - 1967

Chapter One

I spent the afternoon snorkeling in a cove in Laguna Beach. Laguna has some great little spots packed with seaweed, coral and fish. The bottoms are clear and you can see crab and starfish dotting the bottom. I have been snorkeling for years now and introduced the sport to Chuck. You don't need much to get started, just some fins and a snorkel.

"I wish I could stay down as long as you do." Chuck was treading water.

"Abalone! Take a look." I surfaced near him.

"Abalone? They're tasty!" He was breathing heavily.

"They are, if we were in Mexico we could grab them. Here we have to leave them alone."

"Show me." He asks.

"About twenty feet down and to the right. They are wedged between the boulders."

Chuck runs into trouble and comes back up.

"It's harder than I thought." He says frustrated.

"You need to cup your hands, dig and pull up harder." I tell him."Try"using even strokes."

He gives up!

"I am going to go in and take a rest for a while." Chuck paddles towards the shoreline.

A half hour later, Chuck has dried off and is sitting waiting for me in the passenger seat. He has the top down and the radio is playing.

"This car would be better if you fixed it up." Chuck is sitting on a pillow. It is protecting him from the metal spikes protruding from the seat.

"Yeah, it runs good but the upholstery is a mess!" I agree.

"Yeah the seats are falling apart. How do you explain them?" Chuck laughs.

"It's a problem." A loose wedge has jammed its way up my butt again. It makes me squirm.

"I think I will get them fixed in Tijuana. Do you wanna go?"

Chuck pops a stray pimple and stares out the window. "I'll bet your mom's friend Bud could help. He has connections in Tijuana, right?"

I don't get along with Bud and Chuck knows it, but he keeps bringing it up. Bud smuggles birds from Central America and brings them into Mexico. I don't like him. I am dead set against accepting his help for anything.

"I bet he'll know where to get a cheap price." Chuck goads me.

"Yeah but I don't like the idea of being in debt to him. The less I have to do with him the better."

"You should fix this car. It'll be a winner if you do." Chuck winks at me.

"Maybe I will, are you doing anything on Friday? Wanna go to Mexico?"

"Road Trip, now, you're talkin." Chuck was jazzed.

I estimated our driving time would be three hours. Chuck sat on a thick pillow eating a piece of jelly pastry. His voice was almost evangelical in tone.

"What if the earth was like sugar pastry? What if it is about to be swatted like a fly."

"What the fuck?" I wasn't sure if I heard him right. The wind is whistling.

"That's absurd." I said. What was he talking about? Why was he talking about God? What was all this crap about god swatting a fly? Chuck was eating a sugar donut! He had bits of pastry on his cheek. I could see the jelly on his chin.

"Well, the Christians talk a lot about the end of the world. " He smiled at me.

"Yeah so?"

"What if it is closer than they think? What if it is right around the corner. Maybe God's getting ready to end our world. Maybe we are no more important than a sugar donut. Perhaps we need swatting!"

"Yeah I guess they do talk about the "end of times" a lot. But that is total nonsense" I answered.

"Think about it! What do you know about the great flood?"

"Was he serious?" I could not be sure.

"A sugar donut, a flyswatter, or a flood, maybe God can just take his pick of anything he wants. He said it in an off handed flippant.

"You know there never was a flood covering the earth. It is a geological fact. Try telling that to your average Christian! Tell them the Great Flood is nothing but a myth." Chuck and I share a sly grin

He was bullshitting me again. I am not a Christian and he was making fun of their faith and belief in fantastic stories. That was why he was bothering me with stuff about the flood and fly swatters. I ignored him and kept my eyes on the road. After all, I didn't believe in the great flood either.

In fact I chuckled at it, knowing at one time some scientists thought the reason elephant skeletons were found in Mongolia was because they were all washed up from Africa. In that version of reality elephants were not part of a long train of evolution.

"I got accepted at U.C. Santa Cruz." He yelled at me over the wind.

"I had never heard of it. "Where's Santa Cruz?"

Most everybody else was headed to one of the Southern California schools, UCLA or USC. It was the thing to do. Of course it required your parents to have money and mine didn't. At least not anymore. Not since the divorce.

"It's up north, just south of San Francisco." He answered. "I'm going to borrow the money."

"That's not for me. I'll go to junior college. It's dirt cheap." The idea of borrowing and going deep into debt did not appeal to me.

"The Santa Cruz mascot is the Banana Slug!" He cheered, yelling with enthusiasm. "Go Slugs!" "Go Slugs!".

"Slugs?" I had never heard of them.

"How hard does a slug fight?". Silence ensued, I digested the news Chuck was going to be a fighting banana slug.

The bright sun glared in my eyes as we cruised through the various beach towns. A line of makeshift shacks appeared in the sand right on the beach. The shacks were wood crates stacked high to protect the inhabitants from the wind. They had cardboard roofs.

"Who lives in those?"

"Surfers, they freeload." I answered.

Their "homes" sat right on the beach, next to some of the best surfing in the world. It was rent free. A day was coming when they would be labeled a menace. When that day finally came they would vanish and no one would lament their passing.

Chuck and I continued to talk about religion and politics. Our drive under the warm friendly sun was uneventful. My radio blared in the background with Casey Kasem playing the top forty hit parade. We crossed the border into Mexico without any questions asked.

"This is the first time I have been out of the country." Chuck remarked.

"It's my first time in Mexico on my own." I answered back. "My family used to visit friends down here."

I crossed into Old Mexico without a plan. I ended up driving around Tijuana looking for a place to have the upholstery work done. I had assumed the correct shop would be easy to find, sort of like a gas station is easy to find. I had made a mistake. Then wham! the window the window

A familiar Cadillac appeared right next to me. Bud was following me. He rolled down the window and leaned his head out.

" There are two shops on the same block. You should go to the one across the street. I know the owner." Bud was here to help.

Fate knocked and two shops on the same block, right across from each other. I turned into the one with the easiest access.

"Luke, you need to haggle with him." Chuck pointed to a short stumpy brown man with a cowboy hat who was approaching my side of the car.

"I know Chuck, I'll handle it." It bothered me that Chuck thought I was so gr .

"What are you doing here?" I was indignant.

"I promised your Mom I would look after you." He nodded his head in the direction of the shop across the street. His double chins were quivering in unison and emphasized his point.

"You sure?" I started to reconsider. I needed a cheap price."

"I'm sure." Bud was certain he was smarter than everyone else.

Bud yelled in Spanish and got the attention of a squat dark skinned man slumping in a chair half asleep across the street. The little man waved back. They knew each other. I decided to trust Bud.

The traffic was coming at me non stop. Crossing over to the other side was daunting. The oncoming drivers were tailgating each other and darting from lane to lane without signals. It was a chaotic senseless tangle. An opening appeared!

I popped the clutch. My tires spun, and I fishtailed through the traffic in a dangerous weave. I avoided a head on collision. I skidded into the lot spraying a wave of gravel and sand down on the frumpy little man who had rushed out to serve me.

"Shit, what was that all about?" Chuck was ashen. We had avoided doom.

"There was no room, I had to do it." I adjusted my "driving" cap and smiled. My car had responded like a champ. It had "guts" and when you needed it to go, it did.

"The traffic almost broadsided me. My side of the car was exposed." Chuck was shaking from his near death experience. "They almost creamed me."

It was true. I had misjudged the speed of the approaching traffic and the MG is a small car. The idea of a crash was frightening."

"All's well that ends well." I said.

Bud was still stuck across the street, I got out and started up negotiations.

"Chuck, get out so he can see the seat on your side." I nudged him.

The passenger side was by far the worst. It had bare springs pointing skyward like spikes. Chuck removed the pillow exposing the harm it could do. The little man shook his head and whistled under his breath. He made it grim.

Bud made it across the street. He stepped from his car. His body fat was rolling out in a stream. He pushed me aside and jumped into the mix with the little Mexican and began negotiating in Spanish. I became a bystander as they haggled. It was my car and my money but Bud had taken over.

"$75.00 US dollars for the whole job and he will get it done today. He's busy, he has some other jobs booked, but they are not here yet. You're lucky, he has some down time. I suggest you do it, you may not find another vendor to do it today. You should have let me book it in advance instead of showing up like this." Bud scolded me.

"Okay. How do I pay?" What were my choices? I had the cash and took the deal..

"Half now, the rest when the job is done." Bud nodded and the upholsterer nodded back. "Si, half now." So it was set. I gave him the money.

"Have any plans? This will take all day." Bud's glasses were dirty, his beady eyes were squinting at me through the hot sun. Since I had no plans I did not answer. I had not thought about it. "You could go to the races, the horse track is open and nearby. I'll get you a cab."

Chuck jumped on board.

If crossing the street was baffling, it did not prepare me for the cab ride that followed. Seat belts were not standard equipment, and our cab had none. We were tossed from side to side like loose cabbages in a crate. The driver veered this way and that, taking a detour onto the sidewalk to pass a slow moving vehicle. He darted out into oncoming traffic missing a head-on collision. It reminded me of Mr. Toad's wild ride at Disneyland. We held on white-knuckle style until we arrived, unharmed and safe at the track. There is nothing like a cab ride in Tijuana, Mexico.

We soon realized the track was all about betting, and since we were close to broke. We had to be content watching the ponies run around the track. Each race consisted of about two minutes running time for every thirty minutes we waited. The time seemed to last forever, but the races were exciting.

"You know we can buy a beer here if you want. It's legal." Chuck nudged me and pointed to a concession stand.

"How do you know that?"

"Everyone knows if you want to drink all you gotta do is go to Mexico." Chuck was right.

I bought us each a beer. Neither of us had as yet developed a "taste" for beer but we sipped several of them.

On a whim I decided to place a bet and get in on the action. I knew nothing about it, I decided the best thing that could happen was to bet a long shot, and win. I had watched a long shot or two do well, so why not me? Why not a horse I picked?

I started imagining a victory, I could see it in my mind, it felt "fated." I convinced myself it was meant to be. I put two dollars on a 99 to 1 long shot named "White Lightning." I was convinced it was a sure thing, I was going to win, it would pay for the trip, and the upholstery work in one fell swoop. It felt like an obvious outcome for the day.

"It's fated, I'm going to win!"

We had had some conversations about the nature of fate, and had decided in some ways every thing might be "fated." It made sense from a high school physics point of view. There was an order to actions, equal and opposite, always determined. My first action was to place my bet with eager anticipation. The "reaction" was going to be a payout of $198.00.

The bell rang, and my heart raced in hopes of a "White Lightning" victory, I had convinced myself it was fated. The horses were bunched in a pack when they came into the final turn. They thundered down the last long straight away. I searched for my horse, and could not find him. The announcer called the race in Spanish and I never once heard the name "White Lightning". The pack passed. Then I saw him, he was more than twenty lengths behind the last horse in the pack.

"White Lightning" was not striding, he was tripping his way down the track. The jockey dangled from the horse's neck. I imagined the jockey was in mortal fear the horse would plunge face first to the ground, pinning him to the track. In no way could this horse be "racing". He was not even trotting. "Drunk dancing" came to mind. "Nice horse," Chuck could not contain himself, belch after belch of laughter peeled out until he had to stop and pick a pimple. After a silence he laughed. "Fated my ass."

The drive home was cold and windy. The car had stopped goosing me, it was still a little lumpy in places, but the goosing action was gone. The new seats were black and shiny. A definite improvement. We played the radio and over the speakers came an advertisement for a music concert. It was hard to make out the details in the windy night air. The DJ was ranting in a loud voice.

The Monterey pop festival was about to happen and dozens of well-known acts were scheduled to appear. The announcer thundered out as if nothing like it had ever happened before in the history of music! It was to be three solid days of live performances! It would last three whole days. A lot of name bands would be there. It would be "historic".

"Hell, we should go." I yelled above the blustery wind.

"Yeah, we should," Chuck nodded his approval.

We were in agreement, We were going to go to Monterey. The "Summer of Love" was about to begin. The Mexico trip was a success and I now owned one of the coolest cars in town. I was driving a virtual babe magnet. I had high hopes for the future of my love life and who knew what was waiting in Monterey.

Chapter Two

I called the radio station and they sent out a full schedule of weekend shows with ticket prices.

"You can buy a pass covering all the shows or buy tickets to see each show individually. The best shows are at night,"

"Yeah but I am not sure I want to see all the shows." Chuck was skeptical.

"Why not?".

"I don't know a lot of these bands and I want to go to San Francisco and check out the Haight. It sounds cool."

"Okay, when do you think we should do this? The Haight is in San Francisco." I stop short of asking how he thinks we can do both.

"The only Saturday group I recognise is Country Joe and the Fish. The rest are a blank slate for me." Chuck said as he read over the list of Saturday bands.

"Yippee we're all going to die". I sang the only line I knew from the Country Joe song.

"Do you know who any of these guys are?" He read the list out loud, "The Paul Butterfield Blues Band, Big Brother and the Holding Company with Janis Joplin, The Steve Miller Blues Band, The Canned Heat or The Quicksilver Messenger Service? I am sure none of them have had a top forty hit."

"Nope, you're right! They are all unknowns." By "unknowns". I meant not one had ever been on my radio dial.

"I can't afford all the shows! The Haight is where it is happening!" Chuck is insistent.

"Big Brother sounds terrible. I bet he will be watching us." I joked.

We saved $3.50 and skipped the Saturday shows.

"I read a story about a "love-in" in Golden Gate Park and I want to see if it is real." It sounded intriguing.

"What are you talking about?" I am wondering what had captured his imagination.

"Well in this story, these two long haired bearded guys face off naked in the park. There is a crowd of hippies watching."

"And? What is the point?" A crowd watching two long haired naked guys stare at each other did not sound like much fun.

"Well, the article claimed they were stoned and throwing love vibrations at each other. I read they each had a long stick of incense hanging out of their butts. They had a stare down and it went on for hours. The whole weird thing was dramatic." he explained.

"It has to be a joke. Why would anyone do something like that?" After hearing this I was back wanting to see the Saturday show.

"It was a test of wills to find out who could radiate the most powerful love vibration." Chuck tried to explain it.

"I can't believe you are buying into this. It's crap."

"Well, I bet a lot of crazy stuff is happening, and I want to go see it for myself. Aren't you curious?" Chuck asked.

I was curious, and had also read a lot of wild stuff. None of it had involved a stick of burning incense in a guy's butt, but I wondered a lot about the girls who had gone there and what they were like. How could I meet one?

"I think we should go to Monterrey by bus." I said, changing the subject.

"I thought we'd go in your car now you have it all cherried out." I could tell he was disappointed.

"I don't want to take a chance. It's in the shop again and I don't think I can trust it for such a long trip." I waived a bus schedule in the air.

"You got a bus schedule?" That settled it, Chuck put up no more resistance and accepted my plan.

"There's one leaving Long Beach in the early evening. It will run all night. We can sleep on the bus." I was young and the idea of a long bus ride was fine.

It turned out the bus station in Long Beach is in a rough part of town. We arrived in the late afternoon and I left my convertible in the station parking lot. Leaving it felt risky but sometimes you must trust fate and carry on.

We spent the next twelve hours traveling. The trip took endurance. It was very hard to sleep. We arrived in Monterey before sunrise. It was dark and we were both tired from the long bumpy ride.

"It will be a couple of hours before it gets light." I say.

We wander around and find a vacant lot nearby. The ground is rocky but no one is around and it's quiet. We laid out our bags and curled up. We both fell asleep. When we opened our eyes Monterey was electric. The quiet night had turned into a bustling scene full of long haired hippies arriving for a music festival.

"The Beatles are coming!" "The Beatles are coming!" It was on every tongue. It was everywhere!

This mantra was repeated by everyone we met. It had caught fire and spread throughout the town. Excited disc jockeys filled the airwaves with reports from witnesses claiming encounters with one or all of the Beatles every few minutes.

"I saw them having lunch on Cannery Row, or I saw John walking on the boardwalk." Was a common testimonial that was broadcast over and over again. They all were honest and sincere.

Complementing the Beatles rumors were numerous "confirmed" sightings of the Rolling Stone guitarist Brian Jones. The local radio station kept putting live callers on the air. Each claimed they had seen Brian wandering the streets. As the rumors grew, it was suggested all these musicians were going to appear and close the Saturday night show together. The Beatles and the Stones on stage together! The idea was toe curling and the anticipation was thrilling. Everyone was talking about it. Chuck and I got caught up in the drama.

"I believe the Beatles will show," we agreed. It was a near certainty. Everywhere there was a feeling history was about to be made, and even if you weren't a Beatles fan you wanted to see them.

"I can't wait." was my comment.

The entire weekend took on a mystical aura. It was fueled by a belief something unique was happening. It was a communal feeling and it was new to me.

The first concert was scheduled for Friday evening, so we had a full day to "kill". We passed it by hanging out in the area known as "Cannery Row". A part of Monterrey made famous by John Steinbeck.

"Did you read the **Grapes of Wrath**?" Chuck wondered..

"Yeah I did."

"One day I am going to write a novel. I want to be able to create a character as memorable and honest as Lenny. Did you like Lenny?" Chuck was staring into space.

"I can't say I liked him. He was a bit pathetic." I answered.

"He was no hero, but that's what I liked." Chuck was pensive and thoughtful.

A plaque on the pier mentioned Steinbeck had a house in Salinas had been turned into a museum.

"I wish we could go see it." Chuck meant it.

"Steinbeck wrote a lot about "common" people." I added. "He had a way of making them feel important."

"Yeah, he had a feeling for ordinary people."

The streets of Monterey were full of people singing, dancing, and getting stoned. Bright colorful clothes were the norm. The smell of incense filled the air along with the sweet sickly smell of marijuana. The words "peace" and "love" reverberated on every tongue and cars were covered with strings of flowers. Peace signs were taped in the windows and on the doors. Music was the message, and the message was "peace and love."

The concert venue was many miles away from the wharf/cannery area. When the hour for the show drew near we decided to hitchhike to the venue. A car stopped and picked us up. It was a middle-aged couple with their son. Their kid was about thirteen with long hair. He talked through his nose in a high whiny voice.

"I can't stand The Association, they are so lame." He offered this opinion in refutation of Chuck who had expressed his enthusiasm and anticipation in seeing the group. It was news to us that they were lame.

"Why do you say that?"

"I can't stand their voices, they are too sweet." his high whiny voice grated on me.

"I think they harmonize well." I tried to defend them.

"They aren't hip." He delivered an even bigger dose of whine. He believed he was in the know about what was hip.

"Do you think the Beatles or the Stones will show?" I changed the subject hoping to find something I could agree with him about.

"Who cares? They can't stay on the stage with Garcia. None of the Beatles can play their instruments." He delivered some more high whine. Neither Chuck nor I had any idea what to say to refute him.

"Who is Garcia?" Chuck fumbled out the words.

"God, you're so lame." He acted as if we were from Mars instead of Huntington Beach. "They're a San Francisco group and will be performing Sunday night."

His father interrupted us and broke in, "You can get there faster by walking. You should jump out now while I am stopped. It's a long line of stop and go traffic."

He was the incarnation of "Father knows best", and I was happy he intervened because I was losing patience with his kid. The little guy was a snot. This was our first concert, and I didn't want my nose rubbed in because he thought we lacked sophistication. The car came to a dead stop. We were more than a mile away from the venue. We got out and started walking.

"What the hell was that about?" Chuck was also frustrated with the attitude of the "kid" and his attitude.

"Hell if I know. He was annoying." We nodded our heads at each other.

The cars inched alongside and we left the "kid" far behind stuck in the line. The mood was exhilarating, the air was electric. Everyone was polite and courteous. A line of cops watched the parade of "hippy" cars making their way to the venue. The cops kept far away, they were not there to engage anyone about anything. It was chaotic but it was an orderly sort of chaos. The police stood back and watched the show.

At first we were trudging, but the pace increased until we were swept up and carried into the venue by a gushing flow of humanity. The people behind us shoved and pushed, we resisted trying not to trample those ahead of us. As we entered an announcer was chatting up the crowd. He exchanged jokes. The stage hands were setting up the equipment.

"Please welcome, from England…" he stopped and Eric Burdon took the stage.

Eric and the Animals performed a unique version of "Paint It Black". He had a deep grinding voice I found both melodic and satisfying. They did all of their hits and finished the set with his version of "The House of the Rising Sun." Throughout the set we stomp our feet and clap. As an opening band they energized the night with magic.

Burdon was followed by The Association whom the "whiner" had criticized and dished with malice. They sang "Windy", a song I later learned was about marijuana. Lou Rawls followed and turned out to sing in a style I found moving. It was the first time I had listened to him and I got caught up in his delivery. It was exhilarating. He had genuine "cool".

"Man, this is fantastic ." Chuck flashed a smile at me. The night wound down and two familiar faces walked into the spotlight. One had an acoustic guitar and the other was a tall thin man with springy hair.

The lighting focused on the small man with the guitar, they sang together:

"Hello darkness, my old friend

I've come to talk with you again

Because a vision softly creeping

Left its seeds while I was sleeping."

Simon and Garfunkel had performed "The Sounds of Silence" and "Homeward Bound." They touched the heart of poetry in all their songs. Later we learned all the musicians had done the shows for free out of love for music and the desire to share the love. It showed.

"They belong together, their voices blend in such a unique way. Beautiful, beautiful."

The sentiment Chuck expressed was so obvious I slapped him on the back in agreement. The first night came to an end as Simon and Garfunkel walked off the stage to a standing ovation.

After it ended, we hiked into the woods and went to sleep outdoors. I was happy that we had made the trip and was looking forward to what was to come. It felt like a miracle that we could expect two more days of this wonderful live music. Neither the Stones nor the Beatles had shown on Friday, but everyone "knew" with near absolute certainty they would close Saturday night. The talk continued to buzz and echo everywhere. "The Beatles" were coming! And we hoped they were bringing the Stones as well.

Morning came and the birds began chirping an hour before sunrise. The dew was wet and cold on our faces, we could smell bacon cooking, it was in the air from someone else's open fire. Hungry, we found a store and bought a quart of milk, plus a roll and a bit of lunch meat. Our "Breakfast" cost us thirty cents apiece.

It was early Saturday morning, and as agreed we were skipping the afternoon show. It was ninety miles to San Francisco. We stowed our gear in a bus locker and headed for Haight Ashbury with our thumbs out hoping to learn what all the fuss was about.

We settled for a series of short rides. It took three hours but we arrived like flotsam on the famous landmark corner. The place was a circus, pulsating with a heart beat all its own. Strange people dotted the street like ornaments covering the landscape in all directions.

I was fixated on the many young women flaunting their breasts and bare legs. Or was it bare breasts and long legs? They became a parade, a carousel of flesh going by in an endless stream drifting down the street. It was wonderful. A visual orgy of sexy women on parade.

We were mingling in the street. The girls were musky, as if they had not bathed for days. We were packed together. I was drowning in their incredible earthy smell. I wondered if they were looking for sex? Nothing but having sexual intercourse filled my thoughts. Everything suggested. free, I wondered it sex could ever be free.

"Luke, get a hold of yourself, you are out of it." Chuck bumped me.

I was startled by the urgency in his voice. We could not walk in a straight line without bumping into someone. Perhaps it was not a good idea. Half dressed bodies blocked my way.

"Luke, you're bumping into people."

"Sorry, I'm a bit light headed."

Strange smells filled the air. I was wide eyed and amazed. The message was "music and love" with a whisper and a promise of sexual fulfillment. It was stimulating.

"So this is the Haight Ashbury district." Chuck stated the obvious.

"I guess we have been fated to visit the Haight." I answer in jest.

"It's nuts, but it's okay." Chuck gave me a thumbs up sign.

Out of nowhere a group of young men, with shaved heads and long stringy ponytails blocked our way. They were dancing to a drum, and chanting "Hari Krishna, Hari Krishna, Krishna, Krishna, Hari, Hari." The meaning of their chants was lost on me. They were dressed in orange robes, each of them had milky white skin with no facial hair. One dancer approached me and pinned a flower on my shirt.

"Please give a donation." he asked in a demanding voice.

"For what?" I tried to hand him the flower back.

"For Krishna. Of course." He smiled a goofy smile. His eyes were out of focus.

"If I want a flower, I'll pick one." He had picked this one a few blocks away in Golden Gate Park. I dropped the flower. He picked it up off the ground.

"It is up to you. Krishna would be pleased if you give, but if not, it is okay."

"Not a chance." I answered.

I was annoyed. I had little money and had no intention of giving any of it to him. Seeing my resistance the dancer backed off. Good thing, I thought, I was not about to put up with his nonsense.

"Come to the park and get darsham. The swami will be carried in a parade today."
He laughed. "Swami likes excitement. Krisna likes excitement too!"

"No kidding, the Swami himself will be there." I wondered what he meant by "carried
through it."

"Do not make fun, he is a perfect master. No one should make fun of a perfect
master." The orange robed bald dancer was serious.

"Krishna is the Hindu name of God." Chuck informed me as the chanter/dancer
vanished. Chuck read a lot and knew a bit about Krishna.

"Okay, I am glad you told me." The crowd of dancers vanished.

"Let's go into that shop." I pointed to a storefront with pictures of the Beatles and the
Stones looking at us. One was from an album cover. It was the Stones on the
"Between the Buttons" album. Their eyes were dazed and red. They were stoned.

At that same moment back in Monterey, Janis Joplin was taking the stage. Her voice
was "heard" and the crowd went crazy. She blew the socks off the music world. The
show was pure Janis, twisting and throwing her hair everywhere. The opening song
was "Down on Me". She made history, but I had saved $3.50 and went to the Haight
in search of free love.

"Welcome man," A thin reedy voice trebled out a greeting as we walked between
hanging beads. He was smoking a pipe. The beads closed behind us and made a
slight clicking sound. They served as a barrier separating the rooms in his tiny shop.

"Are you looking for papers?" he asked.

"Papers?" I knew he meant papers used to roll a marijuana joint, but I pretended to
be ignorant.

"Yeah papers, we got papers." He smiled, his eyes drifted off, he seemed unable to
focus. It was like he was squinting at someone standing behind me. But there was
no one there.

"There's a shortage of papers right now. You're hip to that right? If you need em, we
got em." He kept right on squinting into the void. For a second I wondered if I had a
parrot on my shoulder.

"I have a driver's license, is that what you mean by "papers"? Do I need a passport?"
I grinned at him. I was trying to be funny but I couldn't get a rise out of him. He
moved on without acknowledging my wit.

"Right," he murmured. "Let me know if you need anything. Peace." He made a V sign with his hand and slipped off to the back. I heard a long inhaling sound followed by a loud exhale. I was sure it was him. There was no one else in the store.

We wandered around looking at water pipes, incense, and other paraphernalia we had no names for, one of his offerings including little packets called Zig Zag's. Zig Zag's showed a bearded man smoking a hand-rolled cigarette. He exhaled a long cloud of smoke on the box.

"Nothing but a lot of junk", Chuck pronounced with certainty.

"You got me," I echoed, shrugging my shoulders. "I guess it is all drug gear but who knows for sure?"

We made our way back out to the street. People were dancing in the street, hips were bumping and churning. A blond girl with braids danced up and made a kissy face at me.

"Are you a hippy, man?" She blew smoke in my face. It was not tobacco.

"Peace," I caught a glimpse of her naked nipples peeking out at me. For that moment the world became an exciting experience. I have often walked on the beach and bikinis were common, so I tried to stay under control and keep my cool.

"Hippy? Me?" I knew the word well, I had read about the hippies, and now they were all around me, but no, I was not a hippy. "I don't think so. How does one become a hippy?"

"You get stoned?" It was a question, not an explanation. She blew more smoke in my face.

"Like in the Bible, they throw stones at you for adultery or other sex crimes?" I tried to be cute knowing full well she was referring to smoking marijuana.

"No man, do you smoke dope, or not? Do you? Sex is better if you do." She was persistent and had taken a shine to me. I was hoping for an invitation. I was willing to try pot if it involved getting into her pants. However, as usual, I was not sure how to proceed. I think she saw the uncertainty showing in my face. It was like I was wearing my virginity on my face.

She laughed at me and flashed me the peace sign, it was not a V for Virgin. Then she vanished into the crowd.

"Come on, man, we have to get back for the show tonight, we'll miss the Beatles."

Chuck was tugging on my arm. He had sensed my interest in her, and thought I might try and follow her. He tugged at my arm insisting we needed to leave.

"Let's go and walk in the park, we got some time. Golden Gate park is where it is all happening." I wasn't sure but I was guessing she was headed in that direction.

"Okay but we only got an hour. I don't want to miss any of the music." Chuck was sticking close as always.

The road to the park was blocked off and people were roller skating in droves. We made our way towards where the marine bandstand stood between the art museum and the Natural History museum. I saw the back side of the blond girl who had made a kissy face at me. I was on her trail. My pursuit was interrupted by loud chanting.

"Hari Krishna Hari Hari, Krishna Krishna" The sound was followed by a stream of dancing monks, who came down the street carrying a platform. A fragile looking bald man in an orange robe sat on top of the platform. He was chanting and counting beads. He gazed down on me. It was as if he was floating in the clouds. He was ancient and grim. His face was haggard and lined.

I am not a religious person so I was surprised when an instinctive thought rose from the depths of my consciousness. It was "Bless me father."

It was spontaneous and out of character. I was lifted from my body in a blue light and held suspended in time. I became aware of an overflowing feeling of love sweeping through the essence of my being. For a moment it was eternal and permanent. But it passed. "Eternal" turned out to be rapid and momentary. Bewildered, I looked at the face of my friend Chuck.

"Damn, did you feel that? Did you see the blue light?"

"Feel what? What light?" His face was blank.

For a moment I understood why all these guys were dancing around with their heads shaved bald singing "Hari Krishna". They were all under the influence of a "perfect master". Does he have some strange power? What did it mean?

"You came." The dancer with the flower had returned and was chanting and bobbing. "Krishna is pleased, I am sure."

"Go away, don't bother us." Chuck tried to chase the dancing dervish away.

"Wait, tell me what your master does?"What had just happened and how could I Explain it.

"He chants the name of God 250,000 times a day, every day. He is a mast for Krishna and God's power flows through him and touches all of us."

"Go away and leave us alone." Chuck raised his voice in anger..

The dancer left and never came back.

"They are enchanted. It is a cult." Chuck shook me. "They have given up everything they own and given it all to their leader."

"A blue light filled my mind and I was not in this world. I was in a world of love." I could not believe what I was saying.

"Chanting can create dangerous illusions. I have read all about it." He gave me a stern warning.

"It felt real to me." I was caught off guard.

"Some victims wake up years later with their hair grown down to their toes and no memory of time having passed. Imagine you find one day your fingernails are six inches long and unclipped. Chants and mantras can be powerful and dangerous. Do not give in. Beware."

"It was a good thing you were here to explain it to me. I might have followed them."

"Maybe it was fated." Chuck gave me a little grin. "My being here I mean."

"Let's go" I mumbled, "We can't let the tickets go to waste. The Beatles are coming".

"We can't miss that." Chuck responded.

The trip back to Monterrey was quick and easy. We held out a sign, "Monterey" and a hippie stopped for us.

"Going there myself, hop in." His quick appearance was magical and preordained.

Saturday night opened with a San Francisco band group called the Moby Grape. They had not yet gotten any air time in Los Angeles. They were unknown to us.

"I like them." Chuck nodded. "We should see if they've made a record and get it."

They were followed by an L.A, band we both knew, it was the Byrds with David Crosby. They did a version of the song "Hey Joe". I had a hard time visualizing any of these guys with their sweet high harmonic voices shooting a woman dead in rage. Nevertheless the Byrds were one of my personal favorites and they did nothing that night to tarnish my opinion. They did a rendition of "Turn, turn, turn." It was wonderful to see the Byrds live. They left the stage to thunderous applause.

For a moment the night air was full of the voice of a rough rock angel.

"When the truth is found to be lies, and all the joy within you dies, don't you want somebody to love? You better find somebody to love!"

It was the soaring voice of Grace Slick, demure, beautiful and full of power. The Jefferson Airplane took off and we all got on board and took flight with them. It was the first time I heard the words:

"One pill make you smaller and one pill makes you large,

And the ones that mother gives you don't do anything at all."

The night flew by in the blink of an eye. Headliner after headliner had appeared, but still the tension was everywhere. Who would close? The moment came, I wondered would it be "Is the Beatles? Was it time for the Beatles?

But instead, out popped Otis Redding, a dancing, prancing, musical maniac. He gave a fantastic performance, full of energy and life. Otis knocked it out of the park with "I've Been Loving You Too Long", "Respect" and "Try a Little Tenderness". As great as it was, Chuck and I were disappointed, no Beatles, no Stones. The almost all white crowd went crazy for Otis. There was no disappointment in their reaction to him. It was pure adoration.

"Man, the Beatles will close the concert." Chuck was keeping the faith. "They'll be the last act, for sure. They'll close it out on Sunday."

"I'm sure you're right". I agreed. "It's too early. Sunday night must be it. Has to be Sunday night. Stars always close out the last show."

We convinced each other the Beatles or the Rolling Stones or both would appear together, or apart and make this experience the ultimate music experience. But the truth was, it was already wonderful.

The next morning we awoke one more time in the woods under the tall trees. It was crisp and cool and the smell of fresh pine needles filled our nostrils. I got up invigorated, feeling alive and ready for anything. We headed for the venue.

The only act that afternoon was the Indian sitar player, Ravi Shankar, who was elevated to overnight stardom, when he became the music teacher and mentor of George Harrison. The venue was not as crowded as it had been since he was the only act and was not sharing the stage.

On the sides were private booths I noticed for the first time. I thought they were reserved for band members and the like. For some reason, I sort of wandered up to the entrance and acted like I belonged in the artists box. When we walked in. No one gave it a thought. We waited for Ravi Shankar to come out, while searching his entourage of followers for George Harrison

Ravi came out, bowed with his hands in prayer, Indian style. He had his tabla player by his side. They each played long complicated solos with strange melodies and rhythms. Exotic, but wonderful. The concert had been many hours of non-stop music. Flowers rained down and the moment was blissful. Ravi bowed, acknowledging a standing ovation. He picked up a bouquet and blew kisses to the audience. The applause continued until they convinced him to play an encore. When they finished, they left the stage to a second standing ovation.

"Listen, I don't want to spend another night here sleeping on the ground." Chuck popped a pimple for emphasis. It broke my feeling of bliss.

"How so? Our bus ticket home is for tomorrow morning, we have to spend the night." I reminded him. The bus left for Long Beach at eight Monday morning.

"We have to spend the night."

"I don't want to take the bus, let's hitchhike home. We'll be home before the bus boards in the morning. I am sure of it." He was adamant. "Screw the waiting, screw the long slow bus ride."

Hitchhiking from Monterey to San Francisco in the middle of the day was one thing, it was ninety miles and took a couple of hours. But all the way to Long Beach? It was more than 350 miles away! Plus we would start in the middle of the night. I was skeptical.

"Nah, it'll be easy." Chuck pinched another pimple and cracked a wry smile. "I want to leave as soon as the second show ends. We can sit up in a tree at the back of the venue. I'll give the quickest path out to the highway. We'll make a sign saying "Long Beach". There will be tons of cars going south. Someone will pick us up right away."

Chuck was referring to a huge tree at the corner of the arena. It had an expansive view of the stage. We had seen people sitting in it. You had to be at least twenty off the ground if you sat in the tree. But Chuck was right, we could be among the first to exit the arena if we got a branch in that tree.

"I'll bet it has a fantastic view of the stage." As far as Chuck was concerned it was settled we were climbing the tree watching the last show from there.

"I don't want to sleep on the ground again and I sure don't want a twelve hour bus ride, again do you?" Chuck was intense.

I had to agree he was right about everything. The bus ride had been painful to endure.. I didn't want to do it again either.

"We'll have to be early to get a strong branch in the tree." Chuck gave me a firm look, don't argue. We're doing it."

"Okay, let's get something to eat and grab a seat in the tree."

It was an uncomfortable balancing act. We were hanging in the air looking down at the stage.

"You know, Chuck, if the Beatles do show, they will be the last act, and we will have been up in this tree for a long time."

He popped a pimple, and squinted at me, "If we need to, we can go one at a time. We can save each other's place on the branch."

"We'll be climbing over people, and around them." I tried to argue.

"True hold it, if you can. It would be easier."

We had several hours to show time. The branch was hard. My butt started to ache.

"I can't stay up here all night. This doesn't seem like such a good idea to me anymore. "I decided it was not worth the pain.

"You're such a wimp. This is the best view in the whole arena." Chuck was annoyed with me. The announcer's mike came on with a buzzing sound.

"Ladies and Gentlemen, by popular demand, welcome the stars of the Saturday show back for an encore second performance. Please give a big round of applause to Janis Joplin with Big Brother and his holding company." The announcer's voice boomed out into the night air. The legend of Janis Joplin had been cemented.

She was on stage and bouncing up and down, anxious to get started.

"Thanks very much, we love you all." She was all smiles, while squinting out at the audience. She turned it on, and became a spinning shaking dynamo, propelling her crackly voice out into the night. She was terrific. A half hour passed and we were still sitting in the tree. I forgot about my sore butt. When she belted out "take another little piece of my heart." I want to give her a piece of mine.

Next up, it was Buffalo Springfield with Steven Stills and David Crosby sitting in for Neil Young. They were introduced by Peter Tork of the Monkees who tried to let us all come down from out of the cloud by saying:

"I know there are a lot of rumors about the Beatles. I am sorry to tell you they are not here. For sure they aren't here. Just enjoy the musicians who are here."

A light chorus of boos greeted the unwelcome news he brought. No one wanted to believe him. The idea the Beatles were making a surprise showing was dying a slow hard death.

The Buffalo Springfield played with fury. The classic song "Bluebird" rained a wall of sound that filled the night. They were a terrific group. The nucleus for a future magical act was on stage that night, with Crosby and Stills playing together.

When they finished their set, Eric Burdon came on stage and introduced the Who. They were making their first live performance in the United States. I knew nothing about them, they managed to keep my mind off how hard the tree branch was to sit on. The last song of their set was "My Generation" with the stammering stuttering Roger Daltry jumping around and Peter Townsend whipping his arms as he strummed his guitar. In the middle of a riff they pulled up and started hammering their guitars on the floor of the stage, breaking them into pieces. Smoke and electricity flew into the night air. Keith Moon ripped at his drums, stuck his foot through one of them and put his hand through another. I was dumbstruck, I couldn't believe it. It was as if they had declared a death sentence on their instruments.

"Damn, they destroyed their instruments." I said it out loud, not believing my eyes.

"They sure as hell did." Chuck confirmed I was not nuts.

The Who had destroyed their gear while on stage. They offered no explanation. When they had finished they walked off without another word. It was a wild act of rage and perhaps freedom.

"Ever seen anything like that?" Chuck asked me, even though he knew the answer was "no." There was a long break as they cleaned up the debris. It was hard to see what was happening below.

The delay in cleaning up the Who's debris and getting the stage reset allowed us to climb down and take the pressure off our legs and bowels. I heard the announcer say the next group up was a San Francisco group called the Grateful Dead.

"Yeah it is, they must be good, on the last night."

They weren't. They were hard to hear and fell short of expectations.

"That kid was crazy. He must have been smoking something. Well there's still time for the Beatles to show up. Fuck Peter Tork, what does he know?" I felt a little vindication.

After the Dead left the stage, a black man with a puffy head of hair appeared, walking around testing wires and picking up instruments checking on their readiness. He played a few rifts on the guitar. He was different. He had a new and different sound, and was not at all like any of the others. Then he shook his head to signal all was ready. At the far corner of the stage I saw a face I thought I knew, it was Brian Jones of the Rolling Stones, I was sure of it. I nudged Chuck and pointed him out.

"I'm sure that is Brian Jones." Chuck's eyes lit up and he shook his head confirming that he too recognized Brian. Brian was an original founding member of the Stones. He carried weight. At least the rumor about Brian was correct.

"Quiet please, quiet. No, no we're not going to play tonight. I am the only member of the Stones who is here. The others couldn't get visas, too much drug trouble." The level of noise increased as the crowd recognized who was on stage.

"I'm here to introduce a musical genius. A yank, this is his first show in the U.S. He has been lighting it up in England all year."

The bubble headed black man appeared with two rail thin white guys also sporting bubble hair. It thought they were wearing helmets. I had never seen an Afro before..

"Ladies and gentlemen, this is Jimi Hendrix and the Experience." There was no reaction. No one knew who he was.

It took a little while for people to tune in and "get" Jimi but by the time he was doing his version of "Hey Joe," the crowd had merged with his music. It was hot, passionate Jimi at his best:

"Hey Joe, where you goin with that gun in your hand?

Hey Joe, I said where you goin with that gun in your hand?

Alright,

I'm goin down to shoot my old lady

You know I caught her messin round with another man."

Jimi Hendrix had arrived. It was a long jubilant set full of energy and fire. He introduced and improvised his way through "The Wind Cries Mary", "Purple Haze", and closed with his version of "Wild Thing". At the end of his set, Jimi lit his guitar on fire and threw it into the air. It was his first live show in the United States and he stepped into musical history. One writer later described it as "Jimi discovering his divinity." Perhaps it was true.

The smoke from Jimi's blazing guitar drifted off into the night.The announcer let the crowd recover.

The Mamas and the Papas walked onto the stage together! It was announced they were the closing act.

Michelle was just as foxy in person as she did in her photos. John had a stove-pipe hat of sorts, baggy pants, and a funky jacket. He played guitar and sang. Michelle and Cass wailed on "Monday, Monday", and people went nuts. They went through every hit, plus some that would become future hits. They were billed as the last act of the night and Peter Tork had told us again not to expect anything more.

It didn't matter much because the expectation the Beatles were about to appear was still there. The enthusiasm in the crowd was electric in anticipation. Scott McKenzie came out and sang "If you're going to San Francisco" "be sure to wear some flowers in your hair", and the Mamas and the Papas got the whole crowd rocking with "Dancing in the Street" and the show ended.

The lights on the stage went out. No Beatles. No Stones. Chuck tugged on my sleeve, "Let's get out to the highway."We scooped up our stuff and headed for the road. Out came the sign: "L.A. or Bust. "We need to wait for a ride to L.A. We don't take anything else."

Sure enough within fifteen minutes, we were in the back of a V.W. van heading home. The driver was a long haired, hippy type, headed to Santa Monica. He was smoking a joint.

"You guys are young, do you want a hit?" We decided to try it. "Peace, man," we said in unison. He passed it back. A few long drags and I started to float. He was playing "Revolver" and I fell asleep. We arrived in Southern California and the sun was rising over the pier in Santa Monica. We were almost home.

"That was easy," Chuck grinned at me. "You slept most of the way home."

I decided whatever I thought I knew about drugs had no bearing with what I found happening on this trip. Nothing that had come before in my life fit anything that's happening now. I felt like I could go anywhere and do anything. It was a new world out there and my life in it was only beginning.

Chapter Three

We've been back for a week. I have a river of nervous energy dammed up inside trying to break free. I want to do something, go somewhere. A seed has been planted but the question is what should I do? What was the weekend in Monterey about? There was all of this amazing live music featuring a huge variety of people who all seemed to be singing all at once. What was it they were saying? If there was a message, what was it? I couldn't get it clear in my mind. What was I supposed to do?

The chorus "You gotta go where you wanna go, do what you want to do" was stuck in my head! It kept playing over and over again in my brain. It is the message I brought home from Monterey and somehow it felt right! It is what these times are about.

When basketball season ended I needed some physical activity. I decided to learn how to play golf. After many years of playing a team sport it is interesting to play one that is individual. I managed to break one hundred within two weeks. It required a few mulligans.

Today, Chuck and I are in the park passing time. I have convinced him to learn to play golf and am trying to teach him how to swing a club. We are hitting a wiffle ball. The park is way too small to hit real balls.

"You grip the club in a V handshake and interlock your fingers." I hold the club out so he can see my fingers as they form a V. "This is the correct way to grip a golf club."

"You keep your left arm straight with no bend in the elbow? Right?." He looked over my shoulder and down the length of my arm.

"It is a pendulum swing, no bend." I affirm his understanding.

"It feels unnatural. What happens if you bend your elbow?" he asks.

"If you bend it, it will open up the clubface. You won't hit the ball in the sweet spot. Watch me." I take a full swing and hit two inches throwing up a chunk of grass. I still chunk it a lot. I am learning how to play but I am also trying to teach Chuck.

"Whoa! Did you mean to do that?" I can see from his expression he knows I missed the shot.

"Of course not, it was too much divot."

"Thought so." He shrugs.

"Bud's bugging me." I changed the subject.

"What is it this time? Does he want to buy you something?" Chuck asks.

"Naw, he's trying to get me to work with him."

"He is trying to score points with your mother again." For some reason Chuck thinks highly of Bud.

"He asked me to go to Central America and hunt parrots with him. Eventually he will smuggle them in the USA. He gives me the shits. No matter how rude I am, he still wants to be friends. He won't take "no" for an answer."

"You're lucky. My mom hasn't had anyone in her life since my Dad got into trouble with the law. Having Bud around is not so bad." Chuck's voice is cold and bitter.

"What trouble?" It was the first time I had heard about trouble with the law.

I take another full swing and pop it up. It hooks left. Loses speed until it falls forty feet away. It is clear Chuck doesn't give a shit about golf. He is just spending time hanging out,

"Did he say where in Central America?" is hovering over his ball.

"Costa Rica," I answered.

"You should go, I would." He swung hard and missed.

"That's a whiff," I chided him. "You need to keep your head down. It's bad form to pull your head. You have to follow through and remember don't look until you finish the swing."

"Easy for you to say. You're a natural. But how can you turn down a free trip? Chuck thought I was nuts.

"I couldn't take ten days in the jungle with Bud. He would drive me nuts in ten minutes. I'd be at his throat."

I swing again and this time it fades right. It is a wild shot and if it were a real ball, and not a wiffle ball it would land a fairway or two over. This shot flies about fifty feet, before it stops in the wind and falls.

"I think ten days in the jungle sounds cool." Chuck swings and tops it. It never gets in the air and rolls thirty feet away. "Shit, this is not easy." He stares menacingly at the club as if it is the club's fault.

"Try swinging easy. It is supposed to be one smooth motion. Ten days with Raquel Welch, that would be cool. But ten days with Bud?" I pretend to puke.

The thought of spending time with Bud made me cold while the mere mention of Raquel was curling my toes. Virginity and testosterone do not make for peaceful thoughts. I have heard the average male teenager thinks about sex every thirty seconds. It was about right.

"He'll be disappointed. How are you going to tell him?" Chuck got one in the air. It was a weak effort and came down rolling a few feet away.

"At least you got one up in the air. That's an improvement. I'm going to tell him to shove it." I did a thumbs down sign and added a little grimace. "He's only buttering me up to please my Mom. I don't think he gives a shit what I do."

"He asked you last year too, didn't he?" Chuck was green with envy.

"Yah, I played basketball in the summer league instead of going with him. I can't use that excuse this year. High school is over for me. There is no basketball league this summer."

"I think you should go before he gets tired of asking." It was clear he would have gone in a heartbeat.

"I want to do something, just not with him." I shook my head in disgust.

"Why don't we take a trip somewhere together? See the world!" Chuck spoke up with enthusiasm. "If you leave he can't bother you."

"That sounds like fun. Where do you want to go?" The refrain from the song echoed in my mind. "Go where you wanna go, do what you wanna do."

"How much money you got?" Chuck narrowed his eyes. "I want to get away from this town. This town is killing me."

"$150.00 or thereabouts. How about you?" It sounded like a fortune to me.

I swung and hit the ball in a straight line. No hook, no fade, and it took off like a rocket. It was the first good shot of the day! I completed the follow through and waited for a congratulatory "good shot". It never came. I wondered, was any one watching?

"I could pull together about that much. You got anything you could sell for cash?" Chuck asks.

"I got old Indian head pennies. I think I could get $50.00 dollars for them."

Chuck swung and whiffed again. He wasn't getting any better. He threw the club in disgust. "What's the fucking point?" He yelled in frustration. "This is a stupid game."

"You have to give it a chance. and give it some time." I counsel him.

"You got Indian head pennies you could sell?" I can see Chuck has had enough of golf for the time being.

"They are getting rare but they're still in circulation. I have saved those I got in change. I think I can get two to three dollars apiece for them. Most people sell them when they get them but I kept mine."

"That's cool. Let's get away from this town."

"Where do you want to go?" I stopped playing golf. We were onto something.

"We just got back from San Francisco, it was fun, but I think we should go east. No point in going somewhere we have already been." His voice was intense.

"East? What's in the east?" I ask.

"It is the oldest part of the country. They have history, everything important in history happened there. We'll go to New York first, the Village sounds cool, I have been reading about it. We can figure it out from there." Chuck was on fire with enthusiasm. I think "New York has it all."

"You want to hitchhike to New York? All the way across the country?" For a moment it sounded risky.

"Yeah, it will be fun." He was confident and sure of himself.

"Well it won't cost much, enough food, and a place to stay." I thought a little about it.

"We can eat real cheap and sleep outside." He had it planned out in his mind. He wanted to go!

"Let's do it. I got about four months if we leave right away." It was impulsive and crazy but I didn't care.

"Four months? How do you figure that?" He was disappointed.

"Registration for college is the first week of September. I gotta be back for college" One thing I knew for sure was I needed to register for school.

The draft had become an omnipresent reality. Either you went to college or accepted the alternative. The alternative was forced service in a war I didn't believe in.

"Yeah, for sure. You still have to enroll. I'm already all set up at Santa Cruz." Chuck was going to be a Banana slug and said "I got it covered."

"Yeah you got signed up in advance. They don't do that at the junior colleges. It's done in person, so I gotta be back in time. When do you wanna leave?".

"How about tomorrow?" He was dead serious. "Let's leave tomorrow."

"I need a little more time to sell my coins. How about the day after tomorrow?" It was settled. We cashed out our bank accounts and packed up our backpacks. I sold some coins. My life's savings came to a total of $238.00.

"New York, here we come!" Chuck did a shuffle and jabbed in the air. He was enthralled with the promise of New York.

My Mom pointed out I was seventeen and could get picked up as a runaway. To compensate she wrote me a letter stating she had given me permission to travel. If need be I could show her letter to the police.

"I put my work number in the letter so they can call during the day. Be careful, I want you and Chuck to stick together and look out for each other." I could tell she was worried but she didn't try to stop me.

"Here are the keys to the MG. Start it twice a week and let the engine run for ten minutes to keep the battery charged. It will go dead if you don't." She took the keys and nodded yes.

"Be prepared," the boy scout motto filled my thoughts. When I finished packing I was loaded with sixty pounds of gear bulging on my back. I was bent straining trying to carry it. I was ready for anything.

I bought a highway map and traced out a route heading east. We would hitchhike across Los Angeles and make our way through central California into southern Nevada. I drew a line up through Utah and Wyoming that headed through the midwest to Chicago. From there it was a straight shot to New York. We hit the road early in the morning.

"No point putting out a sign saying New York." Instead Chuck had prepared one with the vague wording: "Headed east."

At first we inched our way across Orange County. The rides were tiny little jumps carrying us ten miles or twenty miles at a time. Each time we were asked, "Where are you boys going?"

"New York City? I'm only going a couple of miles."

Everyone was in awe of the magnitude of our venture. No matter how short the hop, we got in. A ride is a ride. After twelve hours of continuous itching in the hot sun, we arrived in the town of Barstow, a desert town in central California. It was late in the day and it was blistering hot.

The sun was going down, but it was still close to 100 degrees. We were worn out from wrestling with the sixty pound packs. The bad news was we hadn't gotten out of California. I was discouraged, we had hoped for a better result. I could tell Chuck was frustrated, we sat waiting for our next ride. We were perched on a raised overpass looking out at a vast railway transfer station. Trains were arriving, coupling, and moving off in every direction.

Our canteens were empty and I was hungry and thirsty. We both needed to refill them. I took out my miniature portable chess set and opened the board and made an opening move.

"I'm going down to that service station and fill our canteens." Chuck pointed to a station a few blocks off. "I'll see if I can find out how the trains work."

He took the board and made a move. "You know this isn't much fun. You always win."

"Alright. See what you can get to eat." I was both thirsty and hungry.

He left his backpack and took off with my canteen. Fifteen minutes later he returned with tuna sandwiches and full canteens.

"All the trains coming from the east stop here. They come and go all over the country." He was excited. "We could jump on one and ride it." I could see he wanted to try it. I handed him back the chess board. It was his move. I was closing in on another win.

"How will we get on it? If it's moving, it will be hard with these packs, maybe impossible to board it." I tried to envision us running and jumping onto a moving train with 60 pounds on our backs. It didn't seem possible.

"You're right, jumping on will never work." Chuck moved and handed me back the chess board,

"If we got on one, how would we know where it is going?" I moved and handed him back the board.

"Well, we could get on one that is stopped and wait for it to move." he popped a pimple. He was annoyed with my timidity.

"What if it sits for days? What if they see us sitting there waiting?" I started in on the sandwich he had bought. It had celery mixed in it. "The railway has cops to keep people from riding the trains, you know." The chess board went back and forth several times as we talked.

"You wanna sit here?" He was anxious and had a point. We had been sitting in the desert sun playing chess for an hour and no one had stopped. Perhaps the situation was getting desperate.

"Checkmate!" I captured his King in a little over fifteen moves. His face went sour.

"You won again!" He was resentful.

He had never beaten me, and unless he got better, he never would. I thought it was up to him to get better. Just as soon as the thought entered my mind, a truck stopped. "I'm going to Las Vegas, wanna ride with me?"

That settled it, there would be no train rides on this day.

A little over two hundred miles later we were standing on the outskirts of the city Las Vegas. It gets cold at night in the desert. The moon was three quarters full and we could see sage and tumbleweed everywhere. The sky was crystal clear and full of stars. The night lights from Las Vegas flashed in the distance signaling that the town of "action" was close at hand. Unlike Southern California there was no hint of pollution anywhere. We walked off the road into the desert and went to sleep beneath a bright night sky and slept.

Chapter Four

"I'll let you boys out here!"

The truck driver pulled over and let us out. We climbed down out of his cab on the edge of town. The city lights of Las Vegas blinked just over the hill. He waived as he pulled off. We walked out into the desert and found a quiet place to sleep. I got four hours of sleep in total.

When the bold desert sun, with its piercing beams, opened my eyes I remembered him and the long ride that closed out the first day on the road. The city below was coming to life and it was time for us to get going again. I was encouraged we had made it all the way to Las Vegas.

"If we were still in Barstow, I'd feel like shit." Chuck stretched and got on his feet.

"Yeah that's what I was thinking. We covered a lot of miles last night."

At least we were in a different state and neither of us was discouraged. The desert town was intriguing, I had heard stories about it but had never been there. It bustled in the distance below.

We shouldered the heavy packs and walked off the highway. It was our first night sleeping on the ground under the stars. We were both tired but excited. I wondered what lay ahead.

In the morning we found a nearby gas station and relieved ourselves. In a flash a black and white pulled up in a reckless rush. He has his lights flashing and siren blaring.

"ID's please?" His tone was sharp and critical. We pulled out our ID'S.

"Huntington Beach. You're a long way from home, what are you doing here? His tone was harsh and suspicious.

"We're headed east to New York City," I offered.

"You don't say, I think you might be runaways." He gave me a piercing stare.

"Nah, my mom doesn't care. I got her permission to travel."

"Is that so? Says you're only seventeen. I think I should take you in and see what comes up." His voice was threatening.

Chuck was 18, an adult but I was not. I had the letter my Mom gave me but what if they didn't accept it? What if the cops had trouble reaching my mom? I wasn't sure, I knew I didn't want to be taken in and held. I was vulnerable, Chuck was not.

"I don't care what you're doing. I don't want to see you in town. If you come into town and I see you, I will haul you in. Got it? You'll be a vagrant if I see you in town, I'll arrest both of you." He gave us back the ID's. "Stay out of Vegas."

"Yes sir," we sounded off. He got back in his car, turned off the siren and lights and left.

"What an asshole," Chuck grunted.

"Yeah, but he meant it . He'll arrest us if we go into town." I was spooked.

"Why would we do that? We aren't going to Las Vegas. We're going to New York, who needs stinking Las Vegas?" Chuck spit, he was angry . "He was just trying to intimidate us."

"True and it worked. I want no part of Las Vegas at this moment."

We got out on the highway and stuck out our thumbs heading east. We were like bait in the water being nibbled, our thumbs brought an old Plymouth to our sides. It cruised up and a head with thin, dry, scraggly hair leaned out the window. "Where are you boys goin'?".

"New York City." We offered..

"Long ways. You're in luck cause we're going to Pittsburgh. We can take you to Pittsburgh."

I could believe it.

"Hot damn, we're most of the way there!" Chuck exclaimed.

He got out, opened the trunk and stored our gear. We settled into the back seat of the Plymouth.

"My name's Jeb, and that's Wilbur driving. " Jeb was missing many of his front teeth and those he had were discolored. He had a couple of days of stubble and his eyes were bloodshot. "What do they call you?" he asked us both.

"I'm Luke and this is Chuck." I answered. "It's great you're going all the way to Pittsburgh. I never thought we would get a ride that long. Wow and on our second day!"

"What the cop want with ya? " Wilbur asked from the driver's seat. He had a large scar on his face, and a dent in his forehead. His eyes were bloodshot as well. His teeth were almost a carbon copy of Jeb's, bad and rotting.

"He told us not to try and come into Las Vegas. He told us to move on." I mumbled.

"Run you out of town? You guys got any money?" Wilbur looked at us with a glint in his eye.

"No, we're bumming it." I shot back. His tone caused the hair on my neck to straighten up for a second. I was surprised how I had lied about our money.

It was about six in the morning, and they had country western music playing. Patsy Cline was singing..

"Well, you're welcome to ride all the way to Pittsburgh." smiling like a poorly carved pumpkin.

"Great," Chuck chimed in how grateful he felt.

As we left Vegas the highway veered north. I knew the route would pass through Utah and into Wyoming. Much later it would straighten out and cross the middle states going due east to Chicago. From there it was a straight shot to New York. Or in this case Pittsburgh.

"You guys from Pittsburgh?"

"Naw, Jeb has a brother there, we figure to join up with him." Wilbur grinned again, his mouth showing fewer teeth than I thought.

Things slipped into an uncomfortable quiet, the miles rolled by. Jeb reached into the glove compartment and took out a bottle of Jim Beam. He took a swig and offered it to Wilbur, who took a gulp and looked back at me in the mirror. He shook the bottle at me to see if that would entice me to join in. The bloody rut in his forehead got fresher as the day got brighter, it glistened. It was bleeding. I got the idea it was fresh, a recent wound.

"No thanks, man. I'll pass." I never drink early in the day.

They didn't bother to offer one to Chuck. We were rolling along doing eighty miles an hour. Nevada would soon be a memory and fade into the past.

"Fuck we're out of whiskey!" Jeb tilted the bottle back and made sure he got every last drop out of it.

"Damn, that was quick," he complained, lamenting the loss, he tossed the bottle out and watched it break on the road behind.

I had become fixated on the groove in Wilbur's head. I couldn't take my eyes off of it. It was raw and painful. The brighter the sun got, the more the groove stood out. I couldn't help myself, I was staring at it in the rear view mirror. He caught me.

"You lookin' at my head?" he slurred at me.

"No I lied," He knew it was a lie the moment I said it.

"It don't look so good, do it?" He wasn't going to let it pass. He flashed a crazy goofy smile at me. "Looks a mess….. Don't it?"

"Well what happened?" I decided to take the matter head on.

"I got drunk and got in a fight, and a guy hit me with a pipe. He tried to kill me, knocked me clean out." He grinned his drunken toothless grin again.

"That's too bad." I wasn't sure what to say. I wondered what he found funny about getting hit in the head with a pipe.

"Well Jeb got him. Jeb got him good." Jeb had dialed in on me. Without warning out of nowhere, a pistol appeared in his hand. He was staring at me and shaking the gun in the air.

"We don't own this car. The guy that hit Wilbur did. We stole it from him last night. Along with this gun of his'n. " Jeb flashed the gun again. The gun appeared out of thin air. I could not guess where he had been hiding it. "We got over hundert dollars off him and his keys."

"Bastard had it comin'," Wilbur said with fervor. "Jumpin' me like that."

"Did you kill him?" Alarm bells started ringing in my brain. Who the hell were these guys?

"Don't think so, he was still breathin'. I knocked him cold, but breathin'. When we left." Jeb claimed he had not killed the man.

"It;s all good! We got a hundert dollars and his car. There's a bulletin out for this car. We are gettin' near the Utah border. When we get to the border, we're goin' stop for gas." Jeb stopped talking and stared at me waiting for a reaction.

"Right. I guess you stole the car." I couldn't think of what to say.

"Wilbur's goin' pump gas, I'm goin' on in the station and rob em, we'll snatch some booze and stuff, and we'll jump the state line. I need you boys to keep quiet and sit there. Okay?" He

As he finished explaining his plan a sign saying "State Line ahead in five miles" rolled past. They stopped at a gas station, and left us in the back seats. Wilbur got out and started pumping gas. Jeb headed in to rob the store.

"I feel like shitting in my pants." Chuck was white as a sheet.

"They've got all our stuff in the trunk. I'm scared too. Just sit tight, I'll think of something." I had no clear plan, but one soon came to me. Chuck's mouth was twitching as he tried to smile. I hoped he hadn't shit in his pants.

Wilbur filled up the tank and topped it off. Jeb came hauling back in a rush. Both he and Jeb jumped back in. Jeb had a handful of twenty dollar bills. He rolled them in his fingers and waved them. "Piece of cake."

"Car's full of gas" Wilbur pipes up. "How'd it go?"

"Hit him in the head, no shots fired." Jeb gunned the engine and took off. "He never saw it comin. One solid knock and he fell hard."

Silence ensued. We crossed the state line and headed into Utah. They relaxed. New state, new law enforcement. For them every state line was going to be a new start. A place to fuel up. I decided I couldn't allow it to continue.

"I have a lot of family in Utah, in fact I was born in Salt Lake City." I started to put my proposal out there. It was true. I did have relatives in Utah. I had not planned on seeing them. "I've decided I want to visit my Mormon family."

Jeb and Wilbur stared at each other. A long frozen silence followed. They rolled along for a bit and whispered between each other. Jeb turned and looked me in the eyes.

"We got warrants out for us in at least three states." Jeb emphasized the word "warrants" and narrowed his eyes to the size of slits.

I realized they each had a fresh bottle of whiskey.

"Damn boys, I don't know what I want to do with you. I thought you wanted to go to New York. Now you want us to turn you loose. All we did was rob a filling station. Nothing much harm done!" It was Wilbur, he wasn't happy either.

"You boys thinkin' of turnin' us in?" Jeb was worked up and getting angry and upset at the thought of our potential betrayal.

"No, no. My mother was born Mormon, I was born in Salt Lake." I stuck to my story.

"I don't think we can let you guys out." Jeb was chugging on his bottle. His face was contorted. He was getting more and more hostile.

"We won't tell anybody, I promise!" Chuck was desperate.

"I'll think on it a bit." Wilbur was in charge, I could tell it was his decision on what to do with us.

The miles rolled by. The two of them exchanged whispers. They kept talking but I couldn't make out what they were saying. They both kept on drinking, they were draining the fresh new bottle they had stolen. I knew for sure I didn't want to stay with them and rob my way across the U.S. Who knew what they might be capable of doing? I thought of our packs and the cash we had hid in them.

"My uncle's a good guy, in fact I have three Uncles there and many cousins in Utah." I broke the silence.

"Three uncles, what are their names?" Wilbur squinted at me.

"Ray, Jack and Gene." I fired back hoping to instill some confidence in my plan.

"So you want to go see them?" Wilbur wasn't buying it. "Why didn't you want to go see them before?"

"I didn't know you guys before. Now I do." I decided to try telling them the truth. "I don't want to be a part of what you are doing. Robbing people is not my thing. Hitting people over the head is not my thing. I want no part of it."

"Well I guess I can understand that. Tell you what, there's a turn off comin' up soon." He had a road map in his hand. 'I'm thinkin' bout drivin' you out ten, or fifteen miles into the desert and leave you. If I let you go, don't you think about turnin' us in. If you do, I'll get you!"

Wilbur had come up with an alternative to murdering us. He would take us out in the middle of nowhere and drop us in the desert. We would have to deal with the burning hot sun. Thank God, I thought.

It was dry hot terrain, with burnt hills, and a long canyon road. We drove along a narrow dirt road until it dipped down to a dried up river bed. Wilbur stopped and motioned for us to get out.

"We're gonna leave you here." He got out, opened the trunk and let us get our packs.

" You'll be long gone. I like the idea."

Wilbur was proud of himself for having come up with such a brilliant solution to the problem. "It's mighty hot out here, you should take your time, conserve your strength. It's a long way back to the highway."

It was a hundred degrees or more, the packs weighed sixty pounds, we were almost out of water, and hungry. They slammed the doors, took off in a cloud of dust and left us standing there. The hot sun beamed down on us.

"Remember, you Fucks, don't turn us in or else." It was Wilbur's angry voice screaming back at me. Jeb waved a threatening pistol out the window and fired a shot in the air as the car drove off. I could hear them both laughing hysterically.

"Shit! We're screwed."

"At least they didn't shoot us." And they didn't rob us either, I thought with relief. Somehow they did not search us to see what we had on us. It was lucky. We still had our cash!

We lifted up the heavy packs and started the long trek back to the road. We managed to walk a total of three hundred yards when a jeep came speeding around the corner. The driver saw us, and slammed on his brakes.

"What in the hell are you doing out here?" He had on some light clothes, and a visor. It turned out he had been out surveying rock formations for an oil company.

"We need a ride back to the highway,"

"Hop in. You must be thirsty?" He handed me a canteen. "How'd you boys get out here?"

"Long story, I'm glad you came around the corner when you did."

"Where are you going?" He asked a familiar question.

"New York City," Chuck told him.

"That's crazy. This ain't the way to New York, that's for sure. Well I am going back to the highway, and down to Vegas." He answered. He must have thought we were nuts, but he took us right back to the turn off and the highway.

Chapter Five

We stood on the highway with our thumbs out. I knew right away we could not let the criminals stop our trip. I pulled out my board and we began playing chess. There was no further sign of Jeb or Wilbur, they were long gone.

"You wanna do anything about those guys? Do you think we should report them?"

"Well, I do, but when?" We were in the middle of Utah, far from a pay phone and alone. What were our options?

"I am sure they'll be in the next state by the time we get a chance to report them." I said.

"Yeah, where's a cop when you need one?"

We sat waiting and playing chess for over an hour, no one stopped. The cars flew by at high speeds. People drive at much higher speeds in the open desert. Chuck was improving at chess, and was playing a little better. Our games were lasting longer but I still won all three of them. He was irritated with losing, but I couldn't let him win. If he was going to win, he had to do it on his own. Like me he had a competitive nature and losing didn't sit well with him. "Let him beat me if he can." I could not throw a game by not trying. It's not in my nature.

Finally, a trucker stopped and picked us up on his way to Wyoming. He had a sleeping compartment in the back of his cab, Chuck climbed up in it and went to sleep. Thankfully the trucker did not care for conversation. After Wilbur and Jed I was thankful to be riding with a calm, sane working man. Nothing of merit was passed between us except for some road miles. His ride took us the rest of the length of Utah. It was dark when we crossed into Wyoming.

"This is my first visit to Wyoming." I broke a long silence as he slowed down and prepared to stop.

"There's a railway shack off to the side of the road, it's vacant, you can sleep inside if you want." He indicated we were to get out of his truck.

We hopped out. Sure enough, there was a wooden shack only a short distance away. The door was broken, it had been forced open in the recent past. We tried to sleep but every few hours a train roared by, rattling the shack, keeping us awake. The trains came one after another all night long. We curled up in our bags unable to sleep.

"Those guys were real assholes." Chuck was talking about Jeb and Wilbur.

"Yeah I thought they were bad when we got in the car. Smelly, dirty. We should have known they weren't normal guys." I had been thinking about it. "We need to use better judgment."

"Yeah, It makes sense. If we don't like someone, we should think about refusing the ride." Chuck agreed.

"Okay, in the future I'll give you a signal if I think someone might be a problem."

"Yeah, I'll do the same."

I closed my eyes and tried to go to sleep. The trains kept coming and each time they did they jolted me awake. I thought I heard Chuck snoring but then he broke the silence and spoke in a low shaky voice.

"I have something I want to ask you. It's personal." Chuck's voice was vibrating with emotion. "I have been thinking about it for a while and have been afraid to ask."

"Okay, what's up?" He paused and took a long period of silence.

"Do you think homosexuality is inherited?" Chuck's voice had become small and distant in the dark room. He was lying a few feet away but it felt like he was miles away.

"What? Homosexuality? Inherited?" I had never thought about it. "Why are you asking?"

There was another lengthy silence. I waited wondering what was coming. What had prompted Chuck to ask his strange question.

"Remember when I told you my father got in trouble with the law?"

"Yeah, sort of. Yeah, sure I do."

"Well he seduced our paperboy and had sex with him. The paperboy was still a kid, my father was arrested and sent to prison." Chuck's voice was quivering and shaking. He was humiliated.

I was dumbfounded. I lay there silent thinking of what to say. I didn't say anything. I couldn't think of anything.

"My mother moved us to Huntington Beach to get away from the shit storm it all caused. She had to get away from all the gossip. The whole town was talking behind our backs, and it got to where I heard their whispers everywhere I went. But after a while it was to my face. It became accusatory, "You're a homo aren't you?" or "You're the same like your father," It was mean and hateful. People I thought I knew either shunned me or attacked me. My whole family became outcasts."

"That must have been hard to take! I feel for you and your family." A wave of disgust swept over me. I wondered what it was I was disgusted by? By his father and what he did. Or was it by the way those people had reacted? I knew Chuck wasn't to blame. Why did they blame Chuck? For a moment I didn't know and I wasn't sure. It was unknown territory. I had a sinking feeling. Why? I didn't know.

"It was awful. The police broke into our house and arrested him in front of the whole neighborhood. They took my Dad away in handcuffs. Everyone saw it happen," I let Chuck speak without making a comment. I was at a loss for words. "Soon enough, they all knew why. The whole neighborhood knew our story!"

"So that's why you asked if I think it is inherited? Because of what people said.?"

"It is not that simple, I wonder, am I like my Dad?"

Then it hit me. I had never seen Chuck with a girl, never once. I had never thought about it. He knew some of the girls I had dated, but I didn't know any of his. It could not be a coincidence. How had I missed the clues?

"I don't know much about it. They say we're all like our parents. We look like them. We inherit a lot from them. But I don't know about something like homosexuality. I don't think so, but I don't know. Is he still in jail?"

The room was dark and cold. I became aware we were alone in the mountains. At that moment I felt like I didn't know Chuck at all. Where was he going with this? Why had he waited till now to tell me all this?

"He has two more years, but he might get out early." Chuck's voice was flat. I wondered if he cared, if he wanted to see his dad again. His tone had become cold and unfeeling.

"My Dad and mom divorced a long time ago. I haven't seen my father in years. He left and deserted me and I miss him a lot. Now all I got is Bud and he is worthless. At least you know where your father is." I shared some of my own pain.

"At first my mom took us to see him in jail. But later she decided, she didn't want me to see him anymore. She stopped taking me to see him. It's like I said she is all alone. Everyone made life hard for her. Acting like she was to blame. She had to get away, so we moved. We all had to get away. Everyone was treating us so differently.

"Did he rape the kid? Why did they put him in jail?"I struggled with the shock I felt and searched for something to say.

"He was your age, seventeen when his parents found out. It had been going on for a while.They were furious.They went to the police and filed a complaint." Chuck's voice was shaking as he spoke. Then he continued:

"I'm eighteen, been eighteen for four months. If I had sex with you, it would be a crime for me, not you. I'm an adult and you're not. Not until your eighteenth birthday."

"The boy didn't complain?" I wondered how it would be a crime if they both agreed to do the thing.

"I don't think so. I think the boy was queer and my Dad knew it. The kid didn't say much at the trial. It didn't matter what he wanted. He was not on trial. His parents were angry and the law is clear. Adults can't have sex with minors. Men cannot have sex with boys."

"You have feelings for both sexes?" I felt strange asking, Chuck and I were teammates. We undressed side by side in the locker room. It was common for boys to accuse each other of being queer and tease each other about it. I had never known anyone who was gay until now. This was not a locker room joke.

"It's confusing. But yeah I do. I have had these feelings for a long time. My interest in boys has been getting stronger and stronger. But I don't want to end up like my Dad. I am afraid I might."

The room went silent again. I thought about it for a long time. I had no such feelings. I didn't have fantasies or daydreams about other boys. Did he have feelings for me? Did he want to act on them? I felt like I needed to ask but was not sure how to."I am sure you are not alone with this. I don't share your confusion. I don't have those feelings. It's not something I want to explore. But I am sure someone out there does. You need to talk with them. Find someone who feels like you do."

"I went through my father's things when he went to jail. He had books, magazines, things about being queer. My mom tried to hide them, but I found them." His voice had firmed up, and gotten stronger.

"What was in them?" I had an old issue or two of Playboy. They were worn out from use. I was hiding them in my sock drawer.

"I learned most people who are queer try to hide the fact. Especially in small towns like ours. But in some places they don't. They are "out" and let the world know how they feel. There is a huge community like in New York. I read about it. There is a queer community in the Village in New York."

In a flash I understood. It hit me. That was why Chuck had suggested New York as a destination! Of course! Now it was obvious.

"There's a lot of things to do and see in New York, but when I read there are a whole lot of people who are "out" living there. I felt like I needed to see what it is like. I don't like hiding all the time."

"All this time and I didn't know. You hide it well." We both went quiet and listened to the sound of water running down the mountains.

"Well I am not sure I am queer, but I think about it a lot. I decided I had to tell you."

"I'm glad you did." I answered.

Chuck's voice was frightened and weak throughout his confession. It occurred to me he was afraid of what I might do or say. I stayed quiet and tried to understand it. Then he went silent and we drifted off to sleep.

That night I dreamed of running water, and swimming in the ocean. Water has always been in my dreams. Before I fell asleep I thought about Chuck and how we were going to spend the summer together. His disclosure about having homosexual feelings nagged at me. What did he want from me? I I was about to find out. The wheels were turning but what lay ahead was a mystery.

Chapter Six

We woke up early, the birds were chirping, and the sound of water rushing down the mountain side was loud and clear. All night the sound of running water had been gnawing at the edges of my consciousness. But now as I stepped outside the fast moving runoff was everywhere. Rivlets were speeding down the mountain and flowing uncontrolled across the highway. The winter snowpack was melting. Seasonal waterfalls gushed downward forming a central stream right below the shack where we had slept. I felt alive. I took some deep breaths of unpolluted air, and felt my blood pump. This was not Los Angeles or Huntington Beach, for that matter. These were the high mountains. I felt the energy and power of the natural world pulsing in my veins.

"It's great to be in Wyoming." Chuck was up as well. He joined me in savoring the crisp clean air.

"Yeah, I love the mountains." I pounded my chest,

"Listen about last night's conversation, I am not sure what came over me, I want to say," he was looking at me with a frightened look in his eyes. He didn't finish the sentence, but I knew he was worried. Worried I was judging him.

"I'm glad you told me. It was important. Please, we're friends. It is new to me, let me digest it, but please don't worry about it." The details of Chuck's revelations had been sinking in and I was trying to figure out what it all meant.

"Well, we can't stay here," Chuck averted my eyes.

"Of course not, we need to get moving." I thought about exploring but we had to get back on the road. We rolled up the bags and we were ready to go.

The highway was quiet, and had few cars passing by. We were playing chess again. As always, I won, and Chuck took losing hard. No one likes losing, but he was not in my league. After two hours of playing chess with our thumbs out, we got a ride. A man stopped. He was about to cross the mountains into the high plains of Wyoming. We hopped in.

"The roads are slow, there's a lot of water running off. I'll need to be careful."

"Well, we're glad you stopped," I chimed in.

"It's been raining for a week straight and the snowpack is melting. It's dangerous." He gave me a knowing look as if trying to let me know he was a careful man.

The trip through the mountains was slow. Small landslides blocked parts of the road. In spots the water was a foot deep and pouring across the lanes. The bends and turns were sharp and the road was often narrowed. A couple of small boulders had come to rest . He maneuvered gingerly around the obstacles.

In spite of the hazardous conditions it was impossible to ignore the grandeur of the mountain scenery. At some turns the vista opened up and treated us to an incredible panorama of high snow-capped mountains all standing like brothers shoulder to shoulder as if in a group photo. It was awesome. With the windows cracked we were treated to the delicious smell of fresh mountain air flowing in. The cool air kept us all awake and our driver alert.

"There are highway workers ahead. I think the road might be washed out." He slowed the car down to slow grind. He pointed to a temporary road sign. "Slow Workers Ahead".

A crew of highway workers were out and about. They were tending to a spot where a foot or more of water was gushing across the road. It was clear that several big boulders had landed on the road in a slide but the workers had rolled them away. A clear path had been cleared through the pile of debris.

"They got here a while ago, this trip it's been cleared. Last time I had to wait over a day to get through." He grinned at me with relief shining everywhere in his smile. The water was pushing hard against the side of our car. It had real power and force, it lifted the car up a couple of inches and we slid to the rig. The car seemed to glide and slide towards the edge of the road but the danger passed when it began to descend on a downward angle. Relieved we had passed the peaks and were leaving the higher points behind.

After a while we made it through the passes and into Cheyenne. He had been quiet and courteous, a far cry from Wilbur and Jed. Our conversations had been infrequent and slow paced, I liked him. It was dim out, the sun was hiding under the cloud cover. We looked up to see a familiar sign, the golden arches, of a local McDonald's. It advertised a fifteen cent cheeseburger! It was the same price as California. Hamburgers were a dime. They were small, but at ten cents a bargain. A coke, two little burgers each, plus fries for under a half buck. Sold!

As we walked up to the stand, I parked near a familiar car, with two familiar people sitting in the front seat eating.

"Brad, is it you?" It was a pal from Huntington. Kramer was with him. Jeez, what a coincidence.

"Luke, what in the hell are you doing here?" He was amazed. "Small world for sure." His voice was friendly and warm.

"We're on our way to New York. What are you doing here?" I was stunned to see someone I knew from home a thousand miles away. "

We have finished up a fishing trip." He said.

"Well it is incredible to see you."

"I could not think of anything more to say.

"Well, we'll see you." I shrugged my shoulders.

"See you," he answered back.

The burgers were good, it was the first red meat we had eaten for several days. We wolfed them down.

"Strange to see Brad, here in Wyoming." Chuck commented. "I think we should keep going," he spoke with conviction. "There is a lot of daylight left."

Two more victorious chess games later and we landed a ride. A long, slick Cadillac pulled up with a thin nervous man peeking out from behind the wheel.

"Where are you boys headed?"

We told him and he responded, "I'm going as far as Iowa. Wanna go there? I'm planning on driving all night. I am going straight through Nebraska. I need someone to talk to, I gotta stay awake." I decided on the back seat. Chuck could handle the talking for a while. It was late afternoon and I wanted some shut eye.

We rolled and rolled. After a time it became a two lane highway and there was nothing on either side but row upon row of corn. Nebraska is a long flat state dominated by corn fields. There were no other cars on the road, or so it seemed. He was cruising at a hundred miles per hour. I fell asleep as night descended. I was aware of the tires rolling but the sound became monotonous and vanished in the background.

"BANG"- a loud explosion erupted and the car's tires grabbed the road. We skidded and slid right off the road. I was tossed up against the front seats. My light sleep was shattered. A tire had blown and the car had swerved out of control.

"Thump! Thump! Thump!" Something was pounding against the windshield as we flew out into the field.

"Thunk! Thunk! Thunk! It was the sound of ears of corn breaking on the windshield. I raised my head in time to see the oncoming rush of corn smashing against the front window. The front window broke and a foot long crack appeared. We were off the road and had skidded into a field. The car came to a rest in between rows of corn stalks sandwiched up against the side windows.

"Shit!" Our voices rang out in unison!

"You alright?" It was the driver. "Everyone okay?"

"Yeah, how about up there?" I fired back.

"Fuck, I blew a tire again. I knew the damn things were worn down."

I thought, worn tires and he's been flying along at a hundred miles an hour. What next? I felt bruised on my left side.

"Can you get out and help me change the tire? I have a spare left. I think we can get out of here and back on the road. I need your help."

An hour later Chuck and I pushed the car towards the road, he spun out of the field and edged back on the road. I decided to sit in the front seat.

"You should go a little slower," I suggested.

"Yeah, I guess 80 will do, we are closer now. I'm going to make it by morning." He pulled out a little match box and slid it open. There were half a dozen little white pills in it. "Beans, speed, they will keep you awake." His eyes popped out at me. "Want one?"

"No, I think I'm awake now." Nothing like a drive into a corn field to wake you right up. Four hours later dawn broke, the sun was on the cusp of rising. We passed a sign, "Now Entering Tipton, Iowa, population 645."

"This is home to me," he grinned.

"Why were you in such a hurry to get here?" Looking around, I couldn't believe anything in Tipton required urgency.

"My sister's getting married today." He got off the highway and drove into town. He idled the car engine pulling into a small park. It had a restroom, some picnic benches, a horseshoe pit, and a little fountain with water bubbling up.

"I need you to get out here." We did. "Bye." He drove off.

"I could use a bath," Chuck nodded at the fountain. " It's been three days now."

"I see your point. I might smell it a little too." We had slept outside, and in strange cars, we needed to clean up. The fountain water was cold, too cold, I put my hand in it, but decided it didn't matter, I needed to wash up. I thought a light sponge bath would do the trick.

No sooner had we taken off our shirts, and started washing our armpits, when a black and white with its sirens blazing pulled up. The officer came out of his car bent like he expected to take fire. He had his gun drawn. I kept my armpits up.

"Morning officer, nice morning for a sponge bath, don't you think?" I gave him my gentlest smile. He was pointing his pistol right at me.

"What the hell are you doing?" he had a heat on. I could see his temperature was rising fast. There was no telling what he might do. We scared him to death.

"We were just let off here hitchhiking, saw the fountain, and decided to take a sponge bath." I replied. Chuck looked at his feet and kept his mouth shut.

"This ain't a public bath. How much money have you got?" the officer lowered the gun from my head to my gut. I thought, "Great now he'll blow my guts out instead of shooting my head off."

"Money, are you going to charge us for the water we use?" I couldn't believe it. He still had the gun pointed right at me. I squirmed. I could see his face was taunt. He was wound up tight.

"I want to know if you are vagrants, anyone entering town on foot with less than $30.00 is a vagrant. If you are, you're subject to arrest."

Vagrancy. It was news to me.

"We each have far more. If you'll let me get to my pack I can fetch my wallet and show you." With arm pits up I motioned to the packs. He relaxed a bit, and let me retrieve my pack. I found my wallet and pulled out my cash and showed him I was not a vagrant. I had the cash to prove it.

"Well, I'm going to drive you out to the edge of town. You're going to get out of here. Clear out of Tipton." I decided he must be the official welcoming committee for 17 or 18 year olds in Tipton.

"Okay, I was hoping to stop at a store and pick up a little bit to eat." It had been a long time since McDonalds in Wyoming. "We haven't had the chance to eat for a while."

"That's not happening. " He lowered the gun, at least I was not in jeopardy of being shot by accident. It occurred to me neither Jeb nor Wilbur had ever pointed a gun at me. They only fired in the air. I wondered which situation was the most dangerous. I decided it was this one for sure, one slip, one false move and he would have killed me.

The edge of town turned out to be about a mile away. Tipton was not a big town but it was spread out. Right after the officer turned us loose a farmer came by and told us to hop in the back of his pickup and drove us the rest of the way out of town.

I was hungry but we were on our way to Chicago. We short hopped our way to the Illinois border. None of the rides were memorable. A little ways across the Illinois line we got a ride with a guy in his 30's. He was on his way to the Chicago suburbs.

"I'm getting home from a business trip. I graduated from Wisconsin a few years ago, I'm in sales now. You know Madison?" He had on casual clothes, his hair was a little long for a business type. He had a friendly smile and voice.

"Not much, it's the home of the Badgers? Right?" I knew my Rose bowl games. I also knew it was known as a liberal place. That meant he might be "alright".

"Right, right," he said. He soon realized we were a couple of harmless young guys embarked on an adventure. Neither one of us drank and had only sampled a small amount of drugs. We were not hippies or bums. We were young and about to enter college. We were explorers.

"How do you feel about the war?" he asked me out of the blue for no apparent reason.

"I'm against it, it'll turn out badly, and a lot of people will be hurt by it." It was my honest opinion, and I offered it freely.

"More and more people in Madison are starting to feel the same. Why do you feel that way?"

"Well, two years ago, my family moved into a small apartment. Next door was a large Hawaiian family. Grandfather, Grandma, two women, five children, all living in a two bedroom apartment. The husbands were marines, away in Vietnam. Donnie and Ronnie, I guess. I never met them. They were killed together in a firefight and the notice came in the middle of the night. The walls were thin and I heard the women crying all night long."

"Oh," he blinked at me. "That sounds awful"

"Well, Vietnam got on my map that night. I read a bit, and learned the French had been at war there for fifty years. And now we are trying to maintain and prop up what the French left behind." I was up on my soap box again. It was like I was passing out anti-war fliers all over again.

"Ho Chi Minh went to the Versailles peace conference claiming he represented the people of Indochina. The French police hounded him, broke into his room, followed him everywhere." Chuck burst in. He knew the story as well as I did. Neither of us believed in the Domino theory and we did not believe the communists were soon to be poised on our border ready to take over our country.

"I didn't know that," the driver was named Michael, he was a "nice" guy. "That's news to me. The Versailles thing happened in 1919 didn't it? I didn't know Ho Chi Minh went to Versailles."

"Yeah! He appointed himself." I said. "If the French had been willing to give IndoChina its freedom, none of this would have ever happened. But the French refused to give up their colonies! They were hell bent on keeping their empire intact and that resulted in 30 years of Vietnamese resistance. When they began to lose in the 1950's we started helping the French and sending advisors to Vietnam. When the French were defeated, we stepped in." I had Arnold Toynbee's essays at my fingertips.

The conversation continued on into the night, and we all decided the best thing for the U.S. to do was work out a peaceful solution and leave Vietnam to the people who lived there. It thought it was clear, and we "knew" we were right. There was a general warm feeling of agreement in the car. There is nothing like debating with people who agree with you to get to the bottom of things.

"Listen, I want you to come home with me tonight, meet my wife. I have two kids, I'll buy us all some burgers and fries, and in the morning I'll take you back to the main highway. How does that sound?" Michael was having a "nice" attack. It sounded great and I encouraged him.

Mike's house was a two story brick structure with a wooden fence in the suburbs. There was a dog house visible with a sleeping dog who woke when the car arrived. It barked at Mike, jumping on him and licking him when he pushed open the fence gate.

Nice, I thought. Seconds later we exploded through Mike's front door with a load of aromatic burgers, fries and malts in our hands. Mike's wife could barely keep her feet when the three of us came tramping in the door. For a second I thought she might faint. I could see she was not expecting the two of us with our sixty pound packs on our backs, and bags of burgers in hand. How could she have guessed her "nice" husband was bringing home two strange young men without warning?

"This is Chuck and Luke, I picked them up hitchhiking, we had a great conversation about politics and the war. I told them they could sleep over tonight. On our floor. They are on their way to New York City." Mike was sure he knew his wife. But on the subject of bringing home footloose boys he was about to learn he did not.

Mike's wife's name was Madeline, Maddie for short, and she could not hide her dismay. I am not sure how she kept upright on her feet. It was clear blood was rushing to her head. She put her hand out feeling for the wall.

"Okay," she managed. "Mike, can you come into the kitchen?" Maddie asked and Mike went.

They vanished into the kitchen straight away. I felt for her situation, she had two young boys, four or five years old, who were dressed in their pajamas and waiting up late for their Dad.

Chuck was sure to pop a pimple at any time, and neither of us had been able to finish our sponge bath. We smelled bad and the sight of us rampaging through her door unannounced was a shock for sure.

A few minutes later Mike appeared with a sheepish grin on his face. " Listen guys, Maddie is a little unnerved, and doesn't want you here tonight."

"That's okay," I was half way through the burger and many of the fries were already resting comfortably in my tummy. "We don't need to stay here."

Maddie appeared to gather up her children, and whisk them off to safety in the kitchen. She nodded at us, unable to verbalize her horror.

Her television had the news on, and Walter Cronkite gave a figure of twenty eight body bags for the week, all were loaded and on flights back to the USA. The enemy, he assured us, had suffered far greater casualties.

It all served to assure us "Happy Days" were here again. We were winning and could be sure of that tonight. The score was the Viet Cong with many hundreds of dead, and the USA only 28. As always it was presented as "good" news.

The ride Mike had given us had been a long one, hundreds of miles through many small cities. The burger and fries were far more than we expected, so what did we have to complain about?

Mike apologized several times for his wife's behavior, they were a long way from Madison. Her liberal college days were fading for sure. But I had seen the look of terror in her eyes, and was kind of glad I didn't have to deal with her all night. I am not a dangerous soul. I felt good about leaving. We had created terror in her house, so I was happy to go.

"Don't worry, Mike, we are used to this kind of stuff." But in reality it was the first time it had ever happened and the last. I waved at him as the car door closed and he dropped us off in the middle of the city of Chicago. I had no idea where we were, where the highway was, or what the hell was going on around me. There were a lot of flashing neon lights, a lot of noise, and a lot of raggedly dressed old men milling about. Chuck popped a pimple as usual.

"Well, what do you want to do?" as always he expected me to save the day.

I did not have an answer but one appeared. It was right across the street.I pointed to the flashing marquee of an all night movie theater. Pay one admission and you could stay the night. That's what the sign said, and by God when we approached, it meant it. If we bought a seat for 50 cents, we could stay the night.

"Let's go in here, I don't want to sleep on these streets." It was windy, cold, late, and there were no friendly rattling sounds as there had been in the desert. The movie was a gangster movie I had never heard of, but who cared, I intended to sleep, and figure out what to do when the sun came up.

There were only a couple of things wrong with my inspiration. The theater was right on the "L" loop so trains came roaring by on a regular basis in the middle of the night. The seats were cramped with little or no leg room, and our huge packs took up a lot of space as well.

The theater was deserted so there was no competition from other patrons. We were able to spread out a little but it was not comfortable at all. I bought popcorn. It was a force of habit. I always have popcorn when I go to the movies. It was stale, but I munched it and tried to watch the picture. How bad could it be? After all, I had paid for it.

The movie was awful, a man was caught and convicted of a capital crime and sentenced to death in the gas chamber. The doomed man was strapped in the chair, blindfolded (I have no idea why) and gagged. A hand, unattached to a body hidden off the screen kept coming on screen from the side of the camera shot. The hand dropped pellets into a bucket and began to let off an expanding gas. The killer poisonous gas filled the room, the man struggled in his chair and died, choking to death. Every time the "L" train rattled the theater I woke up and this same scene was replayed, again, and again. The criminal died over and over again.

I was forced to wake up each time a train passed, and made to squint out of half-opened eyes. I was treated to this nightmarish scene all night long. I must have watched the death scene ten times. Jeeze. Thanks Mike, thanks Maddie, I couldn't help but think of them. They had sentenced me to a night of watching death by gas chamber.

We had a hard time getting out of Chicago. Mike had taken us to a rough part of town and it was impossible to hitchhike in. It was my first real experience trying to hitchhike in a big city. A city bustles, has a cadence, and two young guys trying to hitchhike out of it were not the norm. Rides didn't come easily. In fact they never came at all.

We were in trouble. I decided we needed to take buses to the edge of town, and walk to the highway. It took a lot of effort and many hours to get out of Chicago. I knew nothing about the idea of rush hour. Getting to work at a specified time, punching in, were not things I had any knowledge of and I was amazed at the thousands of people trying to do it. It took an effort but we were able to get out of town. After having experienced Chicago, I wondered what New York was like.

Chapter Seven

"I want to visit Notre Dame." Chuck made the suggestion out of the blue. We were on the road having left the all night movie theater behind. I pulled out my map and saw that South Bend was close, less than a hundred miles away.

"Why Notre Dame?" We were more than halfway to New York and my anticipation was building. The goal was within sight and I could taste success.

"I have dreamed about it since I was a kid," he said.

"How so? " I asked. "It doesn't sound like you. It's a religious school. You're not religious."

"Well my Mom is Catholic, and we used to go to Mass. Notre Dame has an aura. I have always thought it was an important place."

I was still trying to process Chuck' revelations about his father's confinement in prison and his apparent attraction to men. Why did he now want to visit a famous religious school? It was confusing. I was not sure what to think.

I asked myself "What should I do about this?" There was no answer. He was a friend, and we were on a road trip committed to protecting each other. I decided I needed to honor his request. Visiting a place he had dreamed about did not seem like much to ask.

"It is right on the way. It will be an easy side trip.I guess we can go by and see what's there." I said.

"It has a famous football program.We could see the stadium. A ton of famous players have played there."

I grew up watching a lot of Notre Dame football. They were always on television.They had won several national championships and were good every year. Most years they were great!

"Okay, Let's go pat "touchdown Jesus" on the butt." I said smiling. It was a Notre Dame tradition. I began thinking about the absurdity of someone thinking Jesus was somehow on the sideline assisting a particular football team. It never ceased to amaze me. What could be more arrogant than thinking God's son was on your side and only your side?

The campus was a hundred miles from Chicago and we were there in less than three hours. It was a harsh day, the wind was howling. All the streets were deserted.

School was out and no one was about. The campus was huge and things were a long walk away. We tried to hitchhike on the campus and never got a single ride. We had to walk and tote our heavy packs every step of the way.

At first, we wandered about, but soon found signs marking the way to the football stadium. My mind flashed back to a recent USC game. In the game Mike Garrett scored touchdown after touchdown in the second half and inspired a twenty four point comeback. It was a USC home game, and God was not on Notre Dames' side that afternoon.

Touchdown Jesus did not carry the day for Notre Dame. It was apparent God was not tackling or blocking well because he was having real problems with Garrett. The stadium was empty and locked. There was no one around. I was disappointed, Chuck was crushed. Our visit had been futile, it was not the right time of year. Football season was four months away.

"I was surprised when you said you wanted to come here. If there was one thing I thought I knew about you, it was you did not believe in Christianity." I chided him for wasting time.

"Well, Christianity is a part of my past. My mother's side of the family of course. I admire Jesus and his ethics." He was sheepish and a bit embarrassed.

"Yeah, I guess it is a little like what Mark Twain said, "I admire any true Christian, I hope I get the honor of meeting one, one of these days."

As far as I knew Chuck was not a Christian. It is something we shared. He had often made fun of well known passages from the Bible. Many of which we thought were not credible.

As we headed back to the road my mind flashed back to one such episode from our recent past. It was the night of our graduation party and we consumed a fifth of vodka. The booze hit him hard and fast. It inspired him to reenact his "version" of the conversation between Moses and the burning bush. His presentation was packed with doubt that a burning bush could be a holy messenger and deliver God's word.

"A bush! Try to imagine a talking bush on fire! Where are the lips? In the flames, or the bush?" Chuck was tipsy.

"I never thought about it. Why does there have to be a mouth?" I asked knowing a mouth implied a head and that implied a body. All we have to work with in the bible is a bush on fire. Our imaginations have to fill in the details.

"Talk about ludicrous. How many talking bushes have you seen in your life?" He waited for me to answer. I didn't bother to try.

"None! And it will never happen! It is as irrational as a talking donkey!" Chuck loved to remind me of the obscure story of Balaam's talking donkey. It was his contention the Bible's infamous talking donkey was the true inspiration behind the television character, Mr.Ed.

"Once you establish a talking donkey can be real, the next step up the ladder is a talking horse, and so I give you, Mr. Ed. Mr. Ed is the direct descendent of the Bibles' talking donkey." Chuck took a bow to let me know how impressed he was with the logical headway he was making in explaining the TV show.

"Yeah, not many people know the story about Balaam's donkey. Even fewer connect him to Mr. Ed. Sometimes I think these bible stories were the marvel comics of their day." I acknowledge Chuck's obsession with the donkey story and its probable connection to Mr. Ed.

"If there had been a talking donkey in those times it would have spoken aramaic. When have you ever met a donkey that was fluent in aramaic?" Chuck was determined to keep his argument on point.

Chuck was drunk on vodka! He was barely getting started and I was to be the recipient of his presentation.

"Snap, Crackle, Pop!" Chuck was singing a chorus! The line caused a vision of Mary Poppins to flash through my brain. It was the "Snap, Crackle, Pop!" reference that stuck in my head.

"These are a few of the things a burning bush brings!"

"Snap, Crackle Pop!" The chorus had become a mantra.

"Moses, Go to the Mountain Top!" Chuck's voice took on a deep authoritative commanding tone.

And with that Mary Poppins began singing once again

"… Snap, Crackle, Pop?"

"I'm lost, Lord, it's been forty years in the desert, give me a sign!" Chuck took on an incarnation of Moses, shaking and cowering in fear.

"Forty years, Lord, forty years of wandering in the desert. It's been a long, long time." Chuck's imitation of Moses was on the mark.

"Go up to the mountain top!" The voice of God was back in command!

"I have been lost in the desert for forty years.I don't see any mountains. What mountain? The desert is flat as hell."

"Snap, Crackle, Pop!" Mary Poppins came dancing in a chorus line.

"Snap, Snap, Snap… I am the Lord your God! Snap, Snap, Crackle, Crackle, Pop! Pop!"

He proceeded to do all three voices one after the other. Moving majestically from the commanding voice of God, to the yiddish voice of Moses and finally to Mary Poppins singing Snap, Crackle and Pop. It was classic Chuck weirdness.

Nearly everyone I grew up with told me they were "true believers." They all claimed to know the truth" and when anything else did not fit their beliefs it was "superstition." My whole life I felt I was surrounded by Christians. Many of them were convinced I was a damned soul and didn't mind telling me so to my face. As Chuck did his impersonation of the "burning bush talking trash", I thought of them and how they would be appalled.

"They'd hang you in the middle ages for this." I said bringing an end to the spectacle.

"I've been practicing this routine, do you like it? It needs some polish, I am only getting started. There's a lot more!"

"I'm sure there is." I said, "I got the idea."

When it was over I wasn't sure if Moses was having breakfast or delivering the ten commandments. Mary Poppins was in fine voice and made an erudite bush. I was not sure if God was to be feared or not. It did seem like Moses needed a bit of pity. It was obvious Chuck did not qualify as a christian. Sacrilege was more his thing.

It was a long slow trudge to get off the campus. No one stopped to help us. It was a ghost town. Once it was behind us, New York had begun to sound a siren's call.

"You are not far." "You are not that far away!" Chuck and I were feeling a real sense of anticipation, anticipation of arriving in the greatest of U.S. cities. We were young, and we were enthralled with our quest!

Chapter Eight

As we approached Pittsburgh, a lingering vision of Jeb and Wilbur danced before my eyes. Pittsburg was their final destination. I wondered did they make it? Were they successfully and able to rob gas stations while driving a stolen car all the way across the country? My hope was they got caught but the chances were they were holed up somewhere in Pittsburg.

Pittsburg was awash with pollution, the air was dirty and hard to breathe. The town seemed to be wrapped in a dirty cloud, and surrounded by a dense fog. Driving through the town, a lot of the businesses were closed, evidenced by the many windows that were boarded and shut. We passed through without stopping. Pittsburg was grim and nothing about it called out to either of us. Jeb and Wilbur, if they were there, could have it.

"You know we are close to Philadelphia." Chuck had the map out again and was looking at what we had left to cross to get to our goal.

"Yeah, so what." I asked.

"I want to see the Liberty Bell!" Chuck surprised me again. He suggested another diversion.

The side trip to Notre Dame had been disappointing. It was not what I expected but a part of me wanted to see Philadelphia! I agreed to his new suggestion. If there is a single iconic symbol of American greatness, it is the Liberty Bell.

"I admire Ben Franklin." I affirmed his suggestion. "After the fiasco at Notre Dame, I thought you would be done with suggesting side trips." I watched him fidget as I forced him to accept the blame for how boring the trip to Notre Dame had been.

"Philadelphia is important. You know it is the actual birthplace of America. Everything started there with the Declaration of Independence. The Constitution and the Bill of Rights. The first Congress, everything."

"Yeah, I guess seeing all that would be cool." Why not? New York would still be there waiting for us.

"Who knows if we will ever get a chance like this again." All of a sudden we were in agreement and on our way to Independence Hall!

We arrived in Philadelphia too late to see anything. We would have to stay the night and visit Independence Hall in the morning.

"This is such an important place." Chuck was in awe.

"Yeah, the birthplace of our nation, I am glad you wanted to come here."

We marveled at it all, this was the town and the place where the Declaration of Independence and the Constitution of the United States had been written and signed. We spent the night sleeping behind a well disguised clump of bushes. No one saw us and no one bothered us. We slept and made it through the night undisturbed.

In the morning we got up bright and early, and found we were surrounded by various vendors who were preparing to hawk their revolutionary memorabilia. They were jousting for prime positions on the walk outside the building. We were first in line waiting at the front door when it opened. We ponied up and paid a small cover and gained entry.

We soon learned the famous crack in the bell did not occur until sometime in the 1840's long after it had called Ben Franklin and others to work. No one knew when or how the current crack had occurred. In fact it was becoming evident the bell had nothing to do with the early days of Philadelphia.

"Well the crack in the bell has no social significance. It's just a crack." Chuck had a habit of reading everything out loud and commenting on it.

"Yeah it wasn't even called the "liberty bell" until sometime in the 1830's. It has nothing to do with the American revolution or the writing of the Constitution." We were going from plaque to plaque and reading them together.

"Yeah, sometime in the 1830's the bell became a symbol for groups working to abolish slavery." Chuck had jumped ahead in the narrative. "They adopted an idea from the old testament."

"How about that, it comes from an Old Testament canon called the "Jubilee." The "Jubilee" was an instruction the Isrealites must free their slaves once every fifty years. The Liberty Bell had become famous as a biblical call to end slavery.

"Yeah, I have to believe the Bible is okay with owning slaves so long as you free some of them once every fifty years." Chuck echoed what I had said.

"Proclaim Liberty Throughout All the Land"! It was a slogan taken from the "Jubilee' and was first used in 1751. The slogan was in use long before the American revolution was associated with the bell. It was an early call to end slavery." It was starting to sink in.

"Did you know slavery was so prominent in the Bible?" I asked Chuck.

"The Isrealites and everyone else had slaves. Abraham had slaves! Moses had slaves! David and Solomon had slaves! This is one of the few passages where God expresses an opinion on slavery. he expects you to let some go every fifty years to stay on his good side." Chuck shook his head in disgust. "Let freedom ring once every fifty years! Is that Inspirational?"

"You are being harsh." I reacted to Chuck's rant.

"The problem is I am right! And you know it. If God's position is that the Isrealites should free the slaves every fifty years, then he is approving the holding of them for the other forty-nine."

"Well the abolitionists decided the slaves should be free all the time and used this passage to promote the idea. It is a flawed book, with lots of parts. I guess you can find just about anything in it."

It was sobering having learned the "liberty"referred to in the 'liberty bell' has to do with the freeing of the slaves and not the revolt against the King of England. Somehow I had thought the liberty bell was famous for ringing out after the signing of the Declaration of Independence. This visit had taught me differently.

We spent the remainder of our tour reading about the Declaration of Independence and the Constitution and the rich slave owners who wrote them.

"Liberty and Justice for all." Chuck sarcastically put his hand over his heart as we left.

"Well that's what we pledge."

After spending most of the day learning the true history of the famous bell we decided it was time to get back on the road to our final destination. We shouldered our packs and headed for the highway.

"Hey you, yeah you!" An old woman with scraggly gray hair and second hand clothes had set up a card table on the sidewalk outside the Hall. She was yelling at Chuck trying to get his attention.

"What is it?" He turned to her. "Can I help you?"

"I'll read your fortune for three dollars. Believe me you need to know what is coming your way." her stare was intense.

"No way! Three dollars is a lot of money." Chuck shook his head".

"My angel tells me you must have a reading." She had a deck of cards in her hand. "He is insisting I do it."

"I don't care who tells you, it's not going to happen. I am not giving you three dollars."

"He insists I give it to you for free if I have to." Chuck raised his eyebrows and shook his head. "Free is free. What does your Angel want me to know? I'll give him a couple of minutes of my time."

"This is Tarot. You shuffle the cards and let your life's energy flow through your fingers into the cards. They will tell the story after that." She handed him the cards to shuffle. He looked at me as if he were apologizing for being foolish and wasting our time. He shuffled the deck several times.

"Cut the deck and draw three cards. The first card will reveal your past, the second the present and the third is for the future." She was a mess with her scraggly gray hair and second hand clothes. She was down on her luck and dirt poor. The cards had not made her rich or her future bright. If they didn't work well for her, why would they work for her or Chuck? He drew the Three of Swords, the Five of Cups, and the Death Card.

The old woman nodded her head and proclaimed that three of the four horsemen of the apocalypse had arrived and were about to run over and thrash Chuck.

"The three of swords can mean emotional entanglement and confusion. You have some personal issues on your mind all the time. The Five of Cups followed and she claimed it indicated sorrow and hasty decisions. It all caused lost friendship, possibly ending in Death." She let out a long whistling breath, "The Angel was right to pick you out. You need my help."

I helped myself. What had we walked into? Where was this leading?

"Surely you don't think I am going to take this claptrap seriously." He slammed the cards on the table.

"Total nonsense!" I yelled at her wondering what was next. Would she offer a sure fire cure cancer for a hundred bucks? Chuck would never fall for it.

"The cards are always right, they come from a deep primal level of soul." she answered. "You can ignore them but it is at your peril."

"Well, I will take my chances!" Chuck glared at her.

"You are always, "taking your chances" with everything you do! You are heading for some turbulent times and must be careful. It is a warning. The Death card may mean actual death, but it can mean death of a path you are on, or the death of a friend, or friendship. There are many ways it can manifest. Not all of them are bad but all of them require you to pay close attention and not take chances. It is a warning."

"Okay, you suckered me into sitting here but I am done." Chuck pushed forward and started walking in the direction of the highway.

"That was spooky." I said. "She was full of gloom and doom."

"I didn't need it, not right now." I could see Chuck was stewing in it.

"You're not taking her seriously are you?" I asked.

"It was all vague bull shit. Like she said it could mean anything." he said. I could see something in him had been stirred.

"Forget it." I agreed, "It was all bull shit."

We got to the on ramp and began playing chess. Chuck was in a foul mood and was having a terrible game. Up to this moment his chess game had been improving. Our games had become close battles but this time it was over in a couple of moves. He played poorly and I captured his queen without much resistance. He exploded, knocking the chess board in the air and attacked me, driving his shoulder into my chest.

"You took my fucking queen." He screamed, knocking me to the ground.

His rage caught me by surprise and I lost my feet. He pinned me to the ground and was thrusting his hips into mine. I fought to get leverage and began to fend off his attack. He was in my face, breathing hard and swearing. His body was hot and he was grinding me into the ground. So far no punches had been thrown. No real damage had been done. I was unhurt.

"Stop it, what's the matter with you?" I yelled at him, but he raged on.

I struggled and strained to get leverage on him. I turned him on his side and got a grip around his neck and put a choke hold on him. I tightened the grip and squeezed the air out of him. I am far stronger than he is and now we both know it. The air went out of his lungs and he collapsed, losing consciousness for a second.

"Quit it. Just fucking stop!" I said with nervous anger. He didn't move. I had knocked him out. I began to worry.

"Wake up," I shook him. "Wake up dammit. What is the problem?" I panicked, what if I had kept the chokehold on too long?

A few more moments passed and I began shaking him.. What if he did not regain consciousness?

Finally, he stirred. We both lay there unable to speak. We had been in constant contact for six days in a row. I knew he didn't like getting hammered at chess. But I thought this can't just be about a stupid chess game. What made him blow up?

"Sorry man, I lost control, it must have had something to do with what that witch said." He woke up and broke the silence.

"Shit man, you need to get a grip." What was this about? Why had he become so angry? Would it happen again?

"Yeah, I'm sorry. I am back in control. You okay?" He asked me.

"Yeah, I'm fine, just surprised. I didn't know you had that in you."

"Neither did I," He answered.

A short time later we got a ride out of Philadelphia, the City of Brotherly Love. We couldn't talk to each other much for several hours. When we did start talking again we decided to put the "fight" behind us. We agreed it wasn't much of a fight and we would never discuss it again. Nevertheless the incident nagged at me. I kept wondering what had triggered his anger. I suspected it might be about his sexual fears.

Chapter Nine

As we approached New York, my inner voice was nagging me around the clock. Our stay in the all night movie theater delivered a harsh lesson. The woods, the desert and the mountains are places to roll out a sleeping bag, but those things will not be waiting for us in New York. There will be no unlocked cabin door to give us shelter. Our stay in Chicago made it crystal clear that the streets of a big city are cold and unfriendly. Even if we got lucky and found an all night theater again, we couldn't stay in it every night. We will soon be in desperate need of a place to stay. In anticipation of this crisis I started asking the drivers who picked us up for their advice.

"Can you recommend a place where two young guys can stay?" I got the feeling they thought I was a little crazy.

I had begun this adventure with a blind faith believing something or someone would guide us. My faith affirmed the world is good, and we could expect things to work out well for us. I assumed there was a "protecting hand" that would guide us and arrange things favorably for us. My faith was about to be tested as we urgently needed to find a place to stay. .

Someone suggested that we try the "The Young Men's Christian Association" better known as the YMCA. I knew nothing about the organization. There wasn't one in Huntington and I am not a Christian. I would say more like an "earth boy." The seasons, the moon cycle, and the long slow circling of the stars all mean something to me. It's the way I was raised.

I was uncertain about the YMCA but was willing to try anything, if it was cheap. I wondered if the YMCA was just for Christians or can "earth boy" and his "gay" friend stay there? In a flash I realized Chuck was gay even though he himself was not yet convinced of it.

"If the YMCA is a Christian organization. We'll have to tell them we are straight." Chuck chimed in.

"Why do you think they'll care?" It seemed strange and irrelevant to me.

"They hate all homosexuality, and believe it should be punishable by death." His tone was grim.

"Death? You think they will kill you?" I was shocked.

"Well that's what it says in the Bible. God despises homosexuality."

"The YMCA wants to kill gays?"It did not seem possible. "What about love thy neighbor and all the stuff Jesus says?"

"Killing is in the law. The Bible says God destroyed a whole valley and he killed everyone in it, including the women and children. He must avenge the crime of sodomy." Chuck was not kidding.

"I guess I need to read the whole Bible and not just parts." I was stunned.

"I have read it cover to cover. The condemnation of homosexuality is real and it scares me." Chuck was nervous and agitated.

"It sounds like we will have trouble at the YMCA." I didn't like it at all.

"Maybe, maybe not." Chuck gave me a funny look as if he knew something he had not yet told me.

Chuck was well read and he had a straightforward way of handling himself but at this moment I was not sure of what he was thinking.

"I may have to lie if they ask." He said. I wondered if he was lying or not.

"I hope they don't ask. The YMCA is our best chance to find a cheap place to stay. I am worried."

As New York got closer, the skyline seemed to grow until it was looming over our heads. It made us feel tiny and insignificant.

"I have never been to a big city before." I said to Chuck. He nodded in agreement.

New York was so unique, it was one of a kind. Breathtaking! Chicago and Los Angeles were no longer my definitions of a "big city." They were now big "towns".

Our trip to the big apple had cost almost nothing so far. We had arrived healthy and in good physical shape. We were ready to see and explore New York City. When we crossed over the Hudson River into Manhattan it had taken under seven days. The skyline was towering above us like a colossus. Once we were under its cavernous shade it became hard to see the sky.

We crossed the bridge and I could not contain my enthusiasm. I felt an unbridled joy and pride in having reached the goal. An Italian named Mario had picked us up in his bread truck on a whim. He shouldn't have stopped for us, he could have lost his job if he were caught. Somehow he had squeezed both of us, including our huge backpacks, into the front of his truck. He was delivering fresh warm bread. There we were wedged in between long rows of warm bread.

It was difficult to maintain my balance as the truck darted around, stopping and starting without any warning. I felt like a twisted pretzel. The smell of fresh bread was an aphrodisiac feeding my brain with feelings of happiness.

Mario knew the city well. The towering buildings and the dark morning sky had no effect on him as he weaved his way down a plethora of one way streets. He snapped off turns without giving it a thought. It was as if he had a road map in his head and then he stopped, jumped out and made a delivery. It was impossible to see the sky. It was dark and forbidding.

I was floating, feeling high and exhilarated. My survival instincts were churning. The sidewalks were teeming with people. A multitude of trucks had double parked each one making deliveries. Together they all blocked the road creating a mess amid heavy traffic. Horns were honking and loud voices were barking out orders no one considered ever following.

"Move it, you can't stop there..." Honk, honk, honk...an angry face appeared for a moment to glare in our side window.

"Shove it." our fearless driver yelled out his window at his attackers! He put the truck in park, and turned on flashing lights and delivered another stack of loaves. He was oblivious to the commotion.

"How far is the YMCA? Do you know the way?" I asked when he returned.

"Sit tight. I got a delivery two blocks from there." And then he winked at me. "I told you. I got you covered."

"Fuck off," Mario yelled out the window one more time in response to an angry cabby who was contesting the right of way.

Four deliveries later and we were climbing out of his truck staring at an old building marked "YMCA." We showered him with thanks. We were "home" and hoping to find they had a place available at the inn for two heathens from the west coast.

"Let me do the talking". I led the way to the registration desk.

"Okay, but I can speak for myself." Chuck reacted.

"I know but for now let me handle it." I was beginning to worry. Chuck believed he had a flashing neon sign on his forehead that read, "I am insecure about my sexuality, and may be gay!"

His fears were groundless. They never mentioned Christianity or homosexuality at all. I was relieved it was not an issue. The YMCA turned out to be a bargain. For three bucks a night we could share a room. For one dollar fifty cents apiece we got two small beds, a toilet, and access to communal showers. There were no kitchen facilities.

"At least there are toilets and sinks in every room." I noted. "They promised to clean the rooms once a week."

We had arrived with enough money to stay for a while. I relaxed. There were no questions about our sexuality, mine or Chuck's. I didn't have to tell them I was still a virgin or about my plans to change that soon. Chuck was not an issue and no one cared or grilled us about his current state of mind.

Fate was on our side. Many people had lent a hand in our arrival and we both knew it. I gave mental thanks to each person who had stopped and helped move us along. Some had taken us only a few miles, while others had given us rides covering long distances. A few had fed us and some had even given us a little bit of money.

I sat and counted my cash and found I had more now than we had when we started. Mike had slipped me a ten when he dumped us on the streets in Chicago! There had been some uneasy, dangerous moments but they did not seem important any more.We had arrived and we were safe.

We shared a list of things we wanted to do and see. Years earlier I had bought a copy of Bob Dylan's first record "The Freewheelin Bob Dylan." Its cover showed Bob with a cap, a folk guitar, and a pretty girl. It talked about a place called Washington Square. I learned that Bob had hitchhiked from Minnesota to visit Woody Guthrie on his deathbed. It was my favorite record. I was overwhelmed with the desire to visit Washington Square right away. I hoped I'd get lucky and meet Bob. Chuck declined to go with me.

We had just finished seven straight days in each other's company without a break. Chuck was getting on my nerves and I was getting on his. Our fight in Philadelphia had passed into history but I wondered if and when there might be another storm coming. He hinted that he needed some "personal time". We agreed to take some time apart.

"I'm going to check out Washington Square," I was intent on seeing Bob Dylan's famous "hangout".

"I'm going to stay here and rest," Chuck sighed.

The subway had a map that marked key locations. Washington Square was prominent and easy to find. I paid my fare and arrived in less than twenty minutes. It was a warm, humid summer day. The air was thick, and damp as I walked out of the subway, and into Washington Square, which turned out to be a park.

It was full of people playing speed chess. I was amazed to find every table had a chess board imprinted on it. You didn't need to bring a board to play, one was already provided. Speed chess is a game played with a clock. Players are limited to five minutes playing time for each side. The clock has two timers, one for each player and if the hand drops on your side before the game is over you have run out of time and you lose.

You have to move fast and finish your half of the game in five minutes or less. It creates extra pressure that often causes mistakes to be made. Speed chess is fun to watch, games happen in a hurry. I soon discovered they were playing for money. The minimum bet was a dollar per game! I was sure I could beat everyone I watched. I could spot and see their mistakes.

"Can I play?" I asked the winner as the game ended.

"It's a dollar a game." The winner was skeptical. "Can you pay up if you lose?"

I fished out a little roll of one's and flashed it in the air. Just like that I was in. If you win, you have control of the board and you play again if you want. I won. I won four games in a row before I lost. I made a net of $3.00 dollars in less than an hour. It was enough to cover the first day's room rent plus some for food.

The game where I lost, I was too slow. Five minutes passed and the speed hand dropped on me. It was a close game, with practice I would learn how to play faster. I formed a plan to play every day and make as much money as I could.

On my subway ride back, the man in front of me vaulted over the bars. He just lifted himself over them, and there was no one around to stop him. I learned that with a little risk, I could ride for free. All you had to do was lift yourself over the bars when no one was looking. I decided to try it. I lifted myself over the turnstile. I did not have to pay.

I was $3.00 on the good side for the day from the chess victories, and now with this new revelation, all future transportation appeared to be free. What a fun city, I thought. I vaulted turnstiles and did so from that day forward. Later I was told about the huge fine you faced if you were caught jumping the rails and took precautions. Luckily for me, I was never caught.

When I got back to the Y, Chuck was lying shirtless in his whites, asleep on top of his bed. I moved around trying not to wake him. He woke up anyway.

"Hey, Luke, what's up?" He was disoriented. He did not make eye contact.

"I went down to Washington Square and won some money playing chess." I flashed the bills with pride. "I made $3.00 in an hour."

"Yahoo , I'm sick of playing you. Glad you found someone else to slaughter." He was pale and tired.

"What did you do? You look beat." I asked.

"I went to the shower, and I washed some clothes." He sat up on one elbow. His hands shook.

"You okay?" I felt something was off kilter.

"I'm a little drunk, I had a couple of drinks." He was shaking so I knew it was more than a couple.

"How'd that happen?"

"I went to the showers to clean up. I was standing there letting the water run over me when an older guy came up to me and started talking." Chuck paused and did not speak again for a while. He gave me a funny stare.

"Okay, he started talking and then what?" Chuck was stalling, not finishing his story,

"He was friendly and told me he had a bottle of Vodka in his room and asked me if I wanted to share it with him."

"Yeah so you had some drinks?" It sounded cool.

"We drank a lot, almost the whole bottle, fast. Then he said he wanted to blow me. At first I didn't say anything, and nothing happened. But then he offered me $10.00."

In a flash I knew his "question" had been answered. He had found what he was looking for. The "old guy" had given Chuck a blowjob.

"You're kidding, right?" I was incredulous. "He paid you? He paid you for sex?"

"Yep." Chuck held up a ten dollar bill. "Funny thing is he's not the only one. This place is crawling with them, and it turns out they are all looking for the same thing.The YMCA is a crazy place."

I was floored. "So you did it? Just like that?" I wasn't sure why I asked again. It was clear the first time he said it.

Ever since the night in the mountains where he had first made his revelation we had avoided talking about the subject. It had not been allowed to come up in our conversation again until the fight in Philadelphia. We found ourselves sidestepping it and not talking about it. But now it was back front and center.

"Yeah, and I liked it. It was easy, it was nothing like trying to get a girl to fuck you. This was no hassle at all."

He had reminded me again of my own trials chasing after girls. It was not going well for me and it was certain no girl would give me $10.00 for a roll in the sheets with her.

The Rolling Stones put it best, "I'm on a losing streak." and I was getting "no satisfaction." My portfolio was a long parade of virgins, all of whom wanted to stay that way. If it was that hard for me what was it like for Chuck?

He had never been able to get a date. One thing I knew for sure was that "good" girls didn't let you take their clothes off. After years of trying both Chuck and I were still virgins. Then I thought to myself, that at least I have been trying for years.

"I wonder if you are still a virgin?" I asked him out loud.

"It isn't the same thing as screwing a girl. But it is sex." He responded.

"Is there a rule about it?" I asked to be clear.

"What's with you and all these rules? The guy asked me if he could blow me and I said yes. We had sex. So guess I am not a virgin anymore."

"Did you cum?" Chuck did not answer. There was a silence as he considered what to tell me.

"It took awhile, but I did. Hell yes I did. He knew what he was doing."

Chuck leaned back savoring the recollection of the moment. "It was great." He smiled a huge smile.

I couldn't believe it. On our first day in New York Chuck got his cock sucked and made ten bucks. On top of that he had had an orgasm that was not self induced and "lost" his virginity. My chess victories had become small and meaningless.

"I couldn't do it. No way. Not with a guy." At that moment it was clear to me. The idea of having sex with another man didn't appeal to me. In fact, it left me cold. I was certain.

"Well, Once I let my guard down, he took over and did all the work. It felt right. He has a "young guy thing." And he has friends, lot's of friends. This place is crawling with guys like him.``

"Then I guess you found your answer today." For a second the whole thing gave me the willies. Then my revulsion passed and I thought it might be the right thing for Chuck.

This became our pattern for the next few days. I played chess, often winning, and Chuck got regular sex, and banked some easy money. My finances were going in the wrong direction. New York was turning out to be expensive, even with the cheap living at the Y. Chuck was showering several times a day, meeting new guys and expanding his clientele. He was making more and more money. It had started to become a little business.

All he had to do to attract attention was linger in the shower. That same shower was now spooking me. I got in and out as fast as I could. I treated it like it was haunted. I found myself less and less willing to venture into it. I didn't want a confrontation. I got clean with my showers taking less than five minutes and I picked the time when I went.

"You know you got the wrong idea, it is not that important" Chuck seemed to be trying to soften my idea about his routine.

What I didn't know was one of Chuck's clients had seen me and Chuck together and was pressing Chuck to introduce us. "You don't got to do much, just go with him and let him pull down your pants. He'll do the rest."

"Not a chance. Not me. I ain't interested." Chuck made several more approaches to get me to give it a try. I stood firm and let him know I was not up to a sexual escapade with a strange man. I wondered why he thought I would be. The more I thought about it, the clearer it became to me.

"Is someone paying you to try to get to me?" I asked.

"Well, if you did do it, there'd be something in it for me too." Chuck averted his eyes.

"Chuck, you're trying to pimp me."

"Nah, don't think of it like that, think of it as opening a new door. There are a lot of guys around here who want to open that door for you."

"I don't want to hear about this again." I scolded him. "Enough is enough. No is no."

"Suit yourself." He picked up his wallet, it was bulging with cash. "But like I said, it ain't as bad as you think."

Chapter Ten

Spending money for entertainment was not possible. I had to find things to do that are free or almost free. I found and fell in love with the Museum of Natural History. It was famous for a massive replica of a Tyrannosaurus Rex. They also had a 94 foot model of a blue whale hanging from the ceiling. They are both stunning. I shared my "find" with Chuck and convinced him we should visit it together.

"You're right I dig the whale hanging from the ceiling. Man, that thing is huge." He winks at me, and gives me a thumbs up. "Love a blue whale!" He held his hands several feet apart. His banter was about the length of the whale's penis hanging overhead.

"My favorite is the dinosaurs." I found myself encouraged and glad he was enjoying the visit.

We wander around the various displays and come upon a section depicting the various races and cultures of mankind. It features imaginary scenes from man's distant past. There are paintings and exhibits of "primitive" people in old traditional dress. They are often hunting or cooking in exhibits that show how primitive life was in a world without modern tools.

We wander into the African section. I stop and study an African plains scene. Chuck meanders and disappears out of sight. I hear him whistling and he struts back into the room acting important and self aware. He made a fancy bow and swept his hand through the air to get my attention.

"Ladies and germs I give you exhibit one: a homely woman." He stopped abruptly in front of a metal bust of an African woman with extended lips. The plaques say plates had been inserted over time and they have made her lips abnormally large. "Imagine a night at the drive in with her!" "You lucky guy!" Chuck winks at me and shimmies like he is cuddling up to her. "Give us a kiss." He laughs uncontrollably.

On impulse he rubs the statue's metal lips with his index finger, ignoring and forgetting the "do not touch" signs. He pretends to stroke her large black lips back and forth. He picks up the pace and is wildly rubbing her lips up and down. He stops and says in a loud stutter worthy of porky pig, "That's all folks."

Just as he began his act an elderly black man with his grandson arrived on the scene. Chuck was so intense he did not see them enter. They watched his whole performance. The grandfatherly old man was shocked. He stared long and hard at Chuck, who shriveled up. Chuck saw the old man and his grandson pleading for forgiveness. He knew instinctively it was wrong. His eyes say." It was just a joke, I meant it as a joke."

The black man's face was tense and filled with obvious pain. He didn't mutter a word. He didn't need to. He and Chuck exchange silent stares. The old man puts his hand on the boy and guides him away. Chuck had meant it to be a joke for my benefit. Nothing more.

"You shouldn't have done that."

"You're right," he says sheepishly "I didn't see them until I was finishing up and by then it was too late. I hurt their feelings. But you know I was kidding around." I changed the subject.

"This exhibit shows there are a lot of different historical roots to the black people.They originated in many different parts of Africa. They have come from many different backgrounds and traditions." The exhibit has taught me something about how they came to be in America. In most cases it is a brutal story.

We finish up in the afternoon and return to the Y. It is Saturday, Chuck will be heading out once again. I will be on my own. I am most evenings.

I decided to pass some time by taking a long walk in Central Park. I mingled with the "hippies", who were "hanging out, communing with nature." They gather in a place called Sheeps Meadow. The meadow is an open space and is also a home base for groups who gather to protest the war in Viet Nam. I stop and chat with the regulars.

The park is full of street musicians strumming their instruments. They keep their guitar cases open hoping for donations. There are so many of them I wonder if anyone makes any money. There are tourists milling around and watching, it reminds me of Golden Gate Park in San Francisco. In the background I hear a group of drummers, there are at least a dozen of them. They are pounding out a steady rhythm. They play without stopping for rest. Young people have come here hoping to get stoned and kill time.

"UGH! UGH! UGH!" a voice screeched out across the meadow.

"UGHA! UGGA! UG!" another voice high up in the trees echoed back.

Two men are making animal noises, while pretending to be gorillas. They are calling to each other across the open field. It is a ritual "stoner game" where you hang from the limbs, and act crazy. They lock in combat! They are rolling out of control down a hill while pounding on each other. It is harmless and strange.

"Why don't you join in and play with them?" The voice belongs to a young girl. She has been watching me watch them.

"I don't know, it's not my thing, wrestling with strangers." I look her over. I decided she is pretty.

"Yah, I guess you would need to know them. You're not from here are you?" She has a thick New York accent "Where are you from?".

"Huntington Beach. What's your name?" I smile.

"I'm Clarisse! Wow! Are you a surfer? Your bleached hair does the trick! Love it! Wow, what are you doin here?" she wanted to know.

"Yeah I get out in the sun a lot. Lightens my hair."

So far I have always been talking at New Yorkers. I am never talking with them. I am asking questions, getting directions, or buying milk. I realizel have had few "conversations",and now she is offering to chat and I am enraptured by her accent.

"You're a surfer dude! I think I'll call you "Surf's Up!" Want to get high, "Surf's Up?" She offers a joint and has been cupping in her hand and hiding it.

"My name is Luke but you can call me "Surf's up" if you want." I take the joint she offers. "The last time I smoked was at the Monterey Music festival watching Janis Joplin."

I name drop hoping to get her attention. It doesn't work. She doesn't react. She doesn't know who Janis is. I take a long drag and try not to cough. I am still learning how to inhale. The smoke burns my lungs.

"I heard all about that in Eric Burdon's song. "Down in Monterrey" that must have been groovy." I was thankful she had heard of Monterey..

"It was three days of music. Simon and Garfunkel were there, they are from New York, you know." I hope I have impressed her.

"Yeah, they are cool."

We sit down in the grass and we talk. I tell her about swimming in the Pacific Ocean and she asks if it is warm like Florida. She has been to Florida with her parents. She lives on Long Island with them. She tells me she has run away from home for a couple of days and is just hanging out. She will have to go back home soon.

"I run away all the time. Drives my Dad crazy." She rolls her eyes and laughs. "He can't handle it."

"The water is not that warm in California. It's in the 60's but once you get in, it feels warml body surf a lot. Newport is the best spot."

"You're not a hippy are you?" she slides closer to me.

"Nah, I don't think so. I graduated high school in June. I am not sure what a hippy is. How about you? Are you a hippy?"

"I got two more years of high school but I don't think I'm going back. I'm staying in the park with a girl friend. A lot of people here say they are hippies. I am hanging out."

We share the joint and it starts taking effect. She snuggles right up next to me. Close, so close I can feel her warm hot breath. She turns her face toward mine and she looks into my eyes. Her eyes sparkle and dance. We have connected. I put my arm around her and draw her into me and we kiss. She lays back on the ground and pulls me on top of her. Her breasts are firm round mounds sliding beneath my chest. She wraps her arms around me and rubs her hips against me and I start to pump. I slide my hand up her leg and grab her rock hard buttocks.

"Clarisse, Clarisse" we are interrupted by a young blond who has appeared out of nowhere. Her voice is harsh and shrill. She is yelling. "Where's that joint I gave you?"

"Shit Helen, why are you bugging in? We smoked it already. This is "Surf's Up". I just met him." I roll over and face the woman who has spoiled the moment. .

"Yeah, Hi Helen, I'm Luke. But you can call me "Surf's Up" if you want." I am annoyed at her for interrupting.

"Damn I can see it in your hair, and hear it in your voice. You're a Beach Boy! I'll bet you're from California!"

"Yeah, I'm from a beach town."

"Far out! You look stoned! Did you smoke my joint? Don't worry I got another one." She pulled out a packed joint and lit it up. She takes a deep drag and hands it to me.

"Back home we have to hide when we smoke joints, we don't smoke them out in the open in the park. Police are heavy on enforcement.There is jail time if you are caught." I say.

"Some places we have to hide them too. But the park is cool." Helen looks at me and says. "What you want with my girl?" .

"We are getting to know each other." I answer. I understand she thinks of Clarrise as her girl.

"Yeah I could see that. But, hey it's cool I share her."

We smoke and I get higher and higher. Helen has wedged herself in between Clarisse and me. I look at Clarisse and want to get back into hugging and kissing. But Helen is in the way. I try to chat but am unable to make small talk.

Meanwhile Helen acts as if she knows everyone in the park. She invites a passerby to sit with us and smoke. It is clear my kissing session with Clarisse is over for now. Helen is dominating the conversation.

"Clarisse, it was fun meeting you. I hope to see you again, but it's time for me to move along." I leave awkwardly. I wonder what it would have been like if Helen hadn't shown up. Disappointment reigned as I headed back to the YMCA.

When I arrive Chuck has finished dressing for the night. He is all "duded" up and getting ready to go out as usual.

"Listen, you want to hang out with me tonight? You could tag along and see where I go and what I do? My routine has changed a little, and you might learn something." He is challenging

"I don't know. Wouldn't I be in the way? I think I'll take a pass tonight. Some other time though." I stay in and read. The truth is I am curious to see how he spends his nights.

Chapter Eleven

Chuck's nights are busy, we keep finding time to spend together during the day. Today is the beginning of our second week in New York.

"I feel like doing something. Why don't we go to the top of the Empire State Building and take a look around." he offers.

"Sure, I've been wanting to check it out." I agree, let's hop on a subway car.

We find the building is open to the public. We marvel at its high ceilings and stunning Art Deco murals. The murals pay homage to the mechanical age with pictures of machines and men hard at work. We stand in front of a mural with greetings to visitors written in more than a dozen languages. It feels like It is like an open doorway to the world.

To reach the top you have to change elevators several times, No single one runs all the way to the top. We got in an elevator with a crowd of about fifteen people.

"Hit thirty, hit the top choice!" Chuck has out how the system works. "We have to change from there."

I hit thirty and we took off. The other riders are going to work. We are the only tourists. The elevator stops for close to a dozen times before we get to the thirtieth floor. When we get to the thirtieth floor we find it will take many elevator lifts to get all the way to the top.

"We're gonna have to change four times. They only go about thirty floors each." Chuck hustles us over to take one that reads floors 31-60. This time we have only a half dozen people riding with us. The ride up is quicker, with less people, there are less stops. When we get out everyone else has gotten off.

"Well, we are the only riders now, we won't have to stop." The thirty floors fly by. It is the fastest acceleration I have ever felt in an elevator. My gut tightens and I feel like I am being pushed down, squashed into the floor. The final and last elevator ride is only twelve floors, it is a quick jump and takes us to the top. It has taken many minutes to reach the top!

It is bitter, cold and windy. We have a startling 360 degree view and can see the city surrounding us in all directions! A nearby plaque tells the story of the many men who died during the construction of the world's tallest building. It was dangerous work. It is a long list.

Chuck has put a nickel in a telescope and is turning the lens around in a 180 degree sweep. He focuses on the river for a moment and on the streets far below.

"I can see every detail. The river is dirty, it's muddy, filthy. Holy shit," Chuck breaks out laughing. " A cop jay walked across a red light. Good lord he's fat, take a look." Chuck chortles and offers me the scope so I can see the fat cop.

"Let me see." I take a turn peeking at the show.

The crowds are all clumped together pushing and jostling their way down the sidewalks like cattle. Most people refuse to wait for lights. Like a herd of cows they cross regardless whether the light is green or red. Back home always waits for every light.

The difference is at home you are always alone, the only one waiting at the light and everyone obeys the law. Here no one obeys the law. At least not the jaywalking law.

Even without the telescopes the view from the top is stunning. It is the tallest building in the world and you can see Manhattan as it stretches out for miles.

"Do not climb on the railing, nets below are provided for your safety!" I read the sign out loud.

The sign informs the public that the platform is surrounded by railings with a net to guard against suicide. If you try to jump off you will end up in the net. I had never thought about committing suicide before. Why would anyone do that? I find myself thinking "It must be a real issue if the building takes precautions to prevent it."

Back home if you wanted to hurt yourself you could consider jumping off the pier in the middle of a storm. No one I knew had ever tried it. Living in New York is different. There is a "pressure to compete" for things, everything involves basic survival! I had never felt that kind of pressure before I arrived here, but now I felt it just trying to walk a straight line on the street. "How strange I am being plagued with these thoughts and I have only been here a short time."

As we leave the building, Chuck decides he must have something to eat. I am also hungry but there is no way I can consider it. I don't have to look. I know it is too pricey.

"Let's go in and get lunch." he peers at the menu in the window.

"Nah, you know I can't do that." I answer harshly.

It annoys me he has suggested it, my bankroll is shrinking, chess is not providing me with much. He knows t don't keep track of Chuck and his sex, we have an agreement. He will never bring anyone to our room. One thing I do see is the ever growing pile of cash he is accumulating. I figure he is having a lot of sex and making money. I wonder if he is rubbing it in?

"No need to get angry. I meant it in a friendly way." He is still reading the menu on the wall. "I am going to get a Pastrami sandwich to go. You can have half if you like." He goes in expecting me to wait. I don't wait, annoyed. I walk off and leave him.

Every day my cash reserves get a little smaller. My trips to Washington Square to play chess are nor producing any winnings. The weak players, the ones I can always beat don't want to play me anymore. Only the strongest players will accept my challenge. The end result is that my income from chess has started to dry up.

On top of that, groceries from the corner store are expensive. I accept that Chuck can treat himself to a movie or a sandwich if he wants it. I cannot and have to pass on things that cost a lot to do. His "new" lifestyle gives him money and freedom to explore things. Things I cannot do.

On the bright side I have acquired a brochure to help guide me to all the museums in town. I have begun exploring new ones. Since almost all museums are free or have small entrance fees, they fit my budget. It is the answer to the question, "How can I pass the time and enjoy myself cheaply? Today I have the guide out and am reading it out loud in the hopes of getting Chuck interested in coming with me.

"The Cloisters is located in Washington Heights. It features tapestries and artwork from the middle ages." I have caught his attention.

"Wow how cool." He perked up and sounded interested. He had come in late and I was surprised he was up and active so early in the day.

"It's way out at the end of Manhattan. It'll take a while to get there." I said, happy to have captured Chuck's interest.

I myself had a quart of milk for breakfast. It costs .19 cents and I felt full for most of the day. We took the subway to the nearest point and we were still left with a long walk. It was located on a steep hill and was an exact replica of a medieval monastery. We entered through a lush garden featuring a variety of flowers in bloom.The air was sickly sweet, and full of the aroma of sweet buds and the sound of buzzing bees.

"This place is beautiful." Chuck said. We agreed and I enjoyed sharing the moment.

"The place has a calm sanity, that is agreeable. I had to agree.

It was a contrast made more valuable after being surrounded by skyscrapers. It was nice to find an exhibit out in the open. Something that was not walled in between towering buildings. The gardens felt like a treat. It had a small entrance fee which we paid with the expectation it would be worth it.

"I have never seen a tapestry before except in photos." I said as we wandered from room to room.

"Yeah but the colors are fresh like they were made yesterday." Chuck stopped in front of a mythic scene of a goddess and a unicorn. Her long blond hair was draped around full exposed breasts. She was riding the mythic horse western style. Her hips were full and round.

"The men who made this liked women." I said.

"Yeah," Chuck agreed. In the corner of the piece was a winged cupid firing an arrow at an unsuspecting young warrior who was ogling the goddess.

Chuck prods me. I laugh and nod he was right. I hoped I would be struck by a bolt of lightning and infected with love.

"I hope when it happens it will be mutual." I try to joke.

We continue wandering the aisles. Every exhibit has an explanation giving the background of when and where the pieces were made. Many of them have been rescued from castles in Europe and sent out to be enjoyed in museums around the world. A group of them were from the Middle East with Arabian themes. It was a fascinating experience, I was in awe at how much detail could be given in this medium and what a complex art form it was.

"Tapestry is a lost art," I remark. "Something no one does anymore."

"In America we make quilts instead." It is an older woman's voice and she appeared from nowhere, and was standing right behind us.

"Quilts? Who are you?" I was startled.

"Mildred, I'm a docent here. We don't get many visitors from your age group. You caught my eye." She is holding a writing pad, I strain to see her badge.

"Well, we are trying to see the kind of things we cannot see back home." Chuck speaks up. He is as polite as he can be. I am amused and make a mental note to myself "He knows how to win an older woman over."

"We love to see people your age enjoying our offerings. If you have any questions please be sure to ask. That's what I am here for. To answer questions."

"I'll be sure to come find you, if I do. Do you mind if we guide ourselves for now?" Chuck enquires in a formal, respectful way.

"Of course, I didn't mean to interrupt your visit. I'll leave you to explore as you wish." She turns and leaves us alone.

"She began trailing us right after we walked in. She has been following us I think." Chuck said in an annoyed voice.

" I did not see her until she spoke up." I was amazed.

"Well you should be more aware of the people around you and what they are doing. I have to because I stick out in a crowd." Chuck's tone was bitter.

"Why is that?" I was surprised.

"Well, I'm different. I'm queer." He looked away as he said it.

"It's not stamped on your forehead. No one notices you. It's all in your imagination."

I grab him and give him a friendly shake.

"You're right. Let's get back to the exhibits. This is some amazing stuff!" he chimes in weakly. He was a bit worn, I think his late night habits are showing. I wonder what he is doing out until late every night?

I stop before a picture labeled John D Rockefeller. He was the chief financial benefactor of the Cloisters, and founded the museum in the 1930's. It was a far cry from anything ever found in "Surf City".

Unicorns playing with blond goddesses did not exist in our little beach town. In the "Cloister" they had a life of their own. They were as real as images stitched in cloth can be. We spent the better part of the day moving from room to room in awe of what the men who had gone before us had made.

The visit to the Cloister left us both feeling peaceful and at ease. We walked back to the subway in silence. Each of us reflecting on the wonders of the day. We jumped the subway rails and rode home. The subway was not crowded and I was relieved to have a seat after a long day of walking and standing. Once again I notice Chuck is strained and tired.

"Are you alright?" I ask him. "I need a break, I'm taking the night off". When we arrived at the Y Chuck crawled up in his bed and pulled the covers up over his head.

"What's up with you?

"I feel stretched and raw." He says weakly.

"How can that be?" I had no idea what he was hinting at..

"Well, you remember Jack, I told you about him. He was the first man I met when we came here." Chuck's voice was timid.

"Yeah I remember what you told me about him." I had never met any of Chuck's "friends". It was part of our deal. We kept his new life separate.

"Well he paid me to screw him in his butt and I did it. It's a lot like sexual intercourse, but different." Chuck mumbled sheepishly.

I had heard some talk about this kind of sex. No one I knew had ever done anything like it. It was a blank slate for me. I knew nothing about it, how could I?

"Does it fit in there?" I tried to imagine it.

"Well, yeah, it can be a little tight. It's hard to put it in, you need to use a lubricant. He got me hard and showed me what to do. I put it on him and he loved it. He went nuts."

"I believe you, If you say so, I don't have any experience." I fumbled for words.

"The first time I mounted him he moaned and groaned like crazy. I fucked him for a long time. As long as I could without a climax. I think it lasted for thirty minutes before I went off." Chuck rolled his eyes as he pretended to have anal sex.

"It is like a long time to stay hard!" I marveled.

"Yeah it is, he got dry and I had to lube several times. He whimpered the whole time." Chuck's voice had gotten intense in the telling.

"So why is your butt sore?" I was beginning to put two and two together.

"Later he told me he wanted to screw me too. At first I didn't want to, but he told me how good it felt." Chuck paused. "And offered me $25.00."

"That's a lot of money." I said.

"It is, I had finished screwing him for thirty minutes and now he wanted to put his dick in me. I was beat and sore. But one thing stood out! The whole time I was in him he was moaning and making noises like an animal. It made him crazy, so I decided to try it."

The lights were off and the room went dark. I could no longer see Chuck's face. I could only hear his voice.

"How was it?" I asked in the dark.

"I let him do it to me for as long as he could. He lasted about ten minutes. He is old and lacks stamina. But I liked it. He hit my spot until I was on fire. My eyes bugged out a little."

"Wow. That's quite a story. So that's why you are sore?"

"Yah, he was my first for everything but I have let several others do me since. There is real money in it. I can be a bottom or a top but I have decided I like being the bottom. I got carried away for a while for a couple of days and over did it." Chuck pleaded with me, like he thought my opinion counted, and mattered for something.

"Okay, and I guess you get paid either way." I wondered what it was like hustling sex for money.

"Now you know why my butt is sore.Too much sex." Chuck's voice had an edge. I could hear it. He was expecting me to condemn his actions. I couldn't think of anything to say. I was shocked. It was a world I had no idea existed until now. I couldn't think of what to say. I didn't say a word.

"I think I know who I am now. I wasn't sure before, but I am now." His tone was defensive as if he was waiting to be attacked. "At least nowI know who I am."

"I guess that's good, who am I to judge. " I said. We stopped talking. There was nothing more to say. I thought he must have been lonely in the past.

As we lay there in the dark in silence, I became aware of soft snoring. Chuck had fallen asleep. Who was he becoming? I had no way to understand. It worried me but I decided he was a man and now, he was his own man on his own terms. I knew a lot of people thought what he was doing was wrong. But he was my friend and we had been through and done a lot together. I saw no reason to let anything change our friendship.

Chapter Twelve

At night my pattern is to hang alone at the music venues in the village. There are a lot of them. I stood out and listened to the sounds drift out to the street. I couldn't afford a ticket. Chuck treats himself and does what he wants. He was having a lot of sex and was happy. He has "found" the life he was longing for and his "new" life was taking care of him.

Chuck frequents a part of the "village" that is "home" to the homosexual crowd. Some of it is open to street traffic. He has fallen in with a couple of young guys, and hangs out with them.They hustle sex for money, and are all close to my age. Chuck wants me to meet his new friends.

"It's safer when you have friends nearby." he tells me. "I have made some friends."

I learn his "clients" are older men, visitors to the village. They are married. They have wives and families and pay young men for sex on the side. He explains there are "clubs" and he goes to play in them after work. The clubs are social and not for business. For weeks now he has vanished every night and headed to the village to pursue his new life.

It is becoming clear Chuck has become a real hustler. He is spending more and more time cruising the "gay sections" of the village. He is out every night. I still look for things to do together during the time we share during the day. When I arrived Chuck was dressing for the night. He was all "dressed" up and getting ready for the "village" as usual.

"Listen, you want to hang out with me tonight? You could tag along and see where I go and what I do." Chuck was offering.

"I don't know. Wouldn't I be in the way?" In truth, I did want to go and see for myself. I found myself wondering, "What was his new "life" all about?"

"If you keep quiet and "hang" it will be fine. There's a club and it is open to everyone. They know me so if you come in with me, it will be fine."

"You're all dressed up, in your new outfit. I don't have clothes like yours." He was wearing a colored jacket and some white dress shoes.

"Wear your sheepherder's coat. People dig it." he answers. "Don't worry about the money, it will be my treat."

We had never been to the village together. So far we have always gone our separate ways at nightime. My routine is to explore the music clubs, and bars. He hangs out in the gay sections. Chuck's village and mine exist side by side in the same town but are in separate universes.

The clubs I know all have cover charges or drink minimums. They are far too expensive. I never go in. I can't afford it. Instead I have to stand outside the entrances or sit under windows left open. The open windows allow the cigarette and marijuana smoke to pour out. I don't like cigarette smoke but I put up with it. A choice spot, one where you can hear the music, is a sought after commodity and I have competition. It can get rowdy, with people pushing and shoving to try to claim a prime spot. Sometimes I have to battle. Tonight I will be visiting a club with Chuck and he will be paying. That is the plan.

"The Stonewall Inn is famous because it offers dancing. Most clubs don't.. It has a cover charge." Chuck taps his coat where his wallet is hiding.

We arrived a little after nine. It is located on Christopher street and there is a short line waiting to get in.

"They have fire rules and a maximum capacity limitation. If it's full you can't get in until someone leaves. There is often a wait at the door." The bouncer at the door is checking ID's, he is wearing a muscle shirt. He recognises Chuck and signals us to come in.

"Hey Charles, who is your friend?"

"This is my roommate Luke from California."

"I'm Luke" I smile and nod.

"Welcome, come on in." He lets the entire short line enter together. Chuck pays the entrance fee and we get two drink tickets.

"Let's get a drink." It is dark and hard to see. The bar is painted black.

"I can't see where I am going." I feel off balance, unable to focus.

"Stick close, I'll get us a beer?" He indicated I should follow.

"A beer sounds good." As we head to the bar my eyes begin to adjust. A lot of people are dancing on an open floor.

"It's early, I don't come till after 12:00. Most nights I try to make a couple of bucks. But tonight you are with me." I count a number of well dressed women in the crowd. A juke box is blaring a familiar song and a number of couples are dancing cheek to cheek.

"There are a lot of girls here." I yell to be heard above the crowd.

"There are no girls here." Chuck yells back. We arrive at the bar and he turns in two tokens. The bartender pours two mugs and hails Chuck.

"Like your friend, Charles," He yells as he passes the drinks.

"My roommate." Chuck yells back above the music.

"Let's sit at the corner table." Chuck leads me to a small table wedged up in the back of the room. He pushes our way up to the table and claims it. Most people are milling together, talking and mingling. A few have found seats. As I try to sit, someone grabs my ass and squeezes it. I swatted the hand away.

"Someone grabbed my butt." I yell at Chuck.

"Yeah, I should have warned you, ignore it." He grins. "It'll happen again soon. They like you."

We slide into the table and I am relieved to have a wall at my back.

"That's not something that's easy to ignore." I say feeling violated.

"They mean no harm. They like you. Someone was letting you know. I don't expect you to stay long. You are here to see what I do. Try to relax for a while."

"Okay, but I can tell I don't belong here and shouldn't be here."

"Yeah well, have a couple of beers and watch a little. This place is well known and is one of the few where dancing is allowed. It happens here every night. There is nothing like it back home." He takes a sip and gestures out to the expansive dance floor.

I sit back and try to relax. I had to see this scene for myself. Some questions are being answered.

"Tomorrow is Sunday. They have sunrise ceremonies in Central Park." I say. " I am planning on checking it out. Are you interested?"

"Is it like Topanga Canyon back home? I liked Topanga when we went." He gives me the impression he wants to come.

"I think so, I am told lots of people gather in the meadow. Everyone gets stoned and watches while the sun comes up!" I wait for Chuck to react.

"Are you asking me to tag along?" He replies.

"Yeah, it'll be fun. We can hang out. We might get stoned and meet some people. I have heard there is always a live band. It's free."

" I'll try to get in a little early tonight. If I knock off here by midnight, we can do it. It's the least I can do, After all you came here to please me." Chuck pats me on the knee. "It's the least I can do."

I sip the beer and watch the people as they carry on. A blonde in a slinky tight red dress appears and heads straight for our table. Even in the dark I can see "she" is stunning.

"Chaz, how are you tonight? Who is your friend and why are you hiding him back here in the corner?" She has come right up to our table and leans over the edge, wraps her arm around Chuck's neck and kisses him. It is a long hard passionate kiss.

"Hi Marla, This is my friend Luke from Huntington. He is shy." Chuck grins at me. "Luke, Marla and I have been hanging out together."

"Well I can fix his shyness. Come dance with me." Marla grabs my arm and pulls me towards the dance floor. "She" has strong hands.

"No thanks, I don't dance." I shake myself loose.

"Don't be shy, I won't bite unless you ask me to," Marla strikes a pose as if she is a fashion model. "You're right Chaz he is a cutie." She runs her hand in my hair and laughs.

,"Marla knows you're straight Luke, I told her all about you. She's having fun with you." Chuck cleared up Marla's forwardness. She was kidding

"Chaz has become a favorite around here in a hurry. He has lots of friends here." Marla sits down and puts her arm around him. She gives him a quick kiss of the cheek. "He's a sweetie."

"I see. I guess. I always thought he could use more friends."

"Well we all love Chaz here. Come on, let's dance!" She takes Chuck's hand and hustles him out on the dance floor.

I sit alone sipping my beer and watching. They dance to the long version of Iron Butterflies In-A-Gadda-Da-Vida. The guitar is deafening:

"Oh won't you come with me

And take me by the hand

Oh won't you come with me

And walk this laaand

Please take me by the haand!"

A strobe light is flashing and I think Chuck and Marla might be smoking a joint. They have been surrounded by several others and have formed a group all dancing together. When the song ends Chuck is motioning for me to join him. I walk towards him but a young man slides in front of me and cuts me off.

"Hi! Wanna dance?" he asks.

"Sorry no, I don't" I push by and join up with Chuck and his group.

" I am leaving." I yell in Chuck's ear. "This is not for me."

"Okay, I'll see you back at the Y. Don't wait for me to come in. I am planning on going to the park with you tomorrow."

I head out onto the street. The village where I have been spending my time is nowhere near as welcoming and communal as Chuck's club was. I think he has "found" something there, an acceptance he would never find in Huntington Beach. It didn't exist in our home town.

"My" village is much colder and far more aloof than the one welcoming Chuck. "My" Greenwich Village has a different feel. It is not a hippie place. It is "Hip" instead of hippy. I have been developing a feel for it. It has a hard edge. "Flowers in your hair" are not the thing in the village in New York. Not by a long shot. I spend an hour alone listening to music in the night air. I decide I have had enough and head back to the Y. I wonder how Chuck is getting along. It has become clear he is not alone in the world anymore.

I didn't hear him when he came at night, but he was up ready the next morning. We got an early start, and headed to Central Park in the dark.

Sheep's Meadow was full of moving bodies. I could see shadow figures dancing and jumping in the early morning light. We picked our way through the open field, walking around mounds of people all snuggled up in blankets. Trash can fires were burning providing us with extra light.

"Reminds me of Monterrey." Chuck appraised the meadow and the free love atmosphere. Pot smoke was floating everywhere. Pipes were passing around for anyone who was interested. If you wanted to get high it was easy to do. We did.

"Hey Surf's Up! Surf's Up! Over here!" it was…. I couldn't remember.. My mind froze..It was her, that hot girl... What was her name again? I couldn't remember her name! What luck running into her again! How could I go blank on her name! I panicked! I froze up! I have always struggled trying to remember names. My heart skipped a beat. Fuck! Now I thought, this girl is so hot!

"Surf's Up." She made me feel unique as if I was the first person she had ever met from the west coast. I liked pretending to be a "beach boy".

"Beach Boy? You? I never saw you do anything but body surf." Chuck laughed out loud at the idea.

He was right, even though I had spent a lot of time at the beach while growing up, no one in Huntington would call me a Beach Boy. It was reserved for the real surfers who spent every day in the sun. I was a dilatant. A body surfer. I surfed without a board.

"Yeah but I am a fine body surfer. I did the Jetty in Newport. That takes balls." I answered remembering how rugged Newport can be. An eight feet wave will take you straight up the face, so you try to stay stable in the crest a few feet below the peak. If you can't maintain the spot in the wave it will throw you straight down and pile drive you into a rocky shell bottom forcing you under for hundreds of feet. You can't come to the surface until the wave releases you. I have been held under until my lungs scream and burst.

"Hey Luke, over here." She stopped calling me "Surf's up" and was using my real name. I headed for her. By now, I was sure her name was Clarisse. I kept searching my memory banks trying to be double sure. One of my greatest fears is to call a girl by the wrong name. I decided hers was Clarisse.

"Hi Clarisse, I'm glad to see you again." Obnoxious Helen was nowhere in sight.

"You came back for me! Have a hit! Want part of a breakfast sandwich?" She offered to share both a joint and a ham and egg sandwich.

Jackpot! I got her name right! I left Chuck standing there and forgot about him. "Yeah, I'll have both." I felt a rush of excitement. My blood raced. My heart was pounding.

She put her arms around me and rubbed her breasts against me, wiggling and jiggling them against my side. Wow! We shared her joint and she started tugging at my hand, dragging me towards the woods. I was relieved I hadn't goofed up. Her name was Clarisse! I had gotten it right!

She pulled on me and aimed me towards a semi private spot almost out of public view in the trees and bushes at the side of the meadow. She had no makeup on at all. She didn't need it. She was glowing! I decided she was pretty. Her hair was jet black and her eyes were pale blue. She had curves. I was excited and breathing heavily.

We lay down side by side, and kissed. She put her tongue in my mouth and was excited too. Her hand felt for my zipper and she pulled it down and put her hand in my pants. I was hard and ready and she squeezed me. She started moving her hand up and down squeezing and pumping my dick. She pulled it out of my pants. Her tongue kept darting in and out of my mouth the entire time. We french kissed with passion and fury. I put my hands on her hips. She had on a granny dress with no underwear. I pulled the dress up and she was naked and exposed. It was a beautiful sight. My heart raced.

She opened her legs and guided my prick until it was touching the lips of her vagina. She rubbed her exposed pussy with my hard dick, lining it up so I could enter her. I pushed a little harder and she was wet and ready. We were lying face to face on the ground. I entered her and slid into her hole. I was up on my elbows trying to keep my full body weight from crushing her. My long quest was coming to an ending. She was taking my virginity! It was magical.

My prick was in her. The ground was hard and unforgiving. I kept the bulk of my weight off her. I kept my mind on the thought of fucking her. I ignored everything but her. We kept at it, she was pumping back at me and speeding up the pace making delightful noises. Noises I had never heard before. It was thrilling. I kept thrusting.

She pumped back and we got into a rhythm. I kept pushing down until my motion was stopped as if I was hitting the inner wall of her vagina. I went back and forth. It occurred to me to change the motion a little, I slowed it down. She gasped trying to pull me deeper into her hole. She dug her fingernails into my back.

Her pussy was on fire! It was grabbing hold of me, clamping around me, squeezing and shaking me. I felt an orgasm coming and it ran over me like a freight train, forcing me to speed up and push harder. I was grunting and shaking, and felt like screaming. I burst into the world of sexual fulfillment. My quest to experience sexual intercourse was over! I had lost my virginity, Clarisse had granted me clemency. Virginity was not going to be a lifelong sentence!

A half hour later we lay there talking about Long Island. She told me she often took the train into the city and liked to stay for a few days. If the weather was mild she slept outside in the park.

"My parents always worry when I am gone. They will be worried. After a day or two they will call the police to look for me. I will have to go home soon." She gave me a coy little smile. I will go home soon.

"But we just met. Do you have to?" I made a little frown to let her know I wanted her to stay with me.

"You can come out and visit me. I have a friend who has an apartment, you could stay there." She suggested I try to visit her.

"I'd like that."

"Can I stay at the Y with you instead?"

"Naw, no women are allowed. It's a men only place. They'd throw me out if I got caught. I could never sneak you in and out. There is only one entrance and it is always watched."

She reached in her pack and pulled out a small writing pad.

"I am going home today, but you should come see me.."

She gave me a folded sheet with her number and asked me to call. I promised I would. I meant it when I said it. Hell yes I meant it! Thanks to her I knew what I had been missing. If having sex with a woman made you a man then I was one now. Funny I thought, I don't feel different

The passion which had caused us to rush to the woods did not ignite again. I had become aware of the crowds and that had cooled my lust. As it started to get late, Clarisse gathered up her things and left for home.

When she left it occurred to me I had left Chuck in the dark, alone in the middle of the meadow. I looked for him but of course he was gone.no The morning had passed and the sun was high up in the sky. I went back to the room and found Chuck milling about.

"I saw what happened! You did it right out there in the open for everyone to see." he sounded agitated.

"Yeah, I did." somehow it didn't matter where we did it or who was there watching.

"How was it?" he asked. "Is everything cracked up to be?"

"Hot! She is hot!" A huge grin covered my face.

"I'll bet. Are you going to see her again?" Chuck sounded a little jealous.

"I got her number, she lives in a place called Plainview on Long Island. There is a train and it goes out there. I am planning on going to see her. I sure hope I see her again!" I pulled out the paper she gave me. There was an address and a phone number. I opened the note for the first time and read it out loud. It read " Come lick me please, Clarisse!"

"Come lick me," I repeated it out loud. "No girl has ever given me a note like that before."

My toes curled up in my shoes. I was still bathing in a warm afterglow of orgasmic bliss. It was a sensation of well being and a closeness with life that I had never felt before. But was it love? Somehow the whole manhood question was on the surface of my mind again. I didn't know the answer. Am I a man now? Did having sex in the park make you a man? For the first time I was starting to doubt this idea.

"Love?" I said it out loud.

"Love?" Chuck heard me and reacted. "You got fucked. Had sex. Hell, she grabbed you by the dick and hauled you off into the bushes. What has it got to do with love?"

"You're right." If it was love it would last. That could only be proven in time. What was this feeling? This feeling pretended everything was perfect in my world? I thought I am just beginning to understand how it all works. I was resolved to see Clarisse again as soon as possible. I longed for more sexual experience. I was almost eighteen and it had been an endless quest.

"Tomorrow, let's go see the Statue of Liberty." Chuck cut into my fantasy by waving a tourist brochure showing the statue on the cover.

"Sure" I decided I should give the experience with Clarisse a little time to settle before I chased after her. I would give it a day and then call.

The following morning we boarded the Staten Island Ferry. The Statue of Liberty was in poor shape and needed repair. The green color was old and faded and had seen better days. It was rusted and the stairway to the top was closed to the public. I had expected it to be dynamic, bursting with power and radiating with an energy of hope, but it was not the case.

"Give me your tired and poor" Did the description fit the statue and the condition it was in. It was "tired and poor." I was disappointed it had been allowed to fall into such a pathetic state. I believed no one cared. What did the neglect say about our country? Perhaps the statue is no longer emblematic of the nation. Perhaps we had stopped caring. The war machine was raging and few wanted to know anything about it. Most eyes were not on the war. Most people were too busy trying to get by to care. Was that the message the statue was carrying in its hand?

Two days have passed since my encounter with Clarisse. I couldn't get her off my mind. I decided to call and set up a date. There is a pay phone in the lobby of the Y. I called and her father answered and asked who was calling.

"My name is Luke.... No you don't know me..... I met your daughter a few days ago in the park.... No! I don't want to stay away from her..... Can I please talk with her.......she's not there? ....She ran away?........No, I don't know where she is... Do you know where she went?....... No! I didn't ask her to come to California with me! .....Can I leave a message?........ Yes, I am living at the Y.......You're calling the police?"....... he hung up on me.

Well I had put my hands on her but it was not in anger. In fact my hands had been all over her. The incident had become complicated. It never occurred to me to worry about her age. She had told me enough I knew she was younger than me without knowing her exact age.

I thought about the rest of what her father had said. I was not ready to go home. The one thing I knew for sure was I wanted to see her again. But did I want her to run away with me? " How could she tell her Dad she was running away with me?" She didn't know my name. Was she telling her Dad she was running away with "Surf's Up. Chuck and I had been together twenty four hours a day while hitchhiking and it had proved to be hard to handle. How would it be with a girl I hardly knew?

Chapter 13

I stopped getting daily reports from Chuck on his enterprise of trolling for men. I had the feeling it might be getting stale, One afternoon I came back to the room to find a note he had left, "Gone shopping." I decided to go down to the Village by myself and hang out for a while. I put on a pair of green and white checkered pants plus a brown corduroy sport coat. The pants were lime green, but it was the white checks that stood out. These were my dress clothes. I was duded out!

I went to my favorite blues club, a place where I could stand near the door and hear the music. I stood and listened. I had done this so many times it had become repetitive and dull. Nothing new. After an hour of hanging out listening, I decided to call it a night and started for the subway jump.

I took a side street and as I did a skinny young black man was coming up the street toward me. His eyes were locked on me and I thought he was coming at me. He zeroed in on me! It made me uncomfortable. He was several years older than me. He bumped into me hard on purpose. I was used to collisions and contact. In basketball I did it dozens of times a day. I slammed him back harder than he hit me. He bounced back surprised.

"Give me five dollars." He said with a hard aggressive stare.

"No." I gave him a quick reply. "No, not a chance."

"You better do it or we'll get you." His tone carried a real threat.

"Fuck no, beat it." I tried to get by him, but he moved up in my face. I lowered my shoulder and jammed it in his chest. I pivoted and threw an elbow into his shoulder.

"I got friends, we'll gut you, if you don't give me the money." His eyes were on fire, "I got some mean friends."

"You're alone." I lowered my shoulder again and brushed him. "Try it."

"You'll regret this, we'll stick a knife in you for sure." He moved aside and let me pass.

"I doubt it." I pushed forward.

I put the incident out of mind. He was another weird character in New York running a game on me. At that moment a delightful blues harmonica floated from a small corner club. I decided to stop and listen. Twenty minutes passed and once I again headed for the subway. I cut down an alleyway and there he was, with two friends, just like he had promised.

"There's the motherfucker!" he saw my green checkered pants from two blocks off. "

Let's get the motherfucker. He slammed me hard." They lit after me. My heart jumped up into my mouth.

"Oh Shit!"

I ran like hell, vaulted the railings, bounced down the steps, and plunged into a waiting subway car. They were still about a hundred yards behind me. There was a black uniformed policeman in the back of the car. I scurried up next to him and stood alone. He nodded unaware of my problem. All of my pursuers made it into the back of the car as the door shut. They were eighty feet away and staring at me. What to do? So far, other than chasing me, nothing has happened yet. Threats had been made, but so what? There was no damage done yet, but if they got their hands on me it would be real trouble.

Should I trust the cop? Tell him my story? Could I? What would he do? What could he do? I thought long and hard about this and decided I didn't know the answer. He was black after all. Would it matter? I was in danger. Was it an issue? How could I prove anything? What would I say? I just stood there next to him. Stops passed and we were in a stalemate. They stayed, and I stayed, we were at opposite ends of the car staring at each other. Ten more stops passed. I did not want to stay in this stalemate to the end of the line. Something had to change.

I walked up to the subway door as the train stopped. The three of them followed suit. The doors opened. I waited, and stood there, after a time I stepped out. They did the same. They were forty feet away. I could hear the car doors starting to shut. Subway doors closed making a sliding sound, I jumped back in the car. They did not. They had quit the chase and gave up! I let five stops pass. When I got out I was lost. Luckily there were maps posted everywhere. I was a long way off course. It took an hour to get back to the YMCA.

On exiting I climbed up the long stairway and there sitting in the stairwell was a Puerto Rican man with his shirt torn open. His exposed chest had a deep slash several inches long. He was bleeding profusely.

Shit! I thought. We made eye contact as I passed. Several people were tending to him and trying to stop the bleeding. I thought there but for the grace of God, go I. It is strange how your mind conjures up conversations with God when you have a rough moment in life.

Upon entering the room I discovered Chuck, all dressed up with a white shirt and tie. He had on slacks and some new black shoes. "What the hell?" I asked.

"I went to a job interview today and they hired me on the spot." He held up a help wanted section from the New York Times on which he had circled a number of ads. "I

want to stay here In New York! I'm going to try to be a runner on the stock market."
He grinned at me.

"A runner, what are you talking about?" He had caught me off guard, I had never
thought of staying and finding work. Instead I was running out of money and getting
ready to leave. I had had enough of New York and was ready for a change. It was
apparent he had other ideas.

"Not sure, but they say no experience is needed. You just have to be able to keep up
a hectic pace. I called and they gave me an interview. I went today and I start
Monday. It pays $475.00 per month." It sounded like a lot of money.

"Just like that? You got a job and you're starting in two days? What about college?
Santa Cruz? The draft?"

My own plan was to eventually return home and start college. Attending college
meant an automatic draft deferment and a temporary pass from being sent to the
jungles of Vietnam. I thought Chuck had been counting on it too.

"The war is no issue for me. I'm queer, I know it for sure and I don't care if they know.
Hell, it's the first thing I'll tell them if they draft me." He gave me a grin. "I don't care if
they give me the acid test."

"The acid test, What the hell is that?"

"Well you know there is no place for a queer in Uncle Sam's army, right? So if you
tell them you are queer, they make you prove it. The military interviewer pulls down
his pants. If you suck him off, you're queer and they can't draft you. It is 100%
guaranteed they don't take queers in the army."

"Is that so?" I had heard there was a policy of no queers in the armed forces but this
was the first I had heard of the acid test. Did it exist?

"Funny isn't it? The guy getting the blow job isn't queer. He's only getting his dick
sucked. He can be in the army, the guy doing the sucking is the problem. Strange
way to look at it in my opinion. But the army doesn't have any room for queers. So if I
get drafted they won't take me so long as I am willing to suck a dick. Which I am."

It was true, it was all he had to do and he would be exempt. Since he had no
problem at all doing it, he had no reason to be concerned. The world gets stranger
and stranger I thought.

"Hell, I've been thinking about leaving. Starting back home." I said. "My money is
running out fast, and I'm not making any at chess anymore. I will be broke soon, and
I've seen enough of New York. I think it's time for me to go."

"Well, I'm staying. By making the money I can cut back on the hustling. It is becoming a strain."

"I am glad you're thinking of cutting back on the nightlife. I think it might be hurting you to do it so much. It's changing you." I answered.

"Yeah, sometimes it is a bit too kinky. I have been in a couple of situations I didn't like."

"I've been thinking about going to Montreal. I want to see the World's Fair. I was meaning to suggest it to you soon."

"It will cost a lot of money. More than here, the fair will be expensive." Chuck had a point. It would cost a lot of money. But if I wanted to do it, the time was now. While I still had some money left.

"A guy in the square told me about it. It sounded so cool. John Glenn's spaceship is on display. The one the Russian's sent up is there too. It's the first manned ship ever sent into space. I knew I wanted to see those space ships."

"Well, I'm staying here. If I don't like the job I will quit."

"What about school? Santa Cruz?"

"I'll figure it out. I may have to work a month or so, and catch a train home or something."

"Shit, man, I guess I'm going to be hitch hiking by myself." I knew I could do it, but it added risk. Two healthy athletic young guys were safer. We had each other's backs. It was like my mother had said there is "safety" in numbers. Hitching all alone would be more dangerous.

Chuck's plan took me by surprise. I wondered how he would adjust to working on Wall street. He was going to carry "buy and/or sell" notices between people managing transactions. I had no idea what that entailed, and I didn't give a shit either.

I studied the map and decided to go to Canada by passing through Vermont. I prepared to go alone. I packed all my excess clothes and gear and went to the post office, and sent it all home. Once I sent it all back my pack was down under twenty pounds. Much easier to handle. I had been hauling way too much stuff. What a relief!

"If I decide I don't like the job or they don't like me, we can meet up again in Montreal."

"Well sure, if it doesn't work out right away. I am planning on taking a peak around Vermont for a few days. I hope to be at the fair in about five days." I hoped he would show but figurered he wouldn't.

"Why don't we plan on meeting at the Russian exhibit in five days, at say 12:00 o'clock. If the job doesn't work out, I will be there and we can meet up again." Chuck was hedging his bet.

"In five days I'll go to the Russian exhibit at 12:00. I will wait twenty minutes, and if you don't show, I will assume you are not coming." We agreed and it settled the matter. We split up. The next morning I left alone. Chuck went to work on Wall Street.

Chapter Fourteen

I was in a dark mood. New York had been interesting, thrilling and disappointing all at the same time. I was no longer a virgin but somehow I felt let down. My encounter with Clarisse hadn't answered all my questions, it hadn't filled in all the blanks. My imagination expected more. A little voice in my head whispered it was the beginning of a quest, and not the end I thought it was. I wondered if there would ever be an end to the quest? How do you know when you have found it? Found manhood? Become a man?

I had not planned on Chuck bailing out. I was annoyed with him for having abandoned our trip together. I felt he had let me down. I believed no matter what life might throw at me, I would find a way to deal with it.

Getting out of Manhattan and escaping New York and its towering skyline was a challenge. I decided to ride the subway until I reached the far edge of the city. From there I was able to get out of New York by thumbing a series of short lifts until I was on the highway leading to Vermont.

"Vermont". I held up my sign. It was the name of a small state not an actual destination. The catalogs made traveling in Vermont become a dream vacation.The pictures in the magazines always came from the fall catalog, and emphasized the dramatic changes of season. It was mid August, the hottest and driest time of year. The leaves had not yet started to change color. Everything was still green, the landscape was a month away from making the transition to fall.

I had no exact destination in mind. I had decided to see the countryside on the way to Montreal. I hope to bum around for a few days and let things happen. A VW van pulled over and stopped for me. I hopped in. A small balding man was driving. The bus had a full load of young people, all of them were about my age.

"I'm Jonathan. Where are you going?" he wondered if he had read my sign.

"I am going to Montreal, to the World's Fair but I want to hitchhike a little around Vermont. I'm trying to see the country."

"Get in, we're going to Vermont. You're not from New York. Where's the accent from?"

"California." I answered. "Huntington Beach."

"That's cool.What are you doing here?" He shot me a quizzical glance.

"I plan to bum around, and check things out." I answered.

"You're doing it alone?"

"I am now, I had another guy with me, but he got a job and stayed in New York..

"These kids are all from New York, our church runs a farm, we provide them with time away from the city. They live for a while on the farm, and work. It gives them a new outlook." He nodded to the five kids sitting in the back of the van. "They are all going to the farm."

"Hi," I waved to acknowledge three girls and two guys, "I'm Luke."

"Hi Luke, I'm........."- five names came back rapid fire one after another. I have trouble remembering names, when they are fired out to a group. I do remember faces and instantly noted a pretty girl in the group. She smiled at me.

"Our farm is near the center of the state, about fifty miles south of Montpelier. Would you like to stay with us for a while?" He made the offer out of the blue.

"What would I do there?" I asked.

"Feed the animals, we have chickens, ducks, pigs, sheep, cows, horses. You could help do some cleaning up, and you could eat for free. Have a place to stay.?"

"It's fun, you'll like it," the young girl spoke up, "We have a garden, we weed, and water the crops. There's lots of things to do. There's a river to swim in. We fish in it, too."

She was a pleasant young redhead girl with bright blue eyes and freckles and was still smiling at me. "Are you Amy?" I wanted to confirm I had her name right. Her warm smile relaxed me. I felt like talking with her.

"That's right." she continued smiling.

"You've done this before, Amy?"

"Yes, many times. I like it, the country is quiet and peaceful. So nice compared to New York." She was calm and pleasant.

"How about you guys? Have any of you done this before?" I asked, "no." Amy was the only experienced farm worker.

"My father's a minister. I've been coming ever since I was young." She had a delightful smile and a twinkle in her eyes I liked, it was her fourth trip to the farm. She was an old hand. I wondered how old she was, I guessed she was about17.

"What do you like best, Amy?"

"I like it all. Swimming, fishing, hiking in the hills. We have campfires, and sing together. Please come visit for a while. It'll be fun."

"Sure, okay, I'll check it out." I had doubts I would see Chuck again. In truth, I thought the money would be appealing. I was almost certain he would be a no show.

Spending a few days in Vermont on a farm sounded perfect. The green hills rolled by, and a number of small streams crossed by dotting the highway. There were a few tiny towns, but most were farms and uninhabited land. It was almost a wilderness, far less populated than I expected.

Many hours later, Jonathan turned off the highway onto a country road. We passed through several old covered wooden bridges like the ones in the photos I had seen. Many miles into the backcountry, a sign appeared, it read "Interfaith Community Farm".

"This is it. We are supported by a number of churches, and many denominations contribute." Jonathan nodded at the sign.

We parked and the boys led me to a bunk house. There were separate sleeping arrangements. Boys in one bunkhouse, girls in another. There were about a dozen boys already in residence. It was near dinner time, and we all cleaned up and they led me to a central building that housed a kitchen and eating hall. Dinner was hot dogs, baked beans, potato chips, with lemonade to drink.

That night there was a campfire, we sang folk songs, and Amy sat next to me. As the night progressed she put her hand on mine, and time passed and she held my hand for the rest of the night. I told her about Huntington Beach, body surfing, snorkeling, and about hitchhiking around. I related some of what had happened. At the end of the night we kissed each other. It was intense.

"You've lived and done a lot compared to most of the boys I know." She had a sweet voice. I walked her to her bunk house and we kissed.. I lingered with her for as long as I could. She was not in a hurry and we stayed on the porch kissing and squeezing each other until someone inside blinked the porch light.

"I gotta go in." She let go of my hand and pulled away.

"You think they knew we were out here?" I thought we were alone.

"There are always eyes watching. You don't have to see them to know they are there."

She opened the door and stood in the doorway. "I'll see you tomorrow."

I made my way over to the boy's bunkhouse and went in.

"Amy's sweet. Be careful, she's a minister's daughter." It was the voice of one of the boy's from the bus.

"Yeah, I know, does it matter?"

"Not if you follow the rules and be careful."

"We just met. Not much has happened." I answered annoyed that I was getting so much attention.

"You sure?" He answered.

"Well trust me, we have only started to get to know each other." I lay down in my bunk and tuned out the comments.

I can close my eyes and fall asleep in a blink. I often snore and I know it. There were at least a dozen or so boys sleeping in the same room with me. I was in dream land almost the second my head hit the pillow.

I wondered who Chuck was sleeping with. and was he alone? By now I imagined the YMCA had given him a roommate or more likely he found one on his own.

"Five O'Clock! Time to Get Up!" It was Jonathan yelling in the doorway."Time to feed the animals."

Everyone rose up as one, and pulled on their pants. I popped out of bed, and followed the line headed to the barn. It was pitch black out and there were no lights. Someone was shining a flashlight on the path and guiding us.

"New guy feeds the pigs " I felt a hand on my shoulder. "Come with me." I followed along behind him.

He led me to a plastic vat full of stinking vegetable matter. There was a short trowel on the vat and two wooden buckets. I began scooping the gruel out of the vat. I could see bits of corn cob and other rotten semi decayed stuff that must have been pumpkin or squash.

"Fill both buckets to the top." The "food" was a soft liquid and it was spilling on my shoes and pants as I tried to scoop it out of the vat.

"This stuff stinks. It's rancid." I was amazed that an animal could eat it.

"Don't worry, the pigs love it. You're spilling it! Take your time, don't hurry. You're moving too quickly, you need to slow down. All you need to do is fill the two buckets."."

It felt like the buckets were too big or the trowels were too small.

"There must be a better way to do this." I complained.

"You'll get used to it. Before you know it someone else will come along and you won't be the new guy anymore. The new guy always feeds the pigs."

"My bad luck!" I complained but I didn't care. Hell I , I was going to feed a pig. How many times would I end up doing a job like this in my life? Ten minutes later I was standing at the pigs trough with two overflowing buckets. I was ready to pour!

"Just dump 'em in, and stand back." My teacher advised me what to do.

The loaded buckets were heavy. I had to strain to lift them up to the edge of the trough. I struggled to get them in the right spot. I tipped them forward and the mush spilled out filling the trough splashing the tub like bathwater. Four huge pigs, each weighing hundreds of pounds, raced forward and competed for the treat. They shoved and pushed against each other hoping to get their noses at the front of the line and were soon buried in the meal.

"Don't put your hands anywhere near them when they're eating. You may lose a finger."

"Are we done?" Fascinated, I watched the show of voracious greed that was unfolding below.

" We still have to wash out and clean the buckets for the next feeding."

After the animals ate, we did. They had stacks of pancakes ready, along with some orange juice. One thing about living on a shoestring and eating small quantities of food everyday is that your stomach gets used to it. It shrinks. I had lost about ten pounds, and these two meals at the retreat were gigantic.They were far larger meals than I had been used to eating.

In the afternoon, Amy came and found me, and led me off to the garden to weed, and trim plants. There was nothing to harvest and since the garden was weeded daily there were few weeds. We walked around rows of corn, carrots, green beans, and tomatoes and picked off little shoots of weeds that had popped up.

"Let's go swimming," she suggested. Weeding had turned out to be a quick short task.

"I don't have a bathing suit." I said.

"Go in your undies or skinny dip, I skinny dip." She laughed. "It's okay, we all do it." I was a little shocked.

"Okay!" I grew up swimming in the waves of the Pacific Ocean. A stream in Vermont should not present a problem. It turned out to be far colder than I expected. I dove in and it was a shock to my system. I came up out of the water with my lungs screaming.

Amy took her top off and went swimming in her panties. I could see she had a lot of freckles and long thin nipples which were rigid and hard in the cold water. They were in a state of excitement. The cold water and air were making them stand up and out. She had a slender waist and rounded hips.

Lovely, like photos in a Playboy magazine, I thought. I could feel my blood circulating and pounding in my veins.

"Do a lot of other people come here?"My first thought was to avoid staring. But she was so relaxed I decided to enjoy the sight.

"Sure all the time, this is a public place, many people swim in their skivvies. Are you shy?" She was so relaxed and at ease, her calm mood took all the sexual tension out of the moment. She does this all the time, and it wasn't supposed to be exciting.

I had kept my underwear on, so I guess I felt shy. We swam for a while and she went to the creek bed, dried off and put on her top. Her nonchalant attitude put all thoughts of sexual adventure out of mind.

"Too bad, I was enjoying the view." I tried to sound cool. The icy stream had cooled my body temperature but not my imagination which I could feel calling in my groin, urging me to take action.

"Do you want to stay here with me? I mean for a while? For the summer?"

It was clear she wanted to be kissed. I kissed her. She was a sweet girl. She kissed me back but there was no hot desire in her kiss. She was not Clarisse. She was not going to drag me off into the bushes. It was not her style.

"Caught you." A voice called, a crowd had arrived. In a blink they were all naked and swimming in the river.

"I am leaving for Montreal tomorrow," I warned her.

"I was hoping I could talk you into staying for a while." She pouted at me.

"I promised a friend I would meet him, and if I am going to keep my promise I need to leave in the morning." I was not sure I wanted to leave. It was a sure bet Chuck wouldn't show, and it wanted to stay and see some more of Amy. The idea appealed to me. But if I wanted to be in Montreal in time to meet up, I had to leave.

"I made a promise. I always try to keep my promises."

"Sit with me at the fire tonight?" She was beautiful, alluring, there was no way I could say no. Part of me wanted to break my promise to Chuck. Her clear bright blue eyes shined. She was calm and inviting but nothing about her was calling out with passion or lust.

Dinner came and the nightly campfire came as well. I put my arm around her shoulders and she snuggled up to me. It felt like we had known each other for a long time, even if it was only the second day. I walked her to the bunk at the end of the night and we kissed long and hard in the moonlight. I felt like I was thousands of miles and endless days away from New York.

"Are you religious, Luke? Do you believe in Jesus?" Her question caught me by surprise!

"Well, my father is a scientist, he raised me to question things, not to accept things blindly." I told her the truth. "I am sure Jesus must have lived on earth. But I am not a follower."

"I see, so do you think you will go to heaven?" She pushed for an answer.

I was not sure what I wanted to say. I had been down this road before, and I knew the routine. If the person asking believes you must believe in Jesus or you cannot be "saved", there are no good answers. I felt trapped, not by Amy, but by things as they are.

"If there is a heaven, I don't see why God would want to deny me access." I said.

"The only way to heaven is through Jesus." She told me sternly. "If you don't believe you won't go." For her that was faith in a nutshell.

"I guess that's the chance I am taking." But the whole idea, the concept of being "saved" is foreign to me.I was raised to question and doubt things. Prove them and verify them. " Can you prove what you say about Jesus?" I pushed back.

"I don't need to. My faith tells me it is true," she said. "Please stay here with me for a while. I'll change your mind." She wanted to be kissed, so I kissed her again. It was becoming habit forming. Her kiss back made it clear she was not looking for me to expand our affair any further than some kissing. She was at her limit of desire and romantic expression.

"Good night", I said and she slipped into the girl's bunk house.

I counted my cash again. I had a little over a hundred dollars left. More than half my bankroll was gone. The room in New York had taken a fair bit, so had the food. Food from small corner stores in Manhattan was expensive. It was clear I was running low on funds.

When I woke, the church gave me breakfast again. I let Jonathan know I wanted to go, and he offered me a ride back to the highway. Amy waved! A part of me wanted to stay but it was not meant to be. I knew that. I think she knew too. We lived on different sides of the country and in different worlds. I was only visiting hers. I had been passing through.

Chapter Fifteen-

I made a sign reading, "Montreal - World's Fair." I refused some short rides and decided to wait for one all the way to the Fair. People going there had to travel down this road if they were coming from Vermont, so I hoped to get one long ride all the way to Montreal. I did. It was from an angular thin man with thinning hair and a mustache. He pulled up in a Lincoln.

"I'm going to Montreal," he rolled down the window and unlocked the door.

"thanks" I got in.

"My name is Henri. I do not often stop for hitchhikers but you look like a nice young man." He had a French accent.

"Well, I'm Luke. I'm glad you did. How many hours do you figure it will take?"

"It's about a five hour drive but we will have to clear customs, which can take a while. Have you ever gone through customs?" he asked.

"No never." I had never thought about it either.

"I am a returning citizen with a passport, so I won't have a problem, but you are young, do you have a photo I.D.?"

"Yes, a driver's license." I answered, "I got it when I turned sixteen"

"That should be enough. They'll be suspicious and ask you where you're going? Why do you want to go to Canada? A lot of young Americans are trying to go to Canada to avoid the draft. You know that, right? They'll assume you are one of them."

"Yes, but I'm only seventeen. I'm not draft eligible yet." I was worried. I hadn't considered this at all. "I haven't had to register yet for the draft. I don't think you have to do anything until you're eighteen."

"OK, well you need to think about it. The policy at the border is to try and stop illegal draft dodgers. So if they think you are coming in to avoid the draft, they'll want to turn you back."

"I had not considered it." I answered.

"When we get to customs I want you to walk over. There is a walk-through line. You can't ride with me."

"What are you talking about?" He had got my attention.

"I can drive right through, I always do. I have a Canadian passport, and a driver's license. They might detain you. If you're with me there is a chance they will detain us both, so I want you to cross by yourself. Either way they will let you in or not. I will be waiting on the other side, but if they hold you too long, I will go on alone."

"What are the chances they will turn me back?" I worried out loud.

"How much money do you have?"

I didn't want to answer, ever since Jed and Wilbur kidnapped me, I had made it a point not to discuss how much money I had or where I had hidden it. I thought it over and I decided Henri was harmless enough.

"About $100.00." I rounded off.

"That should be enough," he nodded. "You may get a limited entry. They'll expect you out within a few days."

Henri was correct, I was questioned, and they counted my cash. I had $107.65. They decided my money would last four days. I told them I could stay much longer and not run out of money. They ignored me and gave me four day's entries.

"Be sure to check out at the border office when you leave the country. We will have a ledger open on you."

I learned no passport was needed. I walked over the border after an hour's delay. When I did, I was surprised to find Henri waiting.

"I thought you were going to leave if I was held up," I said.

"It took me a while longer than usual, the line was long, and I only got through a few minutes ago. I decided to wait for you." He smiled and pulled out into traffic.

"Thanks, I am glad you did."

He had the news on. There were race riots in many major American cities, and the war in Vietnam was getting a lot of coverage as usual. The American body bag counts kept rising, the totals were reported daily. We always managed to kill more Viet Cong than they did American soldiers. It gave the public the impression we were winning. It stood to reason that if more Viet Cong were dying America must be winning. Somehow it was considered to be a reason to be optimistic!

The media narrative made the rebel cause seem hopeless. It was only a matter of time and they would have to quit fighting since they were getting killed at such a prolific rate. Surely they would realize defeat was inevitable and accept their cause was futile. Regardless, even the most callous American was getting sick of the sight of flag draped body bags returning home with dead American boys. It was always hard to watch. No matter how hard I tried I never got used to the widows' swollen eyes as they claimed the remains of their loved ones.

"We don't have a racial problem like you do in America." Henri was reacting to the news. " Many blacks came to Canada fleeing slavery, both before and during your civil war. Some still come to be free of the pressures of your society. We don't have the same history of slavery that you have."

"No slavery? Ever?" I asked.

"No our country wasn't built by slaves.They were all freed when they came here." Henri spoke like a man who was sure he knew the facts.

"So you don't have riots in your cities?"

"No! And many Canadians are opposed to the war in Vietnam. When the Fair opened there was a protest against the war and it was Anti-American. Most Canadians want to let American kids come to Canada, no questions asked. But the border guards, they are a different story. You were lucky they let you in today."

"My plan is to enroll in college, and take the automatic deferment. I have never considered going to Canada." I answered.

"I teach college. French history. It is a part of our heritage. You learn some English history in America, we learn French/Canadian History. The war is discussed daily on our campus. You know it was a French war, one we lost." As the day wore on I learned Henri taught at a university in Montreal.

"I haven't eaten yet, can I buy you dinner?" We had entered the edges of the city proper and several signs advertising fine dining houses had flashed by.

"Of course, One of the first rules of hitchhiking is "never turn down free food."

He took me to a fancy place and I had a steak with a baked potato and sour cream. The steak was huge. It was one of the finest meals I have ever eaten in my entire life. It was the best since the start of the trip.

The conversation stayed with politics, and the racial situation, there was more than enough there to talk about. He was aware of the long French involvement in Vietnam. He wanted to explain it to me, battle by battle. He delivered a lecture about the Vietnamese war of attrition. He explained they were relentless and never gave up. They kept coming back and fighting no matter what. That tendency when combined with the communist party's nationalism gave them a resolve Americans could never understand or appreciate.

"They've been fighting invaders for fifty years. You are the "new wave" of invaders. The Vietnamese will wear you down and you'll leave."

"For sure there is a lot to learn." I knew he was right.

"Death by a thousand cuts." He was adamant and persuasive. "America is trying to salvage the mess we French left. American advisors have been giving advice for over ten years."

He also believed in French separatism.

"Many French Canadians have a closer allegiance to France than they do to the United Kingdom." He made it clear he was one of them. He knew French history well and he chose to focus on the chapters and versions he liked best. He had a long list of reasons the French speaking part of Canada should succeed and align with France.

"We have a long documented history of conflict with the English." He was getting more intense as the dinner went on.

"Vive La Quebec" was his last dinner line, delivered after having drunk several bottles of red wine. He claimed it was the last thing Charles de Gaulle had blurted out while attending the opening of the fair. It created havoc. The press believed de Gaulle was advocating a return to French rule. Many speculated a revolution was implied. "Montreal is a city with strong French ties."

Henri became aware he had been lecturing me nonstop since we sat down to eat.

"I am sorry, where are my manners? I lost track of time and have not asked you once what you are planning on doing tomorrow." He was calculating how best to rescue the situation and make things better.

"Do you want to stay at my house tonight? You can sleep on my couch, and go to the fair tomorrow." It was what I hoped to hear and was perfect. I accepted.

"How far from the fair do you live?" I asked.

"The fair is on two-man made islands and there is a bridge with a tram over to them. I live close by. You can take the tram in the morning."

"That's great!" I was getting excited. Things were working out, I marveled at my luck. I had a place to stay and it wouldn't cost me anything. I convinced myself fate had smiled at me once again.

Henri lived in a large one bedroom apartment in a secure building with underground parking. He had a view of the St. Lawrence river. The city lights were flickering in the night sky when he pulled the curtains closed to give the room more privacy.

"Your apartment is well furnished." I laid my pack next to the couch and took a seat.

"If you would like to shower you could get into some more comfortable clothes." He offered.

"No need, I showered yesterday." It made me chuckle, he thought I had anything like "comfortable clothes."

"Okay, how about some more wine? Red or white?" He asked.

"Sure but do you have something sweeter?" I rarely drank wine, and if I did it was more like fruit juice than wine.

"Sorry, I have a riesling that is sweet. I'll get it" He fetched a bottle and two glasses. "I am glad I had this. I don't drink sweet wine."

"Much better." I said after having a sip.

After a couple of glasses I got tipsy, and wanted to go to sleep. He brought out a blanket and a pillow. I was getting comfortable on the couch when he grabbed my right ankle hard. He was much stronger than I expected. He jiggled it back and forth.

"Please sleep in my bed tonight." He gave me a wicked smile and tightened his grip on my ankle. His grip was like a vice.

"Get your hands off me." I kicked his arm with my free leg as hard as I could. He let go and fell back shocked. His shock turned into anger.

"You ungrateful little bastard. I gave you a ride and bought you dinner. You flirted with me." His face turned beet red.

"You're crazy man, I never flirted with you." I jumped to my feet, prepared to defend myself. He saw I was ready to fight and backed off.

"Get out, I can't have you here if you're going to act like this." He began to rant. "Get out, get out."

I gathered my things and headed for the door.Getting out was all I could think about. He had caught me by surprise and his rage had become venomous without warning. I slammed the door behind me as I left.

I could hear him yelling and screaming as I staggered out into the hallway and down the stairs. Why had he turned on me? I decided you can never tell what people are thinking. I remembered what my mother had told me, "Stay together, there is safety in numbers." At that moment I missed Chuck and wondered how things had turned out for him in New York.

Chapter Sixteen

"You deceived me!" Henri's shrill voice chases after me as I try to escape.

He slams the door in rage. I am flushed with alcohol. I wonder if he had drugged me and suspect he must have. My body is heavy and I was having trouble standing!

I want to lie down and go to sleep. My fingers had gone numb and cold. My mind is dark. I have to close my eyes. I fight to stay awake. In a fog I crawl up in my bag and fall into a dreamless sleep.

When I wake up, the birds are chirping and won't let me rest. Had I passed out? I remember taking refuge in a quiet park. It was light, so I stumbled into a public restroom with a water fountain. I staggered over to get a long drink of cold clear water. My stomach was squeamish and painful. I reflect on how lucky I am to have slept undetected. Once again fortune has smiled on me.

My mind began to focus on meeting up with Chuck. I wonder if he will show? Not likely, I think. He has convinced he wants to stay in New York and carry on with the new life he is developing. It occurs to me the unfortunate incident with Henri could have been avoided and only happened because I was alone. The thought makes me feel vulnerable. I wondered if I needed Chuck? Would I be better off if he showed?

"There is safety in numbers." I repeat my mothers words out loud. There is no one to hear me. I roll up my bag and head off looking for the entrance to the fair. I stop in a corner store to buy a quart of milk and a roll for breakfast.

"Is the fair close by?" I asked the clerk.

"Yes, very close." The young girl behind the counter smiles. "You are close, it is less than a mile."

"Can you give me directions?" I pay for the food..

"You take Montaigne, and go north for three lights," she points to the street outside "and turn right on Claret. After that it is easy, you follow for a few blocks and you'll see the signs. It's not far at all." She is friendly, and anxious to be of help." I can tell you're not from around here. Where are you from?"

"California. I am looking forward to seeing the space capsules. They sound neat."

"Yeah! I loved them. Here take this little booklet, it's free. There's lots to see. There are things from all over the world. Did you drive from California?" she asks.

"No, I hitchhiked. I'm walking."

"Wow, Good luck, enjoy the fair."

I glance at the booklet. The fair is the biggest thing ever to happen to Montreal. It is being held in the center of the St. Lawrence River on two man made islands. It has been under construction for years. The city made a huge investment and its success is a source of immense civic pride. I soon realize it isn't only the city of Montreal swelling with pride. Canada is celebrating in its glory as well.

There are over 90 flags all flying together in unison. It is magnificent! There is one for every country with an exhibit. It is massive. I buy tickets. The entrance fee turned out to be a lot more than I expected, so I decided to buy a two-day pass. I hope it will be enough! If I start early and stay late I can pack the days with action. I am determined to squeeze in as much as possible. The two-day pass has drained my bankroll. I have about $70.00 now

They hand me an official program with a detailed map. I pour over it and locate the Russian exhibit. It is close by so I decided to visit it first. Funny, I grew up in an atmosphere where Russia was vilified. My early school life was one long string of drills highlighting the threats of the cold war.

Once a month we all had to get under our desks and cover our heads to protect ourselves from the threat of being vaporized by an atom bomb. The bomb, if it ever came, would be dropped by the Russians. We all knew Russia was the faceless and terrible enemy that wanted to destroy us. I went through these drills hundreds of times and each time my teachers told me if the bomb dropped in Los Angeles I would be dead in less than a minute later. They offered me false hope, nevertheless I covered up my neck.

From the entrance way on the "Isle Notre Dame" I went straight to the Soviet exhibit. Their exhibit featured pictures of Marx and Lenin and included some of their sayings posted on the walls. They were both grim and serious men and their plaques claimed to be celebrations of "the working class" man.

The most theme was to claim the world exists to serve the "workers." It was not a surprise for me to learn corporations and company advertisements were not present in Russian. They do not exist in Russia. I have learned in school the cold war is a battle between economic systems and ours is capitalism.

Theirs is based on "the dictatorship" of the working man. I found myself disregarding the plaques about labor and its struggles. It was boring. I came to see Yuri Gagarin's space ship. It carried the first human into space.

My interest in space began in our backyard when my Dad tracked the night sky with his binoculars hoping to see Sputnik fly overhead. He picked out a little blip that he saw blinking in the sky and told me it was sputnik. Over the years I followed the "space race" as it developed and am looking forward to the day when man goes to the moon and the planets.

"Remember, Sputnik is Russian and we don't like Russians." A young Mom was talking to her son and I overheard.

"Why don't we like Russians?" The child asked.

"They want to bury us." she answered.

"Bury us, like in the ground? Like you bury me in the sand at the playground?"

"No. They want to kill us all. They have threatened to destroy our country by bombing us until we don't exist." She told him.

"Will God let them do that mom?" his voice was frail and frightened..

"Well, I don't think so." she said hesitantly.

"Well if God won't let them, how can they still do it?"

I marveled at the little boy's logic. Would God let them destroy us? What a question! His Mom didn't answer, instead we turned a bend in the line. And there it was! It was tiny, not much bigger than my 53 MG! My car was okay for a spin around town but I would never want to orbit the earth in it!

"A man has to have real courage to be thrust into space in that tiny little thing." it is the voice of a fellow tourist standing in line next to me.

"Amazing! I can imagine it shaking, and vibrating as it takes off. It would be scary." I answer.

"I wonder how many G's the astronaut gets on liftoff?" He asks out loud.

"A lot, push the button, let's hear the narrative." My new acquaintance pushes a red button and activates the narrative which explains:

"On April 12, 1961 Yuri Gagarin took off on board Vostok 1 for a flight of 108 minutes, during which time he left the earth's atmosphere and orbited the globe. He reached a maximum height of 203 miles or 327 kilometers above the planet. During his flight he experienced up to eight times the pull of gravity. He is the first human to leave Earth's orbit and travel into space."

I picture it moving slowly at first and then faster and faster until he is pinned to the chair. I am overwhelmed. Eight G's! I stood there holding my spot on the line for a long time. People tried to push and hurry past, but I needed to hold my ground. I had to ponder the whole thing. I let it all soak in until I have a full appreciation for the human achievement the pod represents. It is awesome to be standing less than ten feet from such an important monument.

I finished soaking in the glory of Soviet space exploration and followed the path back into the first floor. A flashing sign grabbed my attention! It was an invitation to attend a Russian fashion show! I found a seat and the lights dimmed. A male voice with a heavy accent introduced the women as they appeared one by one.

"Comrade Female Worker Svetlana is always dressed for hard work. Note how useful and well designed for active labor her garments are."

A parade of women follow Svetlana out onto the stage. They are bundled up in factory uniforms and their bodies are covered. There is no skin showing on their arms, legs, or wrists. Their pants are tucked down into their boots. The only visible skin is a bit of neck, and most of it was hiding behind the high collars covering their ears. It didn't matter. They could have been introduced as mummies and I would have been drawn to them like a magnet.

They were gorgeous, stunning women! If the "work" uniforms were an attempt to hide their shapeliness, it failed miserably. They all radiated the same thing! Sex appeal! No matter how austere their uniforms were meant to be, the show left me dazed and confused.

I decide to see what else Russia has to offer. There are lots of photos and charts about farm production and five year plans. The "plans" claim they have all succeeded and everything is working fine. They tell me that if I live in the Soviet Union I will find plenty of food and clothes on the shelves of the local stores.

I soon tire of farms, factories and the loud bombastic boasting about their "military" and its prowess. I find the many pictures of marching men saluting a bandstand full of leaders somber and unsettling. They were ready to go to war, and the message is aimed at the United States. I decided to leave.

The neighboring exhibit belongs to the United Kingdom. I learned that the "United Kingdoms" are England, Wales, Scotland and Northern Ireland. This exhibit features a discussion of the history of the Commonwealth. It made note Canada is a prominent member. Their focus is on the "closeness" exhibited by former colonies and territories to the home country.

The narrative glosses over and takes pains to ignore how the various colonies gained independence. They skip over the frequent conflicts and rebellions of the past. It is as if the U.K. was a benevolent mother who always looked after her children with only their best interests in mind. It implies the Indian quest and revolt seeking freedom, and all those others around the world, such as the uprising in Iraq, where 10,000 Shia were killed by Gurkus, had never happened and were not important.

Most of the attendants presenting the U.K. exhibit were women dressed in mini skirts to accentuate their long legs and see through blouses. In the U.K. "Mini" means "Mini". This exhibit is all about showing skin. The U.K. women all have long skinny limbs, small breasts, and thin bodies. The Russian women in contrast were Rubenesque but mummified.The cultural conflicts are glaring, one features sexuality while the other is trying to hide it. They both have plenty of it but in different ways.

As I toured the U.K. exhibit it became clear why they had invented the saying "the sun never sets on the British Empire." It is obvious it never does or at least never did. The long list of former colonies, most of whom are now members of the Commonwealth form a chain circling the globe. Four hundred years of "ruling the seas" allowed them to dominate the world order for a long time. I am looking at the remaining traces of their empire as I walk through the exhibit. I feel hungry and decide to sit and have some lunch. I will have to splurge and buy a sandwich.

"What is a banger with chips?" I questioned the young man behind the counter.

"A banger is a sausage. Chips are french fries." he answers back. I decide I have to splurge as there is no cheap alternative on the fairgrounds.

"Okay, I'll take an order of bangers and chips. You're English aren't you." I try to make some small talk.

"I am mate. Good of you to notice.""

"I had no idea how many countries your nation once ruled until today. Your country ran the world for a long time. Does it make you proud?

"Well, no! I am afraid we still have much to answer for." His answer surprised me.

I pick up the tray with the bangers and sit down to read the brochure. I learned that in addition to the country exhibits, there are also many "theme" exhibits.

The theme of the fair is "Man and his World". I soon realized these "theme" exhibits were sponsored by big companies and corporations. They have catchy titles such as "Man the Creator", "Man the Provider", "Man & His Health", "Man in Control", and "Man the Producer". There are a total of seventeen individual theme exhibits listed. The brochure paints a rosy picture of a future where all human needs will be met through the application of advancements in science and technology. It gives me the impression my elders are on the ball and the world is in capable hands.

"How odd it is that such an idea has never occurred to me before" I have never given them much credit. I decided to leave visiting the theme exhibits until my second day.

As I read over the list of countries participating I wonder how politics has influenced who is exhibiting and who isn't. I notice there are only a few communist countries in attendance. The only ones there are Czechoslovakia, the Soviet Union, Yugoslavia and Cuba. Where are all the others?

The communist countries from Eastern Europe are not there. Mainland China, the most populated country in the world, was absent. I think it must be because the United States policy has been to pretend mainland China does not exist. Instead of dealing with mainland China, the U.S. has "recognised" Taiwan, or Formosa as the one true "China". Communist China is considered to be a usurper of power and not a legitimate government. America does not bother to speak to them.

Formosa or Taiwan is an island off the coast of mainland China. The defeated general, Chiang Kai-shek fled there when Mao took over China. The U.S. did not approve of Mao and his rebellion and supported Chiang instead. In order to punish Mao it was decided to pretend the country he led didn't exist. The brochure does not deal with the issue at all. It is ignored. I wondered if it ever will.

It made it clear China had been excluded and not invited to the fair. Given its size, population and history, China is the equivalent of having a dragon eating at your table and acting like you don't believe in dragons. If allowed it will smoke and fire until it blows in your face.

These things cause me to ponder the idea of how politics is affecting the fair. I think about the six day war because it has recently ended. In the six-day war the Arabs lost badly. The bulk of Arab fighting was between the United Arab Republic. UAR is the combined union of the countries of Egypt and Syria. I decided to visit their exhibits. What would they tell me about the war? What could I learn? I find the exhibit for the UAR and head for it.

It is a modest one story building. The outside walls feature decorative archways that lend a middle eastern flavor. There are no lines or crowds waiting to get in. There are only a few visitors lingering in the outside room which features a prominent photo of the founder and leader of the UAR, General Gamal Abdul Nassar.

I stop to read the plaque on the wall. It relates how his career began when he was a member of the "Free Officers" brigade. They opposed the role of the British Empire in Egypt and their support of King Farouk in Egypt. Nassar helped depose Farouk and that was the beginning of the end of British domination in Egypt.

"You must be puzzled." A dark skinned Arab man in traditional robes approaches and asks. "Do you have a question?"

"I was hoping to learn something about the war. You have no mention of it anywhere. Why?"

"Well the war happened in June, only two months ago. The exhibit was set up and shipped long before the fair opened in April." The man was baffled. "We couldn't write about it when we put the exhibit together since it hadn't happened yet. What would you like to know about the war?"

"I wanted to learn what your side thinks of it." I asked.

"Well, if you don't know, we were viciously attacked without warning. It was a lot like your Pearl Harbor. Israel has a modern airforce with the latest American planes. Their pilots have been well trained by your best men. They attacked us without warning while our planes were on the ground and caught us defenseless. They destroyed our airforce without a fight."

"Somehow that's not quite the story I read in our papers."

"Well that's the start. The Israeli tanks rolled across the Sinai and hit our forces quickly and killed over 20,000 of our soldiers. We lost hundreds of tanks without a shot being fired because of the surprise nature of the attack."

"Our news reports claimed it was a defensive war. They said Israel fought in self defense." I echoed what I thought I knew. "Arab nations have Israel surrounded and want to destroy it."

"Yes that is what the western news outlets say, but we were caught by surprise. Israel struck first and grabbed huge chunks of Arab land in the Sinai, Jordan and Syria."

"I see, and no one hears your side of the story? Why aren't you telling it here in this booth?"

"There are many nations protesting the unfair representation of the war?" his red face shook in anger.

"No, I had no idea."

"Well, it's true, the western media tells you only the Israeli side of everything. You Americans are so brainwashed." He threw up his hands in despair.

I continue on and wander into a room devoted to the Diaspora. Diaspora is a word describing the exile of Jews from Israel. When the Diaspora happened the Jews were scattered all over the world. During this time they were scattered and their land was lost. They claim it has been taken by force. The land is now called Palestine and is now part of the Ottoman Empire. It has been part of Turkey for four hundred years.

The pavilion offers a room devoted to the development of the "early settlements". These explain the beginning of the return of many immigrant settlers back to the promised land. It is the story of the first Jews who returned "home" to Israel having rejected the separation caused by the Diaspora.

Their reclamation of the holy land started in earnest around 1900 and continued up to the time the holocaust took shape in Germany. The display outlines a pattern, a flow of immigrants coming back to Israel after an absence of many, many years. Their return is a reassertion of the Jews claim to the Holy Land.

Integral to the story is Hitler's takeover of Germany and his attempt to extinguish the Jewish race. I enter a room entitled "The Holocaust". It is a grim pictorial display of the atrocities and horrors wrecked on Jewish population by the Nazi's. I already know the story, but am once again shocked by the stark photos showing piles of skinny rotting bodies in mass graves. I begin to feel ill. It is agony to read about how the world awakened to learn of the horror wrecked by the Nazis.

In response to the horror, those who survived began to return en masse to Israel hoping to reclaim the ancient land now known as Palestine. They were joined by Jews from all over the world and the idea of reclaiming the promised land grew in power. Palestine was soon bursting with new citizens looking for land to claim and farm. They formed the country of Israel.

"All of these exhibits were planned for years before the fair opened in April. The war was not planned although we all expected it. The Arab leaders were giving angry violent speeches threatening Israel on an almost daily basis. They cut off trade lanes and massed troops on our border. They called for the complete destruction and annihilation of Israel every day. There were bombings and terrorist attacks in our cities." he was excited and adamant.

"You expected them to attack?"

"Yes, and they did, setting off bombs and attacking private citizens. Everyday in their speeches they declared war was imminent. Israel is surrounded with hostile aggressors sponsored by the Russians who are egging them on to attack us. Their armies are supplied and trained by the Russians."

"There were frequent terrorist attacks?" I can feel his fear for the lives of the citizens of Israel. I hear it in the way his voice cracks when he speaks.

"Yes and there are many, many oil rich Arab countries all lined up against us. All of them are sponsoring the destruction of Israel. We feel like David defending himself against Goliath. Our leaders decided in order to prevent annihilation we needed to seize the initiative and strike first."

"So you were defending yourself?" I understood. The survival instinct is motivating every word.

"There is a deep, deep commitment to protect Israel and preserve it. This exhibit tells the history of why we as Jews carry a personal responsibility to make sure it survives. Do you know who Ann Frank is?"

"Yes, we did the play at my school." I answer.

"There are original pages from her diary on display here. If you know her story, it is the story of our people. We cannot and will not let it happen again. We will not sit back and let history repeat itself. I promise you that."

"Thanks, I believe you. I'll be sure to see Ann Frank's diary."

As I made my way through the displays I felt the love and passion for Israel and the hope it offered the Jewish people. The history of the holocaust was there and displayed for all to see. Their anguish was evident.

I finished the day visiting various African and Asian exhibits representing the "emerging" countries. These were all places freed in the last few years from European colonial domination. Each tried to tell the story of its history prior to being invaded and conquered by the nations of Europe. These included the African countries of Ethiopia, Kenya and the Congo. The Asian countries included Burma, and Ceylon. There were dozens more I didn't have time to see. It got late and was getting dark, the fair would close and I needed to return to the park to spend the night and rest.

I bought a quart of milk and drank it for dinner. I returned to my park and read under a light for an hour. The park quieted down and I crawled up in the bushes and went to sleep. The next day I intended to see the American and Canadian exhibits and go to the rendezvous spot at the Russian exhibit to meet Chuck. Would he be there? I doubted.

"So did you see the capsule?" The young woman gave me my change of mike and my roll. She smiled

"I saw the Russian ship. It was tiny, and it had a ball shape. I'm going to the American exhibit today." I answered.

"What did you think of the Canadian booth?"

"I haven't seen it yet." I couldn't tell I wasn't sure I would visit the Canadian booth.

"You must, It celebrates our 100th anniversary year as a nation. I'm sure you'll like it." Her voice was firm and sure. "You'll learn a lot about Canada."

"I'll try, I could only afford two days. I am squeezing things in.""The mounted police fire off an old fashioned cannon that loads like a musket rifle. They dress in old fashioned uniforms. It's a hoot."

"Okay, I'll be sure to try to see it."

Chapter Seventeen

On day two I enter the Isle de Notre Dame and head for the monorail. It will take me to the American Pavilion on the isle de Saint Helene's. The monorail system circles both islands and I can ride and see the entire fair. I sit and watch the pavilions glide one by one. It takes over an hour.

The US exhibit is housed in a giant geodesic dome designed by Buckminster Fuller. The brochure features a picture of it at night. The picture is spectacular, towering 200 feet above the ground, it is 250 feet in diameter. There is a lot of translucent air space in the dome that lights up the night in every direction. It features a biosphere with complex shades and windows that are used to control the temperature in a unique way. It is being hailed as a model to be copied for future buildings. It is the only one of its kind ever built.

John Glenn's capsule was similar in size to the Russian version but not as ball-like. Both nations were competing for and claiming possession of space. It is wonderful to be able to see them side by side. In this particular competition the Russians got there first. It made me wonder, did it make them the "winners"? And if so, what did they "win?"

The U.S. pavilion exhibit featured the actual suits worn by the first astronauts when they went into space. It included suits worn by Glenn, Carpenter and Grissom. They are bulky and uncomfortable to wear. My eye catches a sign, "Moon Landing" and an escalator takes me to a model depicting the surface of the moon. It is desolate and dotted with craters.

The model is complete with a landing craft and lunar vehicles. It predicts the US will be the first to the moon. The U.S. aim in the space race is to be the first on the moon. John F. Kennedy declared it a national goal and NASA is in full pursuit of his dream, and are hoping to make a moon landing soon. I wonder, will we win the space race by getting there first? My country thinks the answer is yes.

Conveyor belt helps me to leave space exploration behind. The voice directs me to focus on a presentation now unfolding about the future of robotics. The confident voice asks me to ponder the tremendous progress that has been made eliminating functions once done by human hands. It celebrates the fact robots can do factory line work faster and more efficiently than humans ever could.

It predicts a time when more and more industrial work will be done by machines, leaving men free to pursue leisure. Its claim is that machines will never get tired or bored. They won't go on strike to demand higher wages and they do not require coffee breaks or need extra space to work comfortably. They don't need light or clean air to work at full capacity.

Machines are always compliant with any and all demands and never make objections or critical comments. Best of all they do not have to be coddled or listened to. As I stood there it occurred to me a lot of people were about to be put out of work. The exhibit concludes with the claim goods will be far cheaper in the future, and people will be able to buy them more easily as a result of the huge cuts in wage costs. I wonder "if they don't have jobs, how will they get the money to buy all these things."

Somehow I couldn't resist making a mental comparison. In the soviet display the "comrade worker" was king. He was responsible for all production of material wealth and goods. In the U.S. exhibit machines were the future. I considered the Soviet system had a long history of famine and shortages. The U.S is the land of plenty. How is this all going to play out? It was a lot to consider.

A clock caught my eye and an alarm went off in my head. It was eleven thirty and I was on the wrong island! I had lost track of time! I had a half hour to get to the gate of the Russian exhibit. Luckily the trains ran frequently! The tram stopped at every pavilion. I wondered if I would be better off getting off early and running to the Russian gate. Would I get there faster? The train took too long to load and unload and restart. I decided to get off and run.

The grounds are crowded at midday and I am unable to cut a straight line to the destination. I start and stop trying to avoid the throng who are surging in groups and blocking my way. I fear Chuck has come early and is there waiting at noon! I push harder and try to force people out of my way. I arrive out of breath gasping for air. I am ten minutes late.

It is crowded and there are people surrounding the exhibit. I had hoped he would be visible and standing near the entrance. My eyes comb the crowd and I cannot find him! A crazy desperate thought shoots through my mind. "Is this the only entrance?" Is there a second one or more? I approached an exhibit guide at the entrance.

"Is this the only entrance? The only way in? I was supposed to meet someone here and he is not here." I feel a desperate twinge. I was at the west entrance."

"I see." I circled and found the north entrance. It is a bigger area and has even more people milling about. I cannot survey the entire area, there is no clear line of sight and too many people. He could be tucked away and hidden out of sight.

"Chuck! Hey Chuck! There are trees and benches surrounded by crowds where he could be standing unseen. "Chuck, hey Chuck!" There is no response. I decided he was not at this entrance and headed for the east opening. It is now after 12:30. I checked the other two possible entrance points with no luck. Did we miss connection? I decided it was more likely he had not come. I give up.

I am disappointed and relieved at the same time. The incident with Henri was a reminder that being alone can be dangerous. But as nerve racking as it was, things turned up fine. I would miss Chuck, he was a friend but sometimes he was a pain in the ass as well. His sexual revelations had caught me by surprise and I was still struggling to figure out how I felt about them.

Did it matter? Most of my being said it didn't matter at all but there was a part of me that said it did. Some part of me wanted to reject him. My stronger part, my better part, knew that wasn't fair or right. One thing was clear: we had been sloppy in setting up a meeting place and had failed. If I missed him. It didn't matter at this point, I was alone and likely to be alone for the rest of the trip.

I was starving. I needed to eat something. The smell of meat roasting caught my attention. I was getting sick of milk for every meal. The aroma of meat cooking in spices grabbed my attention and made my mouth water. The sign offered "Lamb Falafel" for $1.10. There was a picture and it looked a lot like a burrito. It was piled full of meat, and the chef had a stack of it chopped and he was grilling it on a hot flame. It was pricey but I decided to try it.

"What's a Falafel? I have never had lamb." I ask the woman taking orders.

"Yes, well it's a sandwich rolled up. They're common where I come from." She had dark hair and dark eyes. "Lamb is delicious, we mix it with beef in some of the sandwiches so you can have some of both if you like."

I ordered one and sat down to eat. A young man close to my age made room for me to sit. I took a bite and realized how much I had missed the taste of meat. The sandwich was juicy, hot and flavorful. I ate knowing it is a treat I will not be able to enjoy again for a long time.

"Have you been to the Iranian pavilion?" The young man wanted to know.

"No, why do you ask?" he is slender and has dark straight hair and olive skin.

"I don't know, you are having a middle eastern sandwich. I thought you knew something about my country." He had a high pitched gentle voice.

"You are Iranian?"

"We prefer to be called Persians. Persia is an old civilization, over 3000 years old. Iran is more of a recent western word."

"I see. You think I should go?"

"Yes, well our countries are close. We are your best ally in the middle east. We are almost partners.You could learn a lot about your best military partner by going."

I decided to go and visit the Iranian pavilion. It is a building surrounded by decorative blue tile columns that are several stories high. Inside the floors are covered by rich Persian carpets. They remind me of the tapestries in the Cloisters museum in New York. There is an exhibit where weavers are operating a loom and making carpets.

I entered a room dedicated to Cyrus, a Persian king from 3000 years ago.

"They are valuable," It is a girl's voice. She has noticed me admiring the carpets being made. "We have many valuable things from the time of Cyrus on display."

"They look expensive." I agree. "It takes a long time to make one."

"Yes and years and years of training." She answers happily.

"You work for the Iranian government?"

"Yes, of course. Why do you ask?"

"Well I was at the exhibit for the UAR and there were no women working in it. Only men."

"Well they are Arab, we're Persian. There is a world of difference. We have different cultures and way different histories. Ours is the first western civilization. We are the root from which all the others grew. The Arabs are nomads who came out of the desert and invaded our country on camels. We are enlightened. The Shah encourages the advancement of women. He is trying to bring Persia into the modern world." Her eyes twinkle as she explains this to me.

"But you are all Muslims. I thought women were not full citizens in Islam."

"Well the Shah is fully promoting the western lifestyle. The clerics oppose him but the people like it. We love everything western."

The exhibit explains that because of its oil fields, great wealth has poured into Iran. This is more true since the Shah took power in the 1950's. The Shah is compared to Cyrus. Both built strong militaries, Cyrus created an empire that lasted thousands of years and the Shah built the largest army and airforce in the middle east. The exhibit's narrative goes on to claim he is guarding the oil fields and is a barrier, a buffer to any potential Russian invasion of the fields. They claim Iran is the strongest and most loyal ally the U.S. has in the middle east. I leave appreciating the world is a big place and there is a lot I have not been taught in school. I learned for the first time where Iran is and why they are important.

I decide to see the exhibits representing places I know almost nothing about. I finish off the day visiting exhibits from places like Tanzania, Togo, and Mauritius. Each is vibrant and has something to offer. My whole being is struck with wanderlust, I want to see these countries for myself. All in all, the fair was amazing but I have spent a lot of my cash on it and as the second day ends, It is time to leave.

Chapter Eighteen-

Chuck did not show, I accepted the future was mine to determine. There would be no more mutual decisions about what to do next. The descriptions of the old city of Quebec with its fortified walls has always captured my imagination. Something about the story of the battle for Quebec called to me. I had an intense desire to see it for myself.

It was intriguing. Some of the original walls from the 1740's were still standing. They ringed the original city protecting it and had made it a difficult target for the English to attack. A famous battle, the Battle of the Plains, had taken place beneath its walls and the English had won capturing the city.

This battle was key to the English defeating the French and taking possession of Canada. I wanted to see it for myself. I left Montreal and made it to Quebec in the middle of the night, and went to sleep beside the old fortress walls. In truth, I had an eerie feeling, a familiar feeling of Deja Vu. What if anything could the feeling mean? It was strong and yet undefined. I felt as if I had returned to a place embedded in my being. A place I already knew well.

In the morning I find myself wandering along the walls surrounding the historic district of Old Quebec. The wall is on a cliff above the St. Lawrence River and overlooks the entrance to the city. I walk from tower to tower noting each is armed with cannons pointing out to the river below. It feels like an old world castle.

The cannons were placed by the French in spots where they could defend the city and hold the high ground. I gaze out at the land where the Battle of the Plains of Abraham was fought. It had been a short lived affair, the entire fight lasted only thirty minutes. Both the English and French generals were killed in the exchanges. The victory gave the English the winning hand and they went on to become the "conquers" of Canada.

In the course of my wandering I came across a monument dedicated to General Wolfe, the English general who had died leading the capture of the city. Visiting Quebec had dredged up memories of a recurring dream I had many times as a child. A dream that was once vivid and full of power, but had been buried and forgotten until now.

In the dream I was wearing a red uniform. A general's uniform! I was leading a charge when I was shot off my horse. I suffered several gunshot wounds and fell bleeding. I died as the battle raged all around me. I had this dream many times as a young boy, and now memories of the dream were resurfacing with a vengeance.

The feelings grabbed me and wouldn't let go. My dreams coupled with the physical reality of being in this place possessed me. It asked me to do only one thing, accept the connection and feel it. I had been drawn to this locale, it was not something I could explain, but I knew I had an affinity for Quebec. As I walked around, I "knew" the grounds I was walking on, they were familiar and important in a personal way. I let the feeling flow through me.

I drifted through buildings still left from the 1800's. There was an armory and a powder magazine, and a prison. They each had a history and were built long after the English took possession of the country. I stumbled on a foundry that had been made into a museum. It had a scale model of Quebec City and was finished in 1808. None of these buildings held any emotional connection. It became clear! The only place where I felt connected was on the Plains where the Battle had occurred. The battle where Wolfe was shot and died.

As the day wore on, I found my way down into the more social, lively parts of town known as the Porte St-Jean. I was of legal drinking age and I decided to have a beer. As soon as I began to drink, a Canadian military man sat down at the table next to me.

"Say Yank, what are you doing in Canada?" He gave me a stare.

"How do you know I'm American?" I answered defensively. I decided he must be a junior officer.

"No offense, I heard you talking at the bar and pegged you for a yank. How do you like Canada?"

"I went to the fair in Montreal and so far I like Quebec."

"Did ya fancy the fair?" he asked.

"I loved spaceships. Never thought I would get that close to them. I could almost reach out and touch them." I shook my head to show my amazement at it all.

"Are you old enough to go into the army!" He sized me up with a glance. "Are you here dodging the draft?"

"I turn eighteen in a month. After that I will have to register for the draft. It's not an issue for me yet."

"Will be one soon enough I reckon. What are you going to do? We got lots of young guys trying to sneak in here." He sounded annoyed.

"I am not in favor of the war. But if I go to college.I will get a deferment for four years.That's what I am planning on doing. Why do you ask?" He was angry with all the draft dodgers hiding in Canada.

"Your government is so stupid. They defer to you if you go to college. It makes no sense. But you haven't got caught in your war. It is a mess."

"Listen, I am not the only one. Married guys are not getting drafted, at least not yet." so some guys get married and get deferred. Lots of people get deferred."

"Our government has refused to send Canadian armed forces to VietNam. First time in our history, we are not on your team. We have fought with you in every war for 100 years, but not this one. "

"I didn't know, I am surprised. I thought you were an ally." I drained my mug of beer.

"Let me get you another one." He motioned for a young woman who was hustling between tables to bring a round.

"Thanks. I am feeling a little floaty so one more but that's it." I said.

"Canada does not support your war. There are a lot of reasons, One is the weapons you are using. We do not condone the use of chemical weapons." He shook his head as if to say "no".

"What do you mean chemical weapons? Why do you think we are using them?" I imagined mustard gas and bodies piled high in the trenches of WWI.

"Napalm. It is a nasty indiscriminate weapon.You are killing lots of civilians. You used it to fire bomb Japan in the second world war and ended up killing more civilians with it than you did with the "A" bomb."

The waitress arrived with my second beer and my new friend paid for it.

"Yeah I've seen the pictures." I hadn't thought of Napalm in that way.

"There is also a rumor circulating you are dropping a chemical agent on the jungles."

"How come I haven't heard about it? Where did you get that from?"

"From your pilots! Some of them don't like it. It is a scuttle butt that we have all heard many times now. It's being used to poison the jungle, to thin it out. Your generals are trying to destroy the hiding place for enemy gorillas."

"Sounds dangerous. Like it might harm lots of people." I took a sip and he continued.

"Word is it already has and they are covering it up. Our military doesn't want to be a part of it. They have said it is a war crime against the civilians."

"Well if I enroll in school I won't be drafted. That's my plan." I put down the empty mug and stood up.

"You want another beer? We could explore the night life together. There are several clubs close by."

"Nah. I can't afford it."

I am starting to feel a little drunk and loose. I remember Henri and decide to decline.

"Two beers are enough! Tonight they feel like a lot. Thanks though!"

I make my way back to the old wall, unroll my bag and fall asleep. Somehow a part of me feels like I belong. When I wake, I recall my legal time in Canada is expiring. I have to leave or be in violation of my entry visa. I decided it's time to go. I decided to see the coast of Maine.

One thing hitchhiking has taught me is if you put yourself on a course and ask for help, someone will come along and help. I make a sign saying, "Coast of Maine" and stand on the highway in Quebec with my thumb out. It is midmorning and an hour passes before two men in leisure suits stop and pick me up.

"We're goin to Baw Hawba- an then on to Bawston." He had a thick accent. "I'm Ced, he's Mike."

"Okay is that in Maine?" I had never heard of Baw Hawba before. I had read the coastline was spectacular and thought, why not see it?

"Baw Hawba juts out in da she. It's a fawthest point ind' east. We'll spen a naiwght. Aan'in the mornin we'll watch the sun cum up," Ced said.

"Why do you want to do that?" I didn't get it.

"Baw Hawba is the fust place the sun shines on America. The fathest point in da east." Ced looked at me. "We wanna be there once. Be the fust person in America to see the sun."

"Sounds like fun. I would like to see the sunrise." I got it. I could be one of the first people in America to see the sunrise tomorrow.

"That's the plan. We'll be the fust to see the sun in America tommraaw. Yaw jus a khad ? Over timeI came to understand that he had called me a "kid."

They were fun guys. As we talked I found out they had been to the fair in Montreal like me, and had driven up to Quebec. I told them my story. For some reason I bragged about my three years of high school French.

"I don't speak a waaad." Ced grinned at me acknowledging my expertise.

They were friendly guys. I felt comfortable. They turned the radio on and picked up a game from Fenway park. Yaz was tearing up the league and they were excited about the Sox. I listened to the game with them. They were intense fans. It had been a while since I heard a play by play being called.

I grew up a Dodgers fan and told them. It didn't matter to them, they hated the Yanks, but the Dodgers were meaningless. I told them about the autographed 1959 Dodgers Team ball I had on my desk at home. It was signed by every Dodger great of the 50's including a young Sandy Koufax. My Dad took me to games and bought it for me. I had seen a lot of good baseball. The Sox won the game and all was well in their world. They beat the Yanks 4 to 3, Yaz had two hits, including a double. They were in a joyful mood in the car.

At that moment an engine light went off, smoke was billowing everywhere.

"There's a station! Pull in there." Ced pointed to a roadside gas station.

Mike pulled the car into the opening and smoke began to flow furiously from the front of the car.

"Tell them what is going on." Ced put the ball in my court. A middle aged attendant approached full of concern. I got out and started to translate our situation from English word by word into a French sentence.

"Nous avons de la fumée dans notre auto. I need assistance" He stopped dead in his tracks and put his hand up indicating I should stop talking. He called out to someone who was in the back room of the station. A younger man came out.

"Nous avons la fume dan notre auto" I repeated what I had said and pointed to the smoke coming from the engine.

"Please, I speak English" he was determined not to listen to my french.

"Okay our car is on fire!" I pointed out the obvious problem in English.

"Yes I can see that. Pop the hood." They were a father and son team. The younger man waved at the air dispersing the smoke.

"You have a broken hose. We can replace it today!".

I recalled my French teacher telling me that the French had little patience with people who spoke their language poorly. I learned she was right. We spent an hour getting the hose fixed. Ced and Mike had fun teasing me about my flubbed attempt at French. Once underway Ced had a question for me.

"Are you a Bozo?"

"What's a Bozo? You mean a clown?" I was baffled.

"Pot, you smoke pot? Bozo's smoke pot, I'm a Bozo," he grinned at me.

"A little!" I wasn't sure how to answer.

"We're gettin near da borda and we have a stick to finish up. Can't try to cross with it in the car. " Ced winked at me. I got it.

"Okay, won't bother me."

"Take some will ya?"

"Sure, why not?" I answered.

Ced was careful not to let any ashes fall, and attended to the debris. We smoked, and I saw a sign that said the border was twenty miles away. I started to feel a little heavy, and things slowed down a little. When the joint was done he ate the roach.

"Had to get rid of our last stick before we crossed. You're with us, and if they ask, give your id. You got an ID?" Mike looked in the mirror at me.

"Sure I have an ID." I started to feel a little paranoid.

Sometimes grass does that to me. It is illegal to smoke it. The penalty if arrested can be heavy and we were about to deal with customs agents. We crossed without incident.

"We'll be there in time for suppaa'hh. Cuda stand fah a bowl of chowdah?"

"They make fantastic chowder in Maine," Mike plugged in.

"Sure, it sounds fantastic." We had it with some bread and butter added, I was satisfied.

They rented a room with two beds and I slept on the floor. We had an early morning wake-up call, and in the dark they drove to the furthest point to the east. We watched as the sun rose in America. It was a full bright sun over an active Atlantic ocean. The sea was busy with small waves pounding on the coast one after another. Gulls cawed and swooped to the sand looking for their breakfast. The ocean air was damp, humid and fresh all at the same time. We were the only ones there.

"To see the sun in America today. Does it feel special?" Mike asked. The truth was it did. We watched together in silence. We watched for thirty minutes, until they took me for breakfast and paid for it. We headed off to Boston.

The Maine coastline was as spectacular as advertised but I saw little to make me want to stop and stay for any period of time. I decided to go to Boston. I hadn't given it a lot of thought, but since they were going my way, why not?

"I love fried claaams." Mike had excitement in his voice as he pointed to a road sign.

"Right up ahead." They both lit up in anticipation. Mike pulled up to the little stand and bought a basket full.

"Ever have fried Maine clams?" His face was lit up with joy as he munched the first bite.

He held them out for me to try. I have to admit they were wonderful.

"Can't come to Maine and not try the clams."

An hour later we stopped again, they bought a second batch and we repeated the worship ceremony. I owe them for introducing me to fried clams.

We arrived in Boston in the afternoon. I had some hours of daylight left. I hadn't done any planning, so I asked them to drop me off in a central location. I was standing on a red brick path in front of the Old South Meeting House, the place where an anti tax meeting had burst into rebellion. It became famous as the incident known as the Boston Tea Party. It is a part of the Freedom Trail, a walk linking famous American monuments from Boston's past.

Like all American children, I had been given a heavy dose of early American history, so this place, complete with plaques and memorabilia was important. I walked the route as far as the end of Paul Revere's house. Boston's old parts are from a different era. Radically different from the beaches of southern California. As I read the literature, I could feel the old city reaching out from antiquity to touch me in the present.

I walked for hours until it became clear the full tour required a car. It was too long to walk. I didn't have enough time to do the whole thing. But I saw enough of it to get a feel for why it was special. It was all the history I was going to get on this visit.

The brochure stated two thirds of the people of Boston were in favor of the revolution when the tea party rebellion occurred. Of course that meant 1/3 were not. I wondered how things turned out for them, for the 1/3 that favored England?

After chatting with some locals, I learned the "scene" was a place called the Combat Zone. It sounded rough, perhaps dangerous. But my curiosity peaked, so I had to check it out.

It turned out to be an area near downtown Boston. I found an area full of music clubs, strip clubs, and bars. It was called the Combat Zone because of the sailors and soldiers who frequented the district. They came in uniform. It was rowdy and loud. The area was designated as Boston's official "Adult entertainment center." It was not the Puritan environment I was expecting.

I walked the streets and went from club to club. I needed to conserve funds. I did not have enough money to do anything more than peek in the doors. I found my way to the door of a strip club named the "Naked I." I had been told this was the stage home of a beautiful woman stripper by the name of Tia. Suggestive pictures of Tia hung from the walls. She was "High Yellow", a racial mixture of black and Spanish blood. She was the star dancer. The "Naked I" was flanked by an adult bookstore and a pizza joint. I got a slice with Pepperoni. The cover charge was $10.00, much too rich for my blood.

I headed to the street. Someone grabbed my arm and was in a vice grip. I was being pulled into an alleyway by a blond with large breasts, high stiletto heels, and a lot of booze on her breath. She grabbed me by the arm and would not let go.``What are you doing?" I tried to pull away.

"Wanna have sum fun?" She was offering herself.I didn't have any money to spend on her and virginity was no longer my problem in life. I was not about to make her the second in my line of sexual adventures.

"Do I look like I have money?" I struggled to get away from her. She loosened her grip.

"Yaah must be a chucklehead. I thought you were milahtary." I hadn't had a haircut in months. I couldn't be military. "Yaah a khad."

"Yes, I'm a kid. I need a place to sleep. I need to get off these streets." I pulled away and stepped back from her.

"A place to sleep?" she echoed back at me.

"Yeah, that's what I need, and I don't have much money." I was surprised she was takin an interest in me.

"Yah know the "boys" take people in and let them sleep overnight. You have thirty dollars?"

"Yeah! Who are the "boys"?" I had no idea who she meant.

"The Boys, the Cops. If you're not a vagrant, they'll let you sleep in jail."

I was astounded! Was it true?

"It's six blocks away. Tahk a raight on the next street, and go six blocks north." She pointed to the turn.

The area was too crowded to try and sleep in, The streets were filled with people and there were no wooded places where I could curl up. I decided to try it, I ventured off to see if the "boys" would put me up for the night.

She had said it was only six blocks, but they turned out to be long blocks. When I arrived, the doors to the jail were locked up tight. There was no "welcome" sign out and it was not warm or friendly. It was dark, it was late, and it was locked. I banged on the doors and a uniformed officer cracked the door and stared at me.

"Well what ya whan?" he sounded upset like I had disturbed his sleep. His was not a friendly voice.

"I am traveling and I was told I could stay the night, rather than sleep on the street. Can I? I'm not a vagrant, and don't want any trouble."

He came out and escorted me into the light. To this day I do not know if it was an actual policy or if he decided to take pity on me. He put me in a cell alone, and I went to sleep in the Boston City Jail, but not before he took my belt to make sure I couldn't hang myself.

In the morning two officers appeared at the door to the cell, with white bread baloney sandwiches stacked on a tray. The shock of seeing uniformed police caused me to remember where I was. In jail.

"How long's this one in fuh?" A heavy set officer asked. He was not the man I had met the night before.

"Twenny daze" The second one blinked at me with an evil twinkle.

"What?" My heart jumped into my throat. Pounding, my blood started racing. "What?"

"Whad he do?" the first one was pulling my chain and had me choking in fear.

"He's vagrant, says heaare." His glare was intense, it was as if I were trash.

"No, that's all wrong. All wrong. I asked to spend the night." I squealed out in desperation.

"No one asks to spend the naght in jail.' It says twenny daze." He pointed at a clipboard.

I was in shock! What to do? They both laughed, Their game had gone on long enough. They had scared the wits out of me.

"Yahr a haf ash, we know ya slept here." He grinned a toothy grin. " Ya seem like a stupid little shit but you're close to broke. We may half to lack ya up soon for real.

You nearly are a vagrant. A vagrant ain't got no money!" He handed me the two stale sandwiches, which I ate, bad as they were, they were free.

I got my belt back and decided to leave Boston. On a whim I decided to head for Washington, D.C. I had an urge to see the nation's capital. Why not? It wasn't far off. Eastern cities are close to each other. I wondered how Wall Street was working out for Chuck. Was he making the money he wanted to make? Was he still living at the Y and visiting the showers? Did he roam the streets at night? I hoped he had given up his street business, I had decided it was doing him harm.

The route I picked let me circle around New York through New Jersey. I was on my way to Maryland and to the nation's capital city. The daily news informed me New Jersey had experienced a race riot in Newark a few days earlier and there was a lot of racial tension in the air.

I avoided the town of Newark. My rides were all short hops, I picked my way across the state. It got late, the sun went down but I decided to hitch as long as there was traffic going by. If you haven't got a comfortable spot to sleep, sometimes it is best to keep moving. I was uneasy with all the talk of race riots and wanted to get to my destination as soon as possible.

A Cadillac pulled up, the driver was an elderly black man in a business suit. He opened the door, "Are you out of your mind?" I had no idea what he was talking about. "You are about to enter Cambridge, Maryland."

"So?" I had seen it on the map, but it meant nothing to me.

"They're trying to burn Cambridge to the ground tonight. It is less than four miles down the road. Get in the back and keep your head down. Stay out of sight." I did as he said.

"Listen, son, twenty-six people died in Newark two weeks ago, and tonight it is happening again in Cambridge. You can't go near the town tonight."

I was lying on the back floor of his car watching the streetlights go by. He locked all the doors.

"You keep down until I get to the outskirts of town, out of the trouble zone. I don't want anyone to see you. Keep down and out of sight."

He had the radio on, an anxious reporter was talking about fire after fire with many important buildings burning and unconfirmed reports of many more said to be burning. The firemen were all white volunteers and they were afraid to go into the areas that were burning. The fires were all in black neighborhoods. A segregated black school was on fire and it was burning to the ground. It was black on black violence. it claimed to be racial protest.

"There was an activist by the name of Rap Brown in town today. He made a speech, and the fires started. People are being shot, it's hell," the driver said over his shoulder.

"I thought he was nonviolent." I recognized the name, Rap Brown.

"Well, he's changed his mind." He sped up the car. I could hear gunshots in the night, they were close. "I'm on the edge of town, the real trouble is about a mile away. Right where you were headed."

"Thanks, I didn't know." I had been headed right into a hot zone and had been blind to it.

Time passed slowly, but he leaned back over the seat, and grinned at me. "I'm Sam, I was visiting my auntie. I'm headed for D.C. Where are you going?"

"The Capitol," I answered.

"I had to stop for you, I couldn't see a young white boy trying to go through Cambridge tonight. Any night would be bad, but tonight? Terrible idea." He shook his head to indicate how bad an idea it was.

"Do you know where the YMCA is in Washington?" I needed to sleep inside. No parks.

"It's close to my home, I could drop you there if you like. You wanna sit up front now? I think we're past the worst of it." He stopped and I moved forward.

"You young people are all so crazy these days. Hitchhiking, going all over. I don't get it." His radio played and we listened to the news. There had been race violence in many cities, a lot of it was about financial inequality.

"Poverty is the problem," he told me. "I got a government job, get good pay and I like my work. No need to cause trouble."

"Tell what do you do?"

"I work for the Dept. of Commerce, in the international trade department. Been there over twenty years. Good place for a black man to be. I earn my money. At least I think so." He flashed a smile again. His white teeth stood out in the well lit night.

He explained to me the city of Washington D.C was almost all black, more than 90%, and all of the whites lived in the suburbs. He told me to be careful and to stay off the streets at night.

"You should not be out wandering around D.C. at night." He shook his head at me to enforce that it was a bad idea.

The radio kept on about the trouble in Cambridge, the announcer claimed that Brown had said something like, "If Cambridge doesn't come around, then Cambridge has got to be burned down." Since it was burning, they were giving him all the credit.

"That's not the way for the black man." Sam said. "It is not the way." He shook his head.

I learned he had two sons, and he wanted them to go to college. His wife worked and they had a quiet suburban life. He was from the suburbs, but he took me into the city. Before I knew it I was standing on the steps to the Y and checking myself into a room. I decided I could afford two nights. I was grateful Sam had come along. I said a silent "Thanks." It was clear he was nowhere "near" his home when he dropped me off.

The rates were similar to those I had gotten in New York, $2.00 per night for me alone. As I signed in, I saw a sign hanging on a bulletin board behind the desk. They were advertising a chess exhibition. A simultaneous match was to be carried out the next evening by a Grand Master.

A simultaneous match is one in which the Chess Master plays all comers at the same time, often dozens at a time. The Master takes on all challengers and they all play against the Master in a lineup of sorts. He walks up and down the rows of desks dispatching the foes. I had heard about it, but had never done it or seen it. I signed up for it. I was excited, I had never played anyone ranked so high in the Chess system.

The desk clerk gave me a little map of the city, which had all the major sites and the walking route to visit them. I went up to my room and planned the next day. It was only a couple of miles to the center of town, so I could walk to many of the famous monuments. I wanted to see everything but since I had only one day and was walking, I had to choose the ones close together. I chose the Capitol building, the Lincoln and Washington monuments, and the White House. It was a six mile walk which I could do with ease..

I went to sleep in a state of high anticipation. The nation's Capitol and a chess game against a Grandmaster were on tap for the next day. I got up the next morning and, as I made my way, I found myself wandering through some of the worst slums I had ever seen. Without a doubt they were among the poorest neighborhoods I had ever walked in. They were poorer than Watts in Los Angeles, poorer than anything I had seen in New York. The houses were in terrible condition, fences barely standing, doors broken, windows broken, sickly black children sitting on porches with nothing to do, and nowhere to go.

I was forced to trudge by house after house. It was painful to see the levels of poverty. I imagined disease on every young face I saw. I was heading for the opulence at the center of the city. No one passed by me as I walked by, it felt like I wasn't there, no one cared or saw a young white guy who was passing through. None of the people loitering in the early morning sun cared about anything at all. They were all alive but there was a sense of death in the air, a sense I had never felt before it was a sense of abject hopelessness.

After a three mile walk, I found myself standing before the U.S. Capitol building. It was imposing and impressive at the same time, a huge dome and the architecture was something that spoke of power as well. Well-dressed people came and went in expensive cars. Some were let off while others were waiting in the front to be picked up.

I sat for a long time, wondering if the people in the limos had ever walked the three miles I had walked through. Wondering if they knew they were surrounded by the poorest neighborhood I had ever been in. The contrast was stunning. I shook it off, and went on to see the Washington Monument, a giant phallus shooting up into the sky, fully erect, a hard rod. The symbol defines Washington? Perhaps a giant erect spike pointing skyward did exactly that, I mused. After all, George was known as the Father of the country.

I hiked to the Lincoln Monument and sat beneath the statue of Lincoln enthroned in a Greek-like structure that reminded me of the pictures I have seen of the Parthenon. Lincoln sitting on a throne, king like. It was majestic and I felt it was meant to suggest royalty, but again, I knew that this man had once been a grocery clerk and had walked five miles to correct a small mistake he had made while making change. Honest Abe, how honest was this monument? Did it really do justice to him? Greek antiquity? Royalty? Thrones? I shook my head at it. Was the poverty surrounding the monument a monument as well? How did they fit together? These questions had no answers.

The city did have a certain majesty, and at the same time it was dark and threatening. It was as if a part of the city was supercharged with the high life of power and politics, while the other was a dark underworld hell of depression and poverty. I kept expecting the two-headed beast guarding the passageway into the underworld at the river Styx to appear barking and growling, snapping at my feet. I was at a loss as to what to know which applied: shame or pride. Perhaps both were called for but the shame side had the upper hand. In fact it was no contest. My stomach was in a knot.

The walk back to the YMCA was more of the same, I had no problems, I was just a young white tourist who passed through a desperate part of town without incident. It was hot, humid, and the feeling of misery was all around me. Several black women with little children at their feet made eye contact with me, and I could not tell if they were greeting me, ignoring me, or letting me pass. Their eyes were vacant but present, and I could not read them. I arrived back at the Y in time for my chess game.

The room was set up for a number of players, at least twenty, all to play one man at the same time. I picked out a chair and sat down. The boards were all ready to go, the Master was given the advantage of white or first move on all the boards. I watched him open each game with different gambits, putting different pawns out, but he was using the Queen's opening or Rui Lopez most of the time. He used the Rui Lopez with me and buzzed by to the next board. Ten moves later, half the boards were empty, he had defeated them without much resistance. I was in an even position, no pieces had been exchanged, we both had established some position. As he eliminated the inexperienced players, he had more time to spend with the ones fighting back.

There were game clocks, so he had to move fast. He eliminated most of the other players. He started standing over my board longer and longer as I tried to mount an attack. I noticed his clock was running a little short, it had run down more than mine as he had spent time beating other players. He was running short on time. I gained a pawn advantage in the center of the board. One by one he beat all of the other players around me. He was now standing in front of me.

It had come down to one game, ours, he was playing only me. I was winning. We were battling but I had gained a small advantage and was able to force a move. We exchanged Queens and I captured another central pawn. I had a strong position in the center of the board, and a material advantage. The game ground on for another hour. I kept my concentration and avoided making any fatal mistakes. As we wound down to the end game, I was able to force a pawn through to the back line and it became a queen. I won, he put his finger on his king and toppled it over on the board. Resignation.

"You're a good player". His bright white hair hung over his forehead.He hunched a bit with a little bend in his back. I noticed the wrinkles on his face for the first time. "How long have you been playing?"

"My dad taught me when I was a kid. I was about five. I have been playing ever since." I answered.

"I do these matches for fun, I'm retired. I used to play on a competitive level, but now it's only fun..". He smiled again."Every once in a while someone beats me." He stuck out his hand to congratulate me.

"It must be hard to play twenty people at once." I said not feeling like I had accomplished much. I had gotten my initial advantage while he was occupied.

"Well most of them cannot play well, so it is only the few who can be a problem. You were one of those. You got ahead and stayed ahead. Most players get careless and make a big mistake. You played without making any errors and kept pushing." I went to sleep that night with monuments on my mind, monumental poverty, and a monumental chess victory. My last thought was about Chuck. How was he doing? Was he making a lot of money? Was he still having a lot of sex? Was he okay?

Chapter Eighteen-

Canada and the world's fair were expensive. I ended up spending more money in a few days than I had been spending in many weeks. If the trend continued I would soon dip below the poverty line and be in danger of being arrested for vagrancy. My encounters with the police had reinforced the message that the men in blue harbored a virulent disdain for poor hitchhikers without resources. I did not want to end up in a confrontation with them and be arrested.

Chuck and I went on our trip hoping to see the USA and experience life in new and unusual ways. We had accomplished some of our goals. If things were to wind up on a successful note I needed to get back to the west coast in time to register for the school year at Golden West College. I was not yet ready to head home and decided if I was careful and a little lucky I could last at least three more weeks on the road. I went to sleep knowing I was not quite ready to head home.

I left the YMCA at the crack of dawn and got a quick ride out of Washington into Virginia. I decided to head south to the gulf of Mexico and the Caribbean sea. I was looking forward to standing on the gulf shore! Once done, I will have seen all of the major bodies of water circling the United States. The idea appeals to me, it has symmetry.

By the end of the day I am hitching in West Virginia. The road is a two lane highway. No one is stopping, the cars go whipping by and I am having a hard time getting a ride.

An hour passed and I stood frozen in the same spot. I knew I was in West Virginia and in the hills but I had lost track of what was ahead. I was not "lost" because I knew I was pointed south. I began walking with my thumb out hoping for a ride. Cars sped by and nothing happened.

Finally a man in his thirties driving an old truck stopped. He was dressed in overalls with a suspender to hold his pants up. He grinned at me. He was fat, with a simple boyish face. He had a childlike quality. His face had retained a shallow innocence.

"Where are you going?" he asked.

"South," I answered.

"Okay, well I'm goin' down the road a bit, you can ride with me." He flipped open the door and invited me to climb up.

When I did, flesh rolled out of his pants, his belt was drawn tight causing his stomach to overflow. His naked belly fat poked out through a shirt two sizes too small. His face was scared. His teeth were yellow and he needed a shave.

"What's your name?" he asked me.

"Luke, what's yours?"

"I'm Jake, where are you from?" his voice had a twang.

"Huntington Beach"

"Wow?" there was a tone of wonder in his voice. "Is that out west?"

"Yeah, California.".

"Wow," he went silent and looked straight ahead. I could see the wheels turning in his head as he tried to think of what to say.

We drove for miles without either of us saying another word. He had both hands on the wheel and was rubbing them in a semicircle. I had the feeling he wanted to say something but was struggling and could not find the right words. Every few minutes he turned his head and stared at me anxiously.

"You want some beer? I can stop and get us some beer. How's that sound?"

"Sure, why not" I hadn't not had one since Quebec. "But I don't have a lot of money."

"Don't worry, I'll pay, I got a job. After all, you come all the way from California." He turned off the road into a truck stop and bought a six pack.

"There's a spot down the way where we can park and drink. No one will bother us. I got some chips." He waved the bag in my face.

He drove down the road and turned off onto a single lane dirt road. It wound around a bend behind a grove of trees. We were hidden and out of sight of the highway. He pulled out two beers, popped one and handed it to me.

"It's cold. Don't that just beat all, me driving by and you were standing out there all alone like that! You goin someplace in particular?" Jake stammered when he sweat as he spoke.

"Naw, I've been traveling for months. I'm getting near the end of my money, and am beginning to head home." I took a gulp of the beer. I decided I was starting to like the taste of beer.

"You said you were headed south. But ain't your home out west?"

"Yeah, but I have enough time to see the gulf and after that I will head west."

"The gulf of Mexico! Wow. I'd like to see the gulf. It must be somethin'. Never been out of West Virginia." He finished his beer and pulled out another. "Want another?"

"Not yet, maybe in a little bit." I replied.

Jake had hammered his first can of beer like it was soda water. He crushed the empty can and threw it in a pile behind his seat. Jake had his window rolled down to disguise the smell of stale beer onto the floor of his truck.

"You must stop and drink here on a regular basis." I ask.

"Not so much. Why do you ask?" He answered nervously.

"I was admiring the stack of empty cans you keep behind your seat." I nod to the pile trying to make a joke about his carelessness. He ignores my attempt at humor

"I got some time comin at the mine. I could go with you and head down to the gulf. What do you think ?" He gave me a quirky smile.

"Well no offense but I like being alone." I glance over and see he is breathing hard. Almost hyperventilating. Sweat had formed on his forehead.

"I hear tell in California you got everything. Everything you want you can get. You even got queers and stuff." His face was stuck in a stupid grin. His eyes were glazed over and he smiled a childish hopeful smile.

"I don't know, I guess so, but I don't know much about it." I answered thinking of Henri, and Chuck. Yeah, I thought, I don't know anything about it, but I thought to say my best friend turned into a gay hustler in New York City.

Jake turned on me and tried to put his arms around me. We started wrestling. I pushed him off, and slapped his face hard. Startled, he came out of his dream. The fact that I was from California, and alone, had empowered him to act on his homosexual fantasies. I was like bait. He was surprised and grabbed his cheek in pain.

"Sorry. Don't know what came over me. You're strong aren't you?" he looked sheepishly at me. I decided he was not dangerous.

"I guess. I played on the varsity, and lifted my share of weights." I wondered what my options were. I had slapped him and he had backed off. I could run back to the road easily enough. Should I insist on him letting me out?

"You know I work in the mines, I could get you a job if you want. They're always hiring in the mines." Weirdly he changed the subject. I didn't answer.

"If you're short on money I could loan you some." Jake was overflowing with goodwill.

"I am not looking for work, I am heading south." I answered. I had had enough beer to make me swirl. I thought again about grabbing my stuff and jumping out of the car.

"I have a sister, do you want to meet her?" He became harmless and less threatening. He was a different person. He had let his feelings out of the bag and now he had somehow got them back in it. He was embarrassed by his latent homosexuality. He had exposed himself. It was like he wanted to crawl away and pretend it had never happened. He couldn't look me in the eye.

"I guess." I wanted to get back on the main road, and if other people came into the picture it would be okay with me. He started the engine and we went off to meet his sister. It turned out she lived ten miles down the road in a trailer park. She had a one bedroom trailer, with two kids.

Her name was Margery, Marge for short. She was on the short side, almost as heavy as Jake. Her kids ran back and forth in the confines of her motorhome, raising havoc, while she smoked and watched television. She was at least as drunk as we were, and squinted at me as we were introduced.

"Luke, meet Marge," he introduced me.

The kids were out of control, climbing, shouting, throwing things, and she didn't take notice. The louder they got the less she cared. I could not judge her age but it was clear she was his older sister. I guessed she was in her late thirties.

"He's from California, I picked him up hitchhiking." Jake made small talk.

"Thas good, why did ya bring hem haere?" she squinted at me through her blood shot eyes.

Why was I there? Sitting in a tiny trailer, in a backwater place somewhere in West Virginia, with two people I had nothing at all in common with, while her two kids were mindlessly raising hell everywhere around me. I decided to leave. The highway was within walking distance. I had my pack on my back and the door was right behind me.

"I'm getting out of here." The whole drama was ridiculous.

"I could open a can of chili, if you want," Marge blurted out. One of the kids started crying loudly and fussing around about his ragged teddy bear. The other was sucking his thumb, and they both smelled like they had soiled themselves. Her eyes focused on me and she was giving me her best "come hither look."

"No, I don't think so, I think I'm going to move on." She was not a good candidate to expand my sexual horizons. She was not going to be on my list. For the time being it was a list of one and it was going to stay that way today.

"You could stay the night with me, if you want." She focused one eye and I cringed. She was thinking of picking up with me where her brother had left off.

"Nope, nope, I gotta get movin'." I picked up my stuff and bolted for the door.

"Take care now." I heard Jake's voice trailing after me. The door banged behind me. The highway was only a short ways away. I got back out there and stuck my thumb out. Not a car in sight. Jake and Marge, what to make of them? A window opened and I saw Marge peered out at me longingly and it then closed. I left, my only regret was it had taken me so long to decide to extricate myself.

There was light traffic and no one stopped. I kept walking and walking. I walked for hours, the road got steep and the hill started to become a mountain. A thick thatch of trees lined both sides of the road and a heavy fog set in. No one stopped so I kept walking. I walked deep into the night, six or more straight hours of walking. It got cold and I was forced to take out my sheep herder's jacket, the only warm piece of clothing I had kept.No cars came down the lonely road, a heavy fog surrounded me.

There were no street lights. It was quiet and dark. I had put many miles between myself and Jake and his sister. I walked into the early morning until it was three, maybe four o'clock.

Then I saw her. At first she was fuzzy, a shadowy ghost-like apparition moving towards me out of the fog. As she got closer and closer, I saw her moving towards me. I realized it was a young woman, she was dressed in a hospital nightgown. There was no light except for a bit of the moon trying to make its way through the fog.

I could see her half naked body outlined through the gown.For a moment it was exciting! She had pointy breasts sticking straight out. Her face was plain, but pleasant. She was unaware of the cold it was or of how scantily dressed she was. She was steaming along oblivious to her surroundings.

"Hello," I ventured forth.

"Hi," she kept walking with determination. I picked up the pace and tried to walk with her.

"My name is Luke," I said. She was pacing, I had to make an effort to keep up. "Who are you?"

"Celia, CiCi, everyone calls me CiCi." She smiled at me, and I could see she was about my age. My mind went to the idea of sex. Her pointy breasts were sticking straight out a foot away in my face. She had on only a light gown but was naked underneath. I could see the curvy outline of her hips and breasts. It was dark but my hormones rushed into my brain, flushing my skin.

"What are you doing out here?"

"What are you doing out here?" she put it right back at me.

"Well, I am heading south." I answered her.

"Well, I am heading to Chill High." she answered back.

"What's Chill High?"

"My home, I live there, all my clothes and things are there." I was having more and more trouble keeping up with her, she was laying them down, and I had walked all day.

"Why are you dressed like this?"

"This gown?" she plucked at the thin cloth gown. "That's all they would let me have. They took all my clothes. I told you I am going to Chill High to get my clothes."

"Who took all your clothes?"

"They did, at the hospital."

"The hospital?" What was wrong with her?

"Yeah, they took my clothes and locked me up. But I got loose and I'm going to get my clothes. After that I am going to hide from them."

It hit me. She had walked out of a mental hospital. I took a deep breath. She kept walking, faster, glancing at me, and looking straight ahead.

"Chill High is down the road apiece. Not far." Her voice was cracking and crisp in the cold night air.

I banished all thoughts of sexual intercourse. I thought about what was the best thing to do. We were alone, walking in the middle of the pre-dawn night down a country road in West Virginia. She had escaped from being locked up in a mental hospital, and couldn't stop talking about Chill High and the clothes she was after. As I walked with her, she told me she didn't like the way she had been treated, and how she was going to hide when she got back home. She expected they would come looking for her, and in fact they most likely were doing so right now.

"Don't want nothin' to do with them people." Her voice was angry and afraid at the same time.

"What did they do to you?

"Took all my things, won't let me have nothin'." She spit out a little fluid as if to emphasize how bad this had been. "Can't have no cigarettes, no candy, nothing I want"

It was starting to get light and the fog seemed to lift a little. I had been walking the entire night. I was tired. It occurred to me that she couldn't take care of herself. She kept repeating over and over again her need to get to Chill High and her clothes.

"Listen," I said, "There a road sign, But it wasn't Chill High was not on it." She was going the wrong way.

"I think we should stop there, and visit the Sheriff. I think he can help you get to Chill High." I had decided to try and turn her over to the authorities.

"You think he'll help?" Her voice had a bit of hesitancy to it. I could tell she wasn't too sure she wanted to meet the Sheriff. "Think he'll help me get to Chill High?"

"I think it would be best if you got some clothes and got out of this cold. I don't think it is safe for you out here." Hell, I thought it was not safe for me out here. What kind of trouble would I get in if they arrested me alone with her? Was I taking a risk in being with her? It was a weird thought, and I didn't know the answer.

"I don't know. They'll want me to go back to the hospital." She was right, but what could I say? She was probably lost. There were no road signs indicating a town called Chill High was anywhere nearby. I was genuinely worried about her safety. I guess she was lost.

"I think you need some help." It occurred to me that if I was found with her, it might be a problem for me. What was I doing with her? How old was she? What were the laws in West Virginia like? I hadn't touched her but what if she said I did?

"If you think they'll help me, I guess I should."

"We'll go and ask, see what they say." I was relieved!

An hour later we entered town as the sun was coming up in the mountains. I found the Sheriff's office, knocked and a uniformed middle-aged man opened the door. He had a partner, I could see him sitting at a desk in the back of their small office.

"What ya want?" He looked me up and down and then his eyes rested on CiCi.

"I ran into her on the road while I was hitchhiking last night. I think she needs help, I think she is lost."

I did not mention the obvious fact she was in a hospital gown, had no underwear on, and was without shoes. I didn't need to. He could see her naked outline in the robe as easily as I could. Both men gasped and the deputy let out a long quiet whistle.

"You come on here, girl." He opened the door wider. He was staring at her. She stepped in the doorway and looked around.

"Where you from?" He was talking to her but I answered.

"California." I responded.

"Chill High." Her high voice spoke over the top of mine.

"Chill High is a hundred miles north of here." She was lost. She had been headed in the wrong direction. "Sam, take a look at what we got here."

His partner got up, walked over, and peered at CiCi, young, half naked, and vulnerable. He made a double take and nodded his approval. Then saw me for the first time.

"Christ. What the hell are you?"He found me as strange as he found her lucious. His harsh stare made it clear I was more of an oddity than she was.

I realized I was unshaven, and my hair was long and uncombed. I was "wild" looking, a lot like someone he had seen on a newsreel dancing in a park in San Francisco. Perhaps I was scary, and someone to be feared. Did he need to defend himself? I was sure I could see all these thoughts running through his mind.

"I ran into her last night on the highway, I thought she should come here for help. So I brought her." I started trying to angle my way out the door. "I am afraid she is lost."

They were hungry wolves about to devour an injured deer. I regretted having brought her to this place. They were interested in her, but I didn't think they cared if she was lost or not.

They were ready to pounce.

"You're not from these parts, are you? Did you say California?" Sam's focus was back on me.

"I'm not from around here, I'm passing through."

"Get on your way then. We'll take care of this girl."

A bolt of electricity jarred my brain.I knew what was going to happen. I could see it in their eyes. I wanted to grab her by the hand and run, part of me said I should try. Another part of me said to leave the matter alone. They were the law. I was the one who brought her there. Where would I take her to be safe? I couldn't take her home with me. It felt like the hand of fate had arrived.

As I left, cold chills ran up and down my spine. I deeply regretted the whole thing. It was impossible to know what to do. Were they were going to lock the door and rape her. They could do as they pleased and nobody would care and after that? Who knows?

I went back to the highway, frustrated, and angry with myself. My plan had made sense when I knocked on the Sheriff's door. I had every intention of helping that girl and it had blown up in my face. I felt ashamed and hopeless.

In a wink I was back on the road. A VW bus with California plates stopped for me.

"Where you going?" the man on the passenger side asked.

"I am headed south." I answered.

"We're going as far as New Orleans. Want to come?"

"Sure." It sounded like a fine destination. I was back on the road. "New Orleans, why not?""

Chapter Nineteen-

Mike and John were from San Francisco. They were in their mid twenties. Each was a bit under six feet tall, with long hair. Mike sported a well trimmed mustache. He had dark eyes and curly black hair hanging on his shoulders. John was a dishwater blonde and was chronically tired as if he hadn't slept all night. They were in jeans and cowboy shirts.

"You guys on vacation?"

"We are searching for the "blues". Mike smiled at me.

"How's that?" He got my attention.

"We're musicians, and have been playin' clubs' around San Francisco for years. Right now we're taking a break and visiting the places where the blues was born.

"What does it mean? Lookin' for the blues?" I was curious.

"We started in St.Louis and went up to Chicago. We finished up in Memphis." Mike answered. "Each town has its own style. When you hear it you know it came from that place. Blues is a form with its roots in several key towns."

"Interesting. How do you know all of this?"

"We opened for some big time guys. Muddy Waters, Johnny Lee. We learned by copying them. These are their towns." Mike had let the famous names roll off his tongue.

"Wow, those are famous guys. You know them?" I was impressed.

"You been hitchhiking alone? " John changed the subject.

"Yeah, New York for a while and I went up to Canada and the world's fair. I covered most of the east coast."

"You got a lot of nerve. I wouldn't do what you're doing." Joe chipped in. "Too dangerous alone."

"Yah I had some trouble, nothing I couldn't handle." I said with swagger.

Mike slipped a tape on his deck. Out came Janis belting out "Take a little piece of my heart" loud and clear.

"I saw her in Monterey at the Pop festival." I nodded towards the sound.

"You were at Monterey?" "We almost played there, it thought like we were goin' get invited to play and it fell apart at the last minute. I'm jealous you got to see it. I wanted to go even if we couldn't play. It didn't happen for us."

"Your band must be good." I said impressed. "What's your name?

Most of the time when guys told me they were musicians it didn't amount to much. It usually meant four guys in a garage playing the same two songs over and over again. But these guys were making a living at it. They must be somebody.

"We're called the Velvet Hand." I had never heard of them.

"Well we played a lot of clubs in northern California. Haven't hit it big yet." John shrugged his shoulders.

As we rolled along they explained how they were trying to discover the roots of American music, especially the blues. Their next stop was the Mississippi delta and after that they would head to New Orleans.

"You're headed to Mississippi? What's in Mississippi?"

"Everyone says it's the real home of the blues." Mike nodded knowingly.

"A lot of rock is based on the blues. You can hear the blues in the Stone's. A lot of their rifts and chords are taken from classic blues tunes." Joe added.

"I had no idea." I thought to myself, the Rolling Stones? Mississippi? Amazing!

"The blues is in everything the early Stones do. I hear it in every song. Of course they are imitators, not the real thing. We decided to hear the real thing for ourselves." Mike added.

"The real thing is in Mississippi?" I was stunned to learn Mississippi had such a history.

"Yup! Next up, we hit Clarksdale, Mississippi, home of the giants. Old timers like Son House and Robert Johnson." Mike let the names roll off his tongue.

"I never heard of them." I said.

"Son House and Robert Johnson are legends. We learned about them when we opened for Muddy at Keystone. Trust us, you'll hear the real stuff in Clarksdale. The Mississippi delta is the true birthplace of the blues."

We rolled through Georgia and a small corner of Alabama without incident. That night we stopped at a roadside rest station and they fed me. It was some beans heated on a burner and hot dogs in a bun.

"We'll be in Clarksdale tomorrow." Mike said, folding up his map.

Mike was in charge of the grass. He was careful about when and where they lit up. Jail sentences for drugs are heavy in the south. The act of having it in the van carries a big risk. Theirs was well hidden. They had welded a compartment to the engine wall, it was worn and old. It had a fake wire that went to the engine for show. It served no real purpose except to hide the pot.

"Had them put in so we could travel. Long hair rock and roll guys are subject to a lot of scrutiny. Can't have pot lying about in the van." Mike winked at me.

We smoked and they took out their acoustic guitars and played. I knew some of the songs and sang along. I have a deep bass voice and can hit low notes.

I loved catching the scenery of the deep south from the safety of their van. The next morning we crossed into the north west corner of Mississippi. I looked out and saw the sign "Now entering Coahoma County." They were both excited.

"Muddy gave us an intro to the owner of an old club where he often plays. They'll all know him there. " Mike's voice was full of excitement.

It turned out to be a little night club with a bar. It could house 70 people tops. It was closed. The sign on the front read "Mississippi Jukes, home of the Crossroads." It would be open at 9:00 PM.

"Let's go see the Crossroads. They can't be far." John's face lit up.

It turned out to be at the junction of hwy 61 and 49. They had it marked on their map. When Mike pulled out the map it turned out to be a bit north of town.

"What's the Crossroads?" I asked. "What's there?"

"The claim is where Robert Johnson sold his soul to the devil. It took place in a meeting at the crossroads. He gave it up to learn to play the blues." John explained.

"The crossroads sounds familiar. I heard it somewhere." I muttered.

"Yeah it's Robert Johnson's most famous song, but a lot of groups have played it." Mike started to tap the tune on the dash and sang:

"I went down to the crossroads

Fell down on my knees,

I went down to the crossroads

And feel down on my knees,

Asked the Lord above for mercy

"Save me if you please."

I went down to the crossroads

Tried to flag a ride

I went down to the crossroads

Tried to flag a ride

Nobody seemed to know me

Everybody passed me by."

Highway 61 is the blues highway! If you head north it goes to St. Louis. Robert Johnson took the blues to St.Louis. Legend has it it goes to HWY 92 and off to a prison. He ended up there for a while too."

"Sounds like he was hitchhiking in the song,".

"Yeah, that's right, he is. Just like you. Did you make a deal with the devil?" We both laughed at the idea.

"Nah, no need. I ain't got any special talents to trade for."

The spot was marked with a plaque. We spent the afternoon milling around in a local park. When the club opened its doors we walked in. Beer was thirty cents. I decided to have a beer and watch. Mike sat at the bar.

"We're from San Francisco. We opened for Muddy Waters at the Fillmore. Muddy sent us and told me to ask for Jimmy."

"Muddy sent you? Have you played with him?"

"Yeah, we opened for him for a week and jammed with him every night. He told us this was the place to go to hear the real Delta sound."

"Yeah, sit back and groove. Jimmy will be in soon. I'll let him know you're here." He poured a round of beers and left us to wait and watch.

The show started at nine thirty. Two casually dressed black men walked on stage and began to play guitar. One played slide and the other rhythm. The club was half full. The slide player led, tossing the notes back and forth. They were joined by a piano player who filled in some texture in the background. The audience was tapping along. Things were warming up. After a bit a short heavy set man wearing dark glasses walked out of the crowd playing a harmonica. He had been sitting at a table near us having a drink. The band was rolling. The harmonica player started singing

"Bad luck and trouble

My only friends!

I been down

Ever since I was ten!

Born under a bad sign

Been down since

I began to crawl!

If it wasn't for bad luck,

If it wasn't for real bad luck

I wouldn't have no luck at all."

Mike and Joe kept time tapping on the table.

They all finished to a rousing round of applause and went right into

"Walkin to New Orleans."

A song I knew well.

"I can't wait to hear Monique. That's her! She's out next. I hear she is too much." Mike nudged me pointing out a sultry black woman who had appeared at the side of the stage.

The harmonica player sang "Walkin" and the spotlight shifted to Monique who slid out on the stage. The small crowd let out a stream of howls.

"They call it stormy Monday

But Tuesday's just as bad

They call it stormy Monday.

But Tuesday's just as bad!

She had an ultra smooth throaty style. She moved with grace from song to song. I tapped my fingers and sipped my beer.

"I'm gonna get some religion,

I'm gonna join the Baptist church

I'm gonna be a preacher

So I won't have to work.

I'm gonna get some religion."

By ten thirty they were playing to standing room only. Except for us, it was an all black crowd. After a half dozen more numbers the set ended and they took a break. The bartender leaned over the bar and whispered. Mike nodded his head "yes".

"We've been invited backstage." I tagged along.

"So you boys played with Muddy, how is he doin? Still playin for all the white folks?" It was the piano player.

"Be kind Walter, you know Muddy still got his roots here. Even if he has been off playing in front of white people for years now. He'll be back sometime." It was Monique.

"He's fine. He sent his regards." Mike nodded to a twelve string sitting up against the wall. "Mind if I play a bar or two?"

"Go ahead, show us what you got."

Mike picked up the guitar and started playing. It was one of their original songs. He had learned it after hearing it once and was now playing it back with some licks he added. They all nodded.

"Is this how you play that last rift?" He asked, acting as if he had played it all his life. He had memorized it and changed it at the same time.

"Not bad, not bad. Why don't you jam with us?"

The second set got underway with Mike playing a slide steel guitar aside Monqiue and her crew. He added pace and volume. The crowd loved it. After that the drinks were on the house and flowed all night.

We spent several more days in Clarksdale. I tried to stay out of the way. My two companions became well known. It was a rural southern town and we had crossed into the music side of town which was almost 100% black. We stood out. Three young white guys hanging out in the black club. Eyes were on us. Who were we? What were we doing there? We stayed out of trouble.

"We're gonna head to New Orleans tomorrow morning." Mike advised me. " But we got a booking. We'll be back in three months with our whole group. They booked us for a week. It'll be great for the band to play in the club Robert Johnson made famous."

Chapter Twenty

The road south ran along the Mississippi River. We arrived in the French quarter in the morning. New Orleans is a unique town, especially the French Quarter. I took an instant liking to the place. The feeling was similar to the one I had gotten in Quebec. A feeling that I belonged there somehow, and that I had been there before.

"We're going to bum around." Mike said. "You can hang with us if you want."

"Thanks, I'll want to wander around on my own.You guys go on." I was running out of money and would head home soon.

"We got a lead on a place to crash tonight but if it don't pan out we might have to drive out of town and camp. If you want a place to sleep, be back here by eight." I appreciated Mike's offer. But I wandered off on my own.

I had gotten used to living out of my sleeping bag, and there is a part of me that likes to let things happen. Besides they had money, a lot more than me and I couldn't sponge off them any more. They weren't rich but they could eat where they felt like eating. I was down to my last ten dollars, way under the vagrancy line. The best I could do was a quart of milk in the morning and a roll. After that I might have to skip some meals.

I strolled down Bourbon street passing a string of open air cafes with outdoor bars full of happy patrons drinking with a vengeance at 11:00 in the morning. Music filled the air and the smell of gumbo boiling on a pot somewhere nearby made me hungry. I came upon a stand selling alcoholic drinks to passersby. There was a sign in the window, it read:

"It's always five o'clock somewhere!" A young woman in skin tight pants that hugged her ass in a tight V crossed her legs with a suggestive dip wanted to pour me a drink.

"What'll it be?" She kept her hand on a tap.

"How much for a draft?" I asked.

"Twenty five cents." She nodded.

"I'm only seventeen,"

"Yeah so what? You're way over 16, I could tell that."

"You'll let me walk off with it and drink it out on the sidewalk?"

"Of course, this is "Norlens'! No trouble, no one will bother you."

I winked and she poured me a beer. It was cold. The special was Crawfish etouffee. I wondered what it was. The price made me laugh, I thought "buy one and head on home" cause you're broke.

I weaved through the crowd. Two blocks down the road a man wearing a loud checkered jacket pounced on me. He had an iron grip he used to grab me by the arm. He deftly yanked me towards some long purple curtains that were hanging loose in the mouth of the club doorway.

"Take a peek!" He shoved my head through the curtains. There was a woman on the stage who reminded me of Jane Russell. She was dancing,and swaying to the music. She was topless and enormous.

"Buy one beer, forty five cents, and you can sit and watch." He let go of my arm and pushed me up to the bar.

I fumbled in my pocket and located forty five cents. A beer appeared to the side of my hand and I was aware of the bartender taking my change. I could not take my eyes off her huge breasts twirling in a slow circle. Forty five cents was a lot, but it felt like a bargain, her breasts were magnificent.

I sipped and wondered if people do this all the time? It was a small beer. I finished it. The bartender would not let me sit and linger. I had to buy another or leave. I left. As I did her magnificent glands were waving goodbye. I got to the door and indulged myself with one long last lingering stare.

I walked out into the sunlight and had to blink to combat the sun. I hadn't meant to drink in the morning. I reminded myself of how destitute I was and that I needed discipline. By now the beers had given me a groove and I was feeling like dancing.

My whole body was caught in a wave of sound. It was the unique sounds of jazz and blues competing with each other. They filled the street. There was music coming from every direction. The venues were so bound they were creating overlapping layers of music mixed together until they became one fluid wave. I was caught in the fervor of Bourbon street. Even at midday it was a party!

I was taught by a deep growly voice churning out the rhythms of Mississippi blues. I thought of Mike and John. A hunched heavy set man with a shiny vest bobbed his head to the beat as he sang. He was white with a deep growly voice. He wore dark sunglasses. I realized he was blind.

"My woman left me all alone,

She gave no never mind,

My woman left me all alone,

It was so unkind."

Mesmerized, I stood through his entire set. When he finished I realized it had gotten late. I needed a place to stay. The streets were now packed with people. They were jammed together making it difficult to walk unobstructed. I was in the habit of going to sleep early. I was ready to turn in and the big easy was just starting to wake up.

New Orleans never closes. The bars close at 4:00 for an hour to clean up a little, but they open again an hour later at 5:00. You can sit at the bar and drink if you want while they clean. I had gotten caught up in the magic of the place and had neglected finding a place to sleep. One thing was certain: there was no privacy anywhere on the streets of the quarter. I knew I could not go to sleep out in the open. No way.

Earlier I passed by two "hotels" within a block of each other. The first was "The House of the Rising Sun" named after the famous song. Or perhaps the song was named after the hotel? It was a mystery. I fantasized about how cool it would be to be able to stay there. It was $2.00 a night. Nor pricey but I hoped for cheaper. I felt broke.

A few doors down the shingle read "The Silver Dollar Hotel." It was priced at $1.00 at night. Sold! To save a buck I passed on a chance to sleep in "The House of the Rising Sun". As tempting as it might be, a night in The House of the Rising Sun was not meant to be.

To say the "Silver Dollar" was sleazy is an understatement. It is worse than that. My room was a small cubicle, about 6' by 10'. with dingy paper thin fiberboard walls. The walls had numerous holes punched in them so if I wanted I could look into the adjoining rooms. They had been dug out by former tenants. I pressed my finger into one of the walls and it sunk in. It would be easy to put a hole or a fist through these walls.

The walls do not go all the way up to the ceiling. They stop after five feet and become a wire mesh. The mesh was tacked to the fiberboard and it continues up to the ceiling. I could stand on the cot and see into the adjoining room if I wanted. I did it and looked over. Luckily, the room next door was empty.

I was relieved, at least I have a room and was not on the street. The cot was rock hard and the bedding was soiled. I decided to unroll my bag on top of it and cover it up. The toilet was making running water sounds in the corner. I couldn't be sure if it was running or broken.

There was half a roll of toilet paper dangling next to one single naked light bulb on a frayed cord. They all hang in the center of the room. I think the bare, bright, bulb is too hot. So I unscrewed it. There is now enough light coming in from the adjacent rooms that will work. I try to sleep but it is still too bright.

There are noises everywhere. People are packed in all around me. I feel like ghosts, faceless and nameless people are in the room with me. Their breathing has become a discordant symphony of sexual arrousal. Loud moans and hot breath are in the room with me, breathing down my neck with uncontrolled passion or at lust. I wonder are they solo flights or are people fucking all around me? I hear a female voice moan with satisfaction, it is a welcome break from the pantheon of male domination. I feel I have become a listening Tom.

The sexual choir is soon accompanied by retching. I hear vomit splattering on the wall right next to me. The sound is repeated a couple of walls down. Several drunks are sick all night long. I'm glad it isn't me. I have never experienced sickness due to alcohol, but I know it when I hear it. Coughing, gurgling, vomiting become a sexual chorus and dominate the night. What can you expect for $1.00?

I fell asleep. When I woke, I decided I had enough of the Silver Dollar Hotel. I have made up my mind to never return to it. I needed to find a better alternative if I was going to stay in the french quarter.

During my aimless wandering that day I had noticed a sign indicating there is riverfront access not far from the Quarter. I locate a small park laid out alongside the river front. It is quiet in the morning. I take the riverwalk and marvel at the volume of water flowing by. It is muddy and moving fast.

The opposite bank is a long way off, too far to swim. Big ships are anchored down the river and I think it must be deep. The river's flow whispers a message of power, immense power. I reflect on the long lineage of witnesses who have stood on this shore and felt its power. It is no different today than it has been for hundreds of years.

Nothing I had read had prepared me to absorb the inevitability of its presence. Its motion licked at the edges of my mind. Barge after barge floated by with only a few hundred yards separating them. They were an endless progression of long flat platforms carrying commerce from the center of the country out to the world.

I discovered the park has several secluded corners with thick bushes providing cover. I could sleep there and hide out of view at night. I decided to stay in town and try sleeping in the park for a while. I hoped for the comfort of warm humid night air. It was already hot and humid, I liked my chances.

It was nine in the morning and I was already sweating profusely. The little park was perfect! I headed back into the magic of the Quarter. The route back passed through a residential section of town. All the homes were old, almost ancient. A couple had signs claiming they were historical landmarks and had been built in the 1820's. They were old but elegant. They had nothing in common with the beach bungalows of California.

I loved the feelings that resonated from the gated gardens. They spoke of a reserved polite welcome and bore hints of a flowing passion, "We make love here" they called to me. As I walked by, I peered through the latticed closed gates and I wondered about the people who called this place home. Who were they? What were they like? I imagined these were exclusive homes and most likely they would not appreciate a long haired scraggly vagabond at their castle walls.

I found my way back to the far eastern edge of the quarter. A feeling of deja vu, similar to the one I experienced in Quebec came over me. I stopped and stared at a mud adobe building standing by itself away from the other buildings. It had the look and feel of true antiquity. A battered wood sign engraved with a portrait of Jean Lafitte swung in the breeze, it read "Serving the drinking public since the 1700's".

I had stumbled upon Lafitte's Blacksmith Shop Bar. A plaque on the wall proclaimed with pride that the old scoundrel himself had once called the place home. I went in and bought a beer for thirty cents. An elderly lady was playing on a piano and singing show tunes. I sat down to listen.

"You always start this early?"

"They let me do what I want." She had a french accent. She smiled at me.

"My mom likes show tunes, she played them all the time when I was young."

"You have a favorite?" she asked.

"Not really."

"Then I guess I'll have to play what I like."Her voice was scratchy and thin. It was interesting to sit with her. I joined in and we sang a familiar song together.

"I live close by. I like to come down in the morning and they let me play. It's no problem if the place is quiet, like now." She nodded and smiled.

I spent the morning with her. Her fingers were bent and moved slowly. It affected her timing but it didn't matter.

"I have arthritis and it's getting worse. Someday I'll have to stop playing, but not today."

I decided to leave thinking it was too early to be drinking. I needed to find something better to do. Something that didn't cost money. The streets were lined with shops. The signs outside promised me things I had never imagined could exist.

I walked into a strange shop selling masks and costumes. Devils, goats and satyrs seemed to be especially prized. Who buys this stuff? Tourists I . What do they do with it? Put it on their walls at home? It soon became clear any one buying a mask needed accessories to complete their ensemble. To go with the masks they offered rows of flowing gowns, capes and robes, each cut to reveal as much flesh as possible. There was a selection of goat costumes, each complete with horns, and a wine flask to sling over your shoulder.

"Interested in buying a horney old goat horn?" The store clerk zeroed in on my shopping.

"Not really, they caught my eye. I'm only looking." I answered feeling pressured.

Next to the goat costume there was a specialty section featuring female mannequins dressed in leather. They had frozen plastic faces with curvy mounds of flesh that could poke your eye out. Some were draped in chains and handcuffs while others had whips and were backed by photos showing women flogging men in dark chambers.

"Is this the stuff you wear to visit Grandma?" I was unable to resist making a comment.

"You'd be surprised who buys this stuff. We get all kinds in here."

"Is there a best seller?" I asked timidly.

"Well the sex toys do well." He nodded towards a shelf in the back. "Bert's Big Blessing does well." For the first time I realized the shelf was full or hard plastic penises. He opened a box and took one out for me to see. "This is Big Bert."

"Wow, that's a big plastic..." I hesitated to name it, I had never seen one that big before.

"Dick! Its' a plastic dick." The clerk named it for me. He waved it in the air.

"Wow, is it supposed to be lifesize?" I could hear my voice get small and timid.

"Only in your dreams. It's twice a normal man. Do you want one? I could wrap it up in brown paper for you."

"What would I do with it?"

"Well if I have to tell you that, I guess you don't want one." He put it back in the box."Are you thinking of buying anything?"

"Well, no not today, I don't think so. Is all this stuff for Mardi Gras?"

"Madi Gras is a state of mind. Not just a week on the calendar." and added " Move along this store is for paying customers." Looking around I saw the place was empty. I left without saying another word.

I continued up Basin Street stopping to look in the windows of an antique store and a music shop. They were well stocked and pricey. I passed on them, there was nothing new and exciting to see.Then it caught my eye! Swinging from the center of an open door was a miniature human skull.

The face was wicked and angry. I reached out and pulled it up close to my face. It wasn't plastic and it wasn't wood. It felt like bone. It had a stale, rancid smell that reminded me of wet dirt. Embossed on the door frame was a picture of a black man with flowing hair and a snake wrapped around his body. His kinky hair was tied in knots and hanging to his waist. His hair reminded me of snakes as well!

The smell of burning incense filled the room. A large black woman in a flowered dress was adjusting vials on a shelf. She turned and saw me in the doorway. She waved, signaling me to enter. I froze and hesitated.

"Well come on in Child, I don't bite." She had an engaging smile.

"Lordy child, you'd think I was the devil hisself." She chided me.

"Well I never been in a voodoo shop before." I stepped in. The sign on the door warned all who entered that they did so at their own risk. I worked up my nerve and entered.

"Are the heads fake?"

"Well that's part of the mystery, isn't it?" She chuckled at my boldness. "What fun would it be if you knew for sure"

I decided the shrunken heads in the windows were fakes, but who could be sure? Could they be real? What did it mean if they were? I knew I didn't want to know. She closed in on me and was standing close enough I could feel her body heat.

"How you doin' today chile?" She was happy I had worked up the nerve to enter.

"I'm okay, jI am shopping around."

"Well, you are welcome." Her teeth flashed and gleamed.

Something drew me to a shelf lined with potions. They were all marked, most were love potions. Others said they could ward off enemies, or keep false friends away, while another promised to make life work better if you were suffering. I read each one and put them back on the shelf with care. Having no knowledge of voodoo, I did not understand self suggestion, or the power of making things real by investing belief in them.

"You see anything you want?" She smiled warmly.

"No, I am passing some time. I have no money to spend." I it would be the end of her interest in me.

"It's not always about money, child."

"What else could I have you want?"

"You've got beautiful wavy hair. Let me have some of your hair and I'll give you a love potion. It'll make any girl you want fall in love with you."

"My hair? How much of my hair?" She caught me by surprise. What would I do with a love potion? But she made me think. Did I need help? Would it help? Why was I thinking about it?

"Like I said, not much, a couple of healthy locks will do." She reached for a little bottle and shook it in the air. "It works, honey child. Slip it in her drink and she will be yours. Any girl you want."

"What the hell, I'll try it." She snipped off two locks of my hair from the back side of my head.

"Once get her to drink it and she'll be yours that same night."

I took the vial and put it in my pocket and left the shop. The old witch had my two locks of hair.

Having the love potion caused me to reminisce about my encounters in the park with Clarisse. But something was missing, was it love? Something in it was not quite right. We had had sex but there was something missing. I could feel it. It all troubled me. Could a potion be the answer? How could a potion bring love? I doubted it but I made the trade anyway.

The moment the shop door closed behind me my mind flooded with intuitions about the Voodoo shop. The old woman as bright and sunny as she was could not hide the fact her place had been loaded with heavy feelings. There were things I could not put my finger on and yet I knew they were present. I had the love potion in my hand and wondered why I had traded for it. Was there something malevolent in the transaction?

I wandered down Decatur street to Jackson where I parked myself on a bench in front of the statue of Andrew Jackson. I decided I needed to assess my situation. I had a little about twelve dollars left. Food ran me a dollar a day minimum, if I slept outside. Beer was costing me a dollar or more a day.

I had passed below the poverty line and could not afford to get picked up by the police. If I did they would charge me with vagrancy if they wanted to. My eighteenth birthday was coming up in the middle of the month. I would turn 18, and I would soon be draft eligible. My enrollment date for college at the beginning of September, a month away. I had to sign up or I would not get a deferment and be in jeopardy of being drafted. I was 1500 miles from home. It would take two or three full days to hitch home. Adding it all up, it was time to head home!

I decided to go clubbing, beer was forty cents a mug, I had enough for a night out on the town. I would party and then pack up and head home! It was my last chance to do the town! Since I had arrived music was constantly filling my consciousness. It was as if the voices of angels and devils were all singing at once. Combined they formed an exotic mixture and became one mighty voice.

It was a wall of sound carrying with the power to engulf me. I felt that if I went under and hit the bottom I might not ever surface again. It was a magical world. I lost all track of time and place. I went from stool to stool sipping beer, listening to the music and watching the shows.

It got late and I found myself in a club called the Dungeon. It had two floors and I was on the ground level. Cocktails were served by a woman wrapped in black and white stripes that crisscross like bars. The swathes of cloth left her skin exposed so her breasts bounced as she moved around the bar. Velvet paintings of scantily dressed women hung from the walls. Music was piped in and a few scattered groups were sitting drinking. Nothing much was happening. It was quiet and tame for New Orleans at night.

On the left side of the room, hidden I saw a spiral staircase that wound downward out of sight. A flashing sign invited me to enter and descend a floor. The basement level promised a dungeon and a replica of a medieval torture chamber.I bought a beer and went on down and sat..

The Dungeon was pulsating with energy. Everything about the place screamed sex! Hot steamy raw sex. Two women, one on each side of the room were pole dancing topless in tiny g strings. They were twirling and offering views of their curvy bodies as they circled the poles.

A cage dropped from the ceiling and appeared lit up under a spotlight in the middle of the stage. The cage door opened and a woman bounced out gyrating in the light. She headed toward me, her hard round naked ass was shaking and across the counter of the bar. She stopped a foot away dripping sweat in the hot lights.

Her butt shook in time with the drum beat. The message was "Sex, sex, We offer sex, that's what we do here!" Her ass called out saying come and get me as it pounded wildly. I realized it was not a drum at all but instead it was my own heartbeat throbbing in my temple lobes.

My body screamed out yes, yes. I have found it here! I was oozing with desire. But nothing more happened. The show went on and on, but I started to cool. Then the music stopped. She collected a few dollars, stuffed them in her "g" string and left.

The night wore on, and I had more beer, but nothing else happened. I thought perhaps I was too shy, or not rich enough or maybe I was too bold. Whatever it was, I couldn't make any contact with anyone. After I tipped her she ignored me. I thought perhaps I needed to try harder but then I thought I should try less. I decided I need to clear my head.

I ducked out on the street and walked up a side alleyway out of the action. The image of her gyrating sweating butt was imprinted on my brain. Her perfect round ass had been six inches from my face and now I felt like it was still there shaking and dripping sweat in my nostrils. I shook my head to clear it. Had I imagined it? Not a chance. Stillness came and I thought no, it was not a fantasy, it was real. Very real. The smell was real. The dripping sweat was real. I was getting drunk.

I leaned back in a doorway to hide. I saw my reflection looking back at me in the glass. I let my body relax and took a deep breath. I rested. I put my dark sunglasses on even though it was night. I started to calm down, I had my sheep herder jacket on and it made me sweat. It was seventy degrees out and late. I felt unkempt and wild. I hadn't shaved all summer and needed a haircut. I thought I might look dangerous.

That's when she came rushing up the street towards me. A young woman was walking so fast she was running. Three uniformed sailors were right on her heels, trying to run her down. She was frantic and a bit scared. They were in hot pursuit, following her down the street. All of them were cooing at her like lechers. It was an awful scene.

"Hey, Baby, you want a good time?" They were all yelling at her.

She had her head down and eyes straight ahead. She plowed right by me without acknowledging me. She never saw me. She was hell bent on getting away, but they were relentless.

"Hey, Baby, we got something for you." They were all right on her heels.

I decided I couldn't watch it. It was going to be three on one, but I decided to move anyway. I took a deep breath, and gathered up my nerves.

"What the hell are you guys doing with my sister?" I used my deepest, most masculine voice! I stepped out onto the street to face them. They stopped dead in their tracks and checked me out.

"That's your sister?" one of them asked. They were dumbfounded, and confused. I could see they were not sure, caught off guard, was she my sister?

"My baby sister!" I answered with as much conviction I could muster. "Leave her alone."

A long silent stare ensued. I wondered about my odds, if I got into a fight with three sailors. Not fair odds for me, but whatever, I had already decided I needed to step up and I had. I was ready to rumble.

"We're sorry." One of them came back at me. They all had their eyes down at the ground. They all knew they were in the wrong and admitted it. I stood firm and waited. One of them kicked the ground. They got sheepish mumbling apologies under their breath. They were shamed and cut bait.

Their sudden departure left me and the terrified young woman all alone in the middle of the night. I was dumbfounded at my luck. She was stunned. She wasn't running anymore, she stood there looking at me.

"You want some coffee? There's a place right over there." She nodded to an empty trolley car sitting right across from the Jackson square statue. It turned out to be a coffee stand with a couple of outdoor tables. She bought me a cup of coffee, and we talked. I told her where I was from and what I was doing. Her name was Valerie.

I liked her immediately. She liked me too. She was about my age, with a sweet southern accent. Sparkling blue eyes, full lips, long blond hair, and a delightful figure that promised perfection. She told me a little about herself. She was in the Quarter on an errand. Her family was from Sweden but she grew up in New Orleans and she didn't remember Sweden. They had moved there before she was three.

"I rarely come to the Quarter, it is a part of town for tourists and outsiders.." She started to explain the errand and stopped short. "No matter why I was down here, I shouldn't have been here at this time of night by myself. Thank you for stepping in, it took courage."

In a flash I forgot all the girls in the bars, she was the one I wanted. She was the real thing, she was magnetic. Somehow fate had allowed me to become her knight in shining armor, what a break for me. I had been foolish and lucky.

We nursed the coffee. Time was of the essence. I wanted to spend as much time with her as I could. Every second became precious! Time flew by and our first cup was gone. They allowed a refill. I had the overwhelming feeling she was going to get away and I would never see her again. My little voice which is usually timid was yelling at me, telling me to pursue her. I could and should not let her leave.

Her voice was magical. When she spoke and smiled, instead of words, little bits of sweetness appeared at the corners of her mouth.

It was as if the words she uttered took on physical form and I could ingest them if I wanted to. I cannot say why, but it was all very sexy. I wanted to kiss her words as they appeared out into the world. I wanted to lick the little bits as they flowed from her mouth. What can I say? I had been struck by a lightning bolt. It doesn't happen every day, in fact it had never happened to me like this before. But now it had, and in the most improbable way. I was awestruck.

The coffee ended and she said she had to go. It was late. She took my hand.

"Promise me you'll see me again tomorrow. You must promise to meet me here at 7:00. At this cafe." Her words were a dream coming true. She wanted to see me again!

"Yes," with my throat in my mouth. "Yes." We would meet again the next night, at the same spot at 7:00. in the evening.

When she left I fell into a haze. I bought a beer from a local corner store and headed for the river bank spot where I would spend the night.

My hiding place was only a few blocks away. In the dark I found my comfortable corner and laid out my bag. I had gone on a binge and was down to my last $5.00. I was too drunk and too overwhelmed to care. Somehow it didn't matter!

I turned on my side and watched the barges float down the mighty Mississippi. All I could hear was the water making a lapping sound as it touched the shore. It was soothing. I felt alive. Valerie was a fire in my mind! Her beautiful face, her curvy shape, her southern drawl. She was perfect!

The sun opened my eyes. The river was in the same place I left it, flowing endlessly to the sea. Life felt really, really good. I had one problem! A whole day of waiting lay ahead. Thoughts of Valerie were consuming me, proving desire and anticipation are fierce friends. Our reunion was fourteen hours away. To me it was an eternity!

I consoled myself with the idea the French Quarter was there to help me pass the time. It offered a continually changing scene. It was the most interesting place I had ever been. It offered a constant flow of jazz, blues or rock around the clock!

The unfortunate truth was I was down to my last five dollars with a date ahead. My good sense knew I should be heading back to Huntington. My pocketbook was insisting I go home. I listened to my heart. But how long could five bucks last? What if I got checked for vagrancy?

I wandered around the Quarter, in and out of every place I had visited plus some new ones. I began to realize how small the Quarter was, less than a dozen square blocks. There was a lot of action packed into a small space! The clock kept ticking and the day dragged its way into night. The rendezvous time had arrived and I went to the little coffee shop at Jackson square. Valerie arrived on time at 7:00 as promised.

"Luke, I'm so glad you came!" She wrapped her arms around me and hugged me. My heart raced. She had on a one piece polka dot dress with an open v neck and short sleeves. The dress flowed and hugged her curves.

"I'm happy to see you too." I blushed at her touch.

I took her hand and we walked off chatting, our hands swinging in rhythm. She appeared to float as if she were walking on a cloud.

"I told my friends what you did and they all said you were really brave. They all want to meet you." she said.

"I figure most people would do the same." I responded truthfully.

"Nah, the truth is most people would look the other way. But not you. That makes you special. Not many guys would do what you were doing, travel around the country all alone."

"I guess I am one of those guys who has to see what is on the other side of the mountain. But I wasn't always alone. I had a friend with me when I started out."

"Yeah but you're alone now, I think it takes courage. What else are you planning on doing with your life?"

"Well the plan has always been for me to go to college. I'm gonna register when I get home." I thought, in order to do that I have to be home in about a week. Should I tell her that too?

"Wow! None of the boys I know are going to go to college. Isn't that expensive?" She asked.

"Not in California. We have a lot of two year schools and they are cheap, almost free." I answered.

"Here it costs a lot. Plus you need to be smart and have good grades. You got good grades?" She focused on my college plans. I wondered why.

"Yeah good enough, but what about you, what are you looking to do?" I asked, squeezing her hand.

"I want to meet someone exciting.Some one different from the rest and have adventures with them." She squeezed back.

The world seemed to be conspiring to sweep me away. For a brief moment it felt unreal as if the whole affair was imaginary. Was I somehow deceiving myself into making her real? It couldn't be possible that a girl that beautiful was out with me, holding my hand and looking into my eyes the way she was.

We stopped in front of a "Lucky Dog" hot dog stand. Their cart was shaped like a long plastic hot dog in a bun dripping in mustard. The middle of the cart is a hot dog steamer, and they offer many different condiments. "Lucky Dog" stands are located all over New Orleans and can be found on most of the street corners.

"I've been wanting to try one ever since I got here. Ever have one?" I asked her. "I want mine with Chili and onions and cheese."

She smiled agreeably.I bought a foot long Lucky Dog, fully loaded. She suggested we share, it was perfect for me because I was flat broke. The vendor scooped a full ladle of chile and poured it on the middle of the dog until the chile spilled over the edge of the bun. He piled on a large topping of cheese and handed it to me. It was messy. I took a bite and tried to give it to Valerie.

She reached for the dog and lost her balance and the dog slipped. It was as if some lusty force had pushed her into me. I had become clumsy, almost magically and without warning. I grabbed her and pulled her close. We kissed hard, long succulent kisses. Our juices, tastes and smells mixed together. Excitement, magic and lust were in the air. My toes curled up in my shoes, my hands stroked her ass. It was fantastic. I dropped the hot dog. It slid off its paper plate, and bounced on the sidewalk.

"Sixty second rule." I mumbled. She looked blank, I picked it up and put it back in the bun. "If it is on the ground for less than sixty seconds it is unharmed. There's a rule that applies here!"

"Never heard of the sixty second rule before, I like it." She took the dog from me. Her fingers were covered with cheese and chili. She licked them clean.

I was relieved. My budget had one dog limit and I had to salvage this one. I didn't want her to go hungry and I didn't feel like I couldn't afford another.

"It was exciting." She leaned over and put her tongue in my ear. Her breath was warm, and sweet.

"Dropping the Hot Dog was exciting?" I joked.

"Nah you silly guy, the kisses!" Her eyes were intense. There was a quiet moment and I felt overwhelmed.

"I know you are almost out of money. But I have an idea I hope will help." I could tell from her tone she was sincere.

"I am desperate, since I met you, I have thought about nothing else." It was true I was infatuated. She was a prize.

"I think I can get you a job. My brother has a friend. And his friend always needs a capable man to pound nails." Valerie had a plan.

"Nails, pounding nails? Carpentry?" Was that what she meant? Me, become a carpenter?

"Yes, I think I can get it set up." I believed I saw love in her eyes. It was something I had never seen before.

Was this it? The answer? It was so different from what had happened with Clarisse. Valerie cared about me and I was getting to know her. I liked the person she was.

"Yeah, I would like to stay." It felt overwhelming, I had a deadline and the draft was slooming. It would be impossible to manage.

According to the news clips the war was becoming more intense. I knew I must get into college or face the draft. I was running out of money. Still, I knew I wanted to stay with Valerie? Impulsively, I agreed to try it.

A voice in my mind whispered, if you do that you will not get a deferment, you will be drafted, inducted, and shipped off to Vietnam. The more my mind played out the scenario, the more real the jungle became. My rational mind was telling me, "you need to go to college." But my heart was saying to stay and "pound nails".

"Stay one more day. If I can get you a job, you have to stay." She Made me promise again. "I'll know tomorrow if I can get you hired. You must promise."

We lay on the grass and kissed and petted. My heart was pounding and I was sure it was loud enough to be heard all over town. She was not shy, but she let me know she had limits and it was clear we would not consummate our affair on this day. It didn't matter at all.

We parted company with the understanding she would return the next day and when she did, it would be with a job off. Her taste and smell filled my nostrils leaving me lightheaded. I could hear her voice laughing and giggling long after she left me.

It was never my plan to stay in New Orleans. I am an explorer by nature and I need to know and see what is on the side of the next mountain. Now almost by accident there was a possibility I would make New Orleans my home.

I poured the love potion into the Mississippi river. It was a terrible idea, but still I had a fantasy that a lonesome fish would fall in love and have extra special little fish babies. But I thought it had dissolved and floated out to sea.

One thing was for sure, I was ready and willing to be with Valerie and wondered if it was possible. My quest to end my virginity had ended in Central Park but my real quest had just begun. I was only beginning to realize the possibilities of love. Imagination or reality, which is better?

I began to think the limits of love were what my imagination thought they could be. I was hoping for more, for something much greater. Had a true lover stepped in and answered the question for me? Has it begun for me?

The wait was more unbearable than it ever was. I had a dollar and fifty cents left in my pocket. It was milk money for a couple of days for sure, but I had to see the end of my road was coming. I refused to see it!

I couldn't get my mind off of Valerie! I didn't want to wait another moment. Now, now, now, I want to see her now. But the clock said she wouldn't be back for ten hours or more. Tick, tick, tick. I had to wait.

I stood on the banks and watched the mighty river roll. It was an old and ancient town and the home of another historic battle in the war of 1812. None of it matters. I knew I was capable of doing many different things in the world. But what were they all? How did this fit in? I had no idea. What was I doing? I knew the answer. I was waiting, waiting for a woman!

Could I convince myself I wanted to pound nails? Her luscious kisses we had, had set me off hoping. But it was not to be.

The time for us to meet had come and Valerie did not show! Perhaps she couldn't get me the job she had promised. All I knew was she missed our date and I was on a short leash. I had just enough money for a few quarts of milk. There was no job on the horizon. I was not going to pound nails. I needed to register for college, get my deferment, and slip back into society. I felt a loss, a sadness. I had been let down but there was no bitterness, no anger, only sadness and an aching feeling of regret. I didn't know her address. Where did she live? I must have been a fool.

Chapter Twenty One:

The trip out of New Orleans was not difficult. I got a quick ride up to Baton Rouge, with a Cajun in an old pickup truck. I imagined him hunting racoons in the forest under moonlight. The trees hung over the road and formed an umbrella that covered the truck.

"I lived out here all my life." His dark stringy hair covered his ears. He had thick bushy eyebrows that accentuated his wild eyes. Long hair jutted out of his nose. "Yessir, Never been no place but here."

"Well I have never been here before either. I hear there are a lot of alligators in those swamps?

"For sure there is, you don't want to swim in them." he advised me.

"Sounds dangerous." I replied.

"Well, it can be, my brother and I hunt em. They're fine eatin."

"You don't say. You hunt em? How do you kill them?"

"After we got 'em caught we split' em open with a knife. We go after the smaller ones. Three to four feet." He grinned at me as he said "split em open."

"I'll bet that is something to see." I tried to appreciate his talents, envisioning him gutting an alligator with a knife.

"Skins bring good money." He bragged.

"You must be strong to do that."

"Got to pick the right ones. Not too big or they'll get you." He held his arm in the air revealing a long dark scar.

It got dark as if we were driving in a tunnel. The branches had grown on both sides of the road until they linked in a mesh at the top. They blotted out the sun. The air was full of a sweet essence. I looked back and saw Valerie in my mind's eye.

She was now the girl I had left behind. What did it mean? I felt betrayed and alone. I was on my way back to Huntington with fifteen hundred miles to travel. It would take at least two or three days if luck was on my side.

I got rides into Texas without any memorable incidents. It was hot and dry. Texas felt like it was a vast desert. I made it to a rest stop in the middle of the state by the end of my first day out of New Orleans.

A rancher dropped me off near a turnoff to his ranch. It was a clear cloudless night, the sky was bright and the stars were overwhelmingly clear. The "rest stop" had a restroom, picnic tables, and water. It was deserted. Not a single car in the lot. The desert night was brilliant.

I soon became aware of the sound of rattles, the sounds were everywhere. The snakes were playing a weird symphony with their tails. I imagined somehow they were making each other aware of their mutual presence. What to do? I needed to sleep.

I crawled up on a picnic table three feet off the ground and pulled my bag over my head. I curled up in it and went to sleep. It was a warm night. I hoped no snake would come visiting in search of heat. I was not bothered. I woke refreshed, having had no snake problem. The night passed without incident.

I spent the day hitchhiking through Texas. It was milk for breakfast and milk for dinner. I was dropped late in the day at the eastern edge of the town of El Paso. In my mind I could almost hear the voice of Marty Robbins singing about Mexican girls with black sparkly eyes. I waited for an hour and decided I had to walk. Everyone was ignoring me. I walked, and then I walked some more, until I had crossed the entire seven miles of the town of El Paso. It took several hours.

El Paso consisted of long rows of adobe houses. There were no landmarks to help me get my bearings. It lacked a sky line. I walked until I reached the western edge. It was a boring town and felt like an unfriendly place.

At the western edge of town, a trucker stopped for me. He was on a long haul to Los Angeles. He intended to drive straight through, no stopping for sleep. He had a deadline and was intent on meeting it.

"I'll give you a ride all the way to Los Angeles, but you got to stay awake and promise to keep me awake." He held up a thermos. "I got a full thermos and can stop for more if need be."

"Okay you got a deal." I would try to stay awake.

Off we went, all he wanted was conversation. He was driving against the clock, and needed my help to ensure he stayed alert. My problem was figuring out what to talk about. I tried telling him about the trip I was completing, but he didn't care and wasn't listening.

"Just make sure I don't doze off." He reminded me.

He grunted when I stopped talking. It was his way to remind me we had a deal. He was a long haul driver and I got the feeling he found my conversation trivial.

"Keep me fuckin awake." He said and I did.

Before I knew it, I was walking down the road a block away from the little apartment my family called home. I headed straight for the parking stall where I had left the mg. There it was with the top down and cover on just as I had left it. It was smaller than I remembered. It needed washing. I slid into the driver's seat and turned the key in the ignition. The engine caught fire and roared to life. I felt a sense of relief and thanked my mom for having kept it alive.

The door to our apartment was unlocked. I walked in unannounced and found my Mom at home. She had an open book in her hands and the tv was on.

"Good God, I'm glad to see you." She flew out of her chair and gave me a bear hug. "I saw Chuck at the mall two days ago, he is in a huge body cast. He had a bad car accident and broke his arm and collar. I heard you split up. I've been worried sick ever since I saw him and found out you were all alone."

The tone in her voice went from joy to anger. She was happy to see me but upset at the same time. "You promised me you and Chuck would stay together."

"Chuck's back already?" I asked.

"He's in bad shape.You should go see him."

She said he had broken bones? What the hell happened? I needed to know.

"He is worried about you. He's been back for three weeks. He thought you'd be here before him. I am mad he left you all alone. How could you go off by yourself like that?"

Mom was right, shit happens in this world. If the summer had taught me anything it was you could not be sure what was coming around the corner next.

I found Chuck trying to read Tolstoy with one arm in a white cast. He was struggling to turn the pages and was having trouble keeping the book steady on his lap. The cast was heavy and hard to manipulate.

"Dude what happened?" Chuck asked in a loud angry voice. "I was standing in front of the Russian exhibit waiting. You never showed."

There were four entrances and I went to all of them. Somehow I missed him. How long had he waited?

"Crap! What happened to you? How'd you get this cast?" I asked.

"You first, why didn't you meet me like we planned?" He insisted.

"I was there at 12:00, and waited twenty minutes. Until I realized there were three other entrances and ran to all of them. But I never saw you at any of them. " It was true. I had been. "You never showed, so I left."

"Well, I was there at the North entrance waiting. I waited an hour." Chuck started to fumble with his words.

"Trust me, So I guess we just missed each other." I tapped his shoulder with a light punch. "I guess we fucked up. I'm sorry."

"Sorry I thought you didn't want to meet back up with me." He said.

"What happened? You look terrible.How did you break your arm?"

"Collar, I broke my collar and my arm. I hated the stock market job, they yelled at me at the top of their lungs. Run here, run there, "hurry up you idiot". No one yells at me like that. I quit in the middle of the first day."

"I messed around, went to a few places, and hung out." You needed to be there to understand. Chuck knew that. If you have spent time living on the road you know what it is like. Things just happen. There is no plan. How do you explain it?

"What about you? Does all this shit hurt?" I asked again about his broken bones.

"When you didn't show I started hitching home. Somewhere in Kansas a guy hauling a trailer full of horses picked me up. He said he was tired and let me drive. I fell asleep and rolled the truck. It was a bloody mess." Chuck spoke in a monotone like he didn't want to remember the accident.

"Christ, that sounds awful." I was shook up.

"One of his horses died. We both ended up in the emergency room. I almost got arrested. He blamed me. Said I killed his horse. Tried to file charges. That gypsy in Philadelphia was right! I had a death in my future. I was in the hospital for days. After that I took a bus home."

As Chuck told me the story of how he had become a horse killer, his face grew tense with pain and anguish.

"Sounds like an accident to me.You shouldn't blame yourself."

"Yeah but I knew I was groggy.I should have pulled over. I didn't". Guilt covered his face as he spoke.

I wondered what would have happened if I had been there? Would I have been the one driving? Would I have crashed the car? Would I be the one who helped kill a horse? I didn't think so.

"How long will it take to heal?"

"I'm gettin better. I will be able to go to school. I got a favor to ask." Chuck had a worried look on his face.

"Yeah what's that?".

"You know all the stuff I did in New York?"

"Stuff? We did a lot of stuff."

"You know what I am talking about. The queer stuff." His face contorted as if it pained him to recall.

"Yeah, what about it?"

"You gotta promise to keep it a secret. No one can know anything about it"

"You said you "found" yourself. Did you change your mind?"

"Well I did, but it is different here. In this little town. People cannot know about it. My life would be hell. Finding yourself works in New York. You are one in a crowd. But not here, here you can't be out in the open. It's dangerous. Here I would be the only one. A target for the religious bigots who'd put a bullseye on my back."

"I guess you are right."

"Crap! You're kidding, the old testament bible says queers should be put to death. God commands it.?" Chuck was stunned.

"But what about love thy neighbor as thyself? Doesn't sound like he's saying kill all queers to me."

"Mercy doesn't apply, As far as they are concerned God has damned us all." Chuck made a gesture of hanging by sticking his tongue out.

"Yeah, I guess it's sort of like what Mark Twain. "I admire Chistians, I hope to meet one someday."

"Mark Twain never lived in this town." He said.

"Okay it's our secret." I agreed.

"I am gonna go away to Santa Cruz and never come back."

"No problem." I knew he was right. His life would be hell.

The local junior college accepted me, I got the standard deferment from college, and started living a "normal" life. Free from worry about the draft.

The pace of life became slow and predictable. Living and traveling on the road you are at the whim and mercy of fate. Life is uncertain and every moment is pregnant with possibilities. Each turn, each bend in the road may offer a new slant on reality, a new and different way to see the world. There are always new people and new challenges.

My days are planned before they start. I get out of bed at a predesignated time. I show up and sit in classes on schedule. I listen to the lectures someone else has planned. Read books picked by the professors and write papers about them. My life has order. I go to work, take movie tickets at the door , and quiet the kids in the third row. I change the marquees every Thursday night, and butter the popcorn. It is all too predictable.

One day at work as I was walking up a row policing the kids when I came upon a kid I knew from school.

"Luke, how was the United States of America?" His eyes glowed, his face shone with anticipation. I paused. What could I say? What did he expect to hear? I knew he wanted to hear something wonderful about the United States. The question implied he thought of the United States as one uniform monolith where everything was good, just, and perfect.

He wanted me to say something about, "Truth, justice and the American Way." It was as if we were a comic book country. I thought about it. My mind raced for a second, I knew I could not give him an answer. How was the United States of America at the end of the summer of 1967? It was impossible to say with any clarity how the United States was doing. I wasn't even sure it could be spoken of in that way.

I only remember what he asked and I was dumbfounded. The nation was an amalgamation of places and people in motion. I had traveled and seen a little bit of it. I was a bit older and felt a bit wiser because of it. I knew for certain that "thinking" "you knew for certain" was an illusion. I had looked into too many faces, heard too many stories, to think it was that simple.

"Fine, the United States is fine. It has a lot of good people living in it." The truth was it felt like I stuck my finger in an electric light socket, and couldn't pull it out."

I thought back to all of the people who had been kind and had wanted the best for me. There had been a huge number of people who had touched my life and nearly every one of them had done so with the best of intentions. It was a blessing!

Made in the USA
Middletown, DE
25 August 2024